# JUST DIFFERENT DEVILS

## By

## Jinx Schwartz

## ACKNOWLEDGEMENTS

As always, my first reader and hubby Robert "Mad Dog" Schwartz, is my rock. His patient tackling of techie stuff that makes me scream at my computer is priceless. Maybe I should give him a raise?

Holly Whitman has been the editor of every one of my books, and she keeps me out of the ditch when my story heads there. The last eyes on the book before I hit the "publish" button, are Donna Rich's. Thanks Holly and Donna.

I have some amazing beta readers! And here they are, in no particular order: Karen Kearns, Sara F. Howe, Lela Cargill, Bonnie Julien, William Jones, Carolyn Bowman, Mary Jordan, Dan O'Neill, Jeff Brockman, Stephen Brown, Jenni Cornell, and Dottie Atwater.

# Books by Jinx Schwartz

## The Hetta Coffey series

Just Add Water, Book 1
Just Add Salt, Book 2
Just Add Trouble, Book 3
Just Deserts, Book 4
Just the Pits, Book 5
Just Needs Killin', Book 6
Just Different Devils, Book 7

The Hetta Coffey Boxed Set, Books 1-4

Troubled Sea
The Texicans
Land Of Mountains

Just Different Devils
Published by Jinx Schwartz
Copyright 2015
Book 7: Hetta Coffey series
All rights reserved.

# JUST DIFFERENT    DEVILS

## By

## Jinx Schwartz

# Chapter One

We're all in the same boat,
Just different levels.
Dealing with the same hell,
Just different devils.
*—Anonymous, paraphrased.*

From ghoulies and ghosties
And long leggedy beasties
And things that go bump in the night
Good Lord, deliver us!
*—Scottish prayer*

Something went bump in the night.

At least I think so, because both Po Thang and I were startled awake—he evidently a nanosecond ahead of me. While I was fighting off the dumbness of a disrupted deep sleep, he was already stiff legged and growling.

I instinctively groped for my Springfield XDM 9mm, found nothing on my built-in bedside table but a Kindle: a jolting reminder I'm on my boat in Mexico, and don't have no stinkin' gun. Rats!

Po Thang's menacing rumble grew louder as he pounced from his two-thirds of my queen-sized bed. Pushing myself upright, I was all ears, taking heed of his familiar route. Toenails scrambled up three teak steps leading to the main cabin, the muffled galloping paws pounded the carpet, then up another five wooden steps. His doggie door whopped as he dove through and claws scraped the fiberglass deck above my cabin in an effort to gain purchase. Then, a second of silence as he went airborne before executing a four-pawed, ten-point plant into my skiff tied alongside the aft swim platform. A small tsunami of displaced water swayed my yacht.

I kicked aside tangled sheets and flipped on a wall switch controlling the deck floodlights, then another for the underwater LEDs mounted on my boat's hull. Peering anxiously out a porthole next to the bed, all I saw was turquoise Sea of Cortez water glimmering, jewel-like, in that eerie glow-in-the-dark effect of a night lit swimming pool.

Within seconds, the lights—an irresistible visual lure—attracted everything from tiny tropical fish to larger predators, their splashes and dashes sending Po Thang into a barking, snapping frenzy. If it *was* some kind of threat that woke us, all that darting sea life quickly obliterated any recollection of it from my dog's fickle little golden-retriever brain.

Higher cognitive processing is not his strong suit.

Seeing nothing scary out there, I convinced myself all was well. Hell, it isn't that unusual to get whacked upside the hull by a fish, or an entire school of them, during the night. Many a morning I've found some feckless flee-er had miscalculated and, instead of escaping becoming a midnight meal for something higher on the food chain, ended up just as dead in my dinghy.

Trudging out on deck in my panties and oversized tee shirt sleep gear, I hissed, "Put a lid on it, dawg," hoping he hadn't woken the entire anchorage. An almost full moon shone on the other residents at *Isla*

San Francisco: five sail boats, two power boats a little smaller than my forty-five-foot Californian motor yacht, *Raymond Johnson*, and a Mexican booze-cruise megayacht on the far north end. The hundred-and-seventy-five footer was still ablaze with lights and alive with laughter in these wee hours. At least they wouldn't be annoyed by our lights and barks. I hit outdoor switches and snuffed all the lights on my own boat, instantly putting the kibosh on Po Thang's merriment, as well.

Fully awake now, I grabbed a bottle of water from my outdoor fridge and climbed to the flying bridge to stargaze. Even in the brilliant moonlight, the Milky Way shimmered in an indigo sky like nighttime traffic on a Houston freeway. On the horizon, a dim halo marked the city of La Paz, Baja California Sur, about forty-five miles to the south.

My boat was snuggly anchored in only twelve feet of water in the sandy hook at the southwestern anchorage of this tiny island. Even without underwater lights, the white sand bottom around us glowed, mottled by moonlit streaks. In the clear water I identified garden eels, their tails buried in sand homes, swaying gracefully with an incoming tide.

Po Thang joined me on the bridge, vaulted effortlessly into the second mate's chair, and whined.

"No way, Sailor Dawg. No walk now. So, avast yer snivelin' ye scurvy mongrel, and get ye to thy pee pad."

He hates that pee pad, which is actually a piece of artificial turf tied to a rail with a piece of line, and easily tossed overboard for a rinse when needed. With all his bad habits, one would think fastidiousness in Po Thang's privy habits might be on the lax list, but this is the one area of his training that actually took. Taking a leak, much less a dump, on the boat deck evidently goes against his personal dogma.

He woofed and looked so distraught that I led him onto the foredeck and took a sympathy squat on the pad. Guilt assuaged, he followed my lead.

The things you do for your dog.

Since I knew there was no way I'd get back to sleep anytime soon, I made a cup of coffee, pulled on lightweight sweat pants, and went back to the bridge. A gentle southwesterly breeze swung us bow-to the incoming tide and a slight swell, saving the boat from rolling on its longitudinal axis, which is boat speak for getting whacked broadside by enough water to roll the boat from side to side and make us toss our cookies.

The refreshing zephyr also kept bugs at bay. If the wind shifted, we'd have to beat feet out of Dodge, because San Francisco Island, in the southern part of the Sea, is famous for no-see-ums wafting out from the island's interior salt flats to make life miserable for woman and dog alike. I am highly allergic to the dastardly little sand flea's bite and actually spike a fever in reaction. The chomp sites itch and ooze for days and leave marks for months. I've tried every anti-bug potion known to exist, but they nail me right through it. For at least another month, until the first norther of the fall whoops down from California and chills the air and sea, I have to be on the alert.

I turned the subsurface lights back on because I enjoy the almost glass-bottomed-boat-like effect. Po Thang immediately headed back for the dinghy as roiling fish returned and he went back to Bonkerland mode, his head snapping back and forth as he kvetched in frustration at the excess of visual riches.

My smile at his antics froze and my heart submarined into my stomach when a large dark shape in the water caught my peripheral vision. It had emerged from under the boat, then quickly disappeared underneath us again. Luckily Po Thang missed seeing it, but I spilled what was left of my coffee in my haste to turn on the fishfinder/depthsounder. It took a minute to spool up and when it did an alarm went off because I had it set at fifteen feet while anchoring a couple of days earlier. Once anchored, I turn it off, relying on my GPS alarm to alert me of a shift in location in case we dragged.

The fishfinder/depthsounder monitor screen was a blur of red, as if we were hard aground, which I knew we were not. Something was blocking the image. Something large that went bump in the night?

Ordering Po Thang to *come* when he was so entranced was useless, so I raced to the swim platform, grabbed his harness and hauled him back to the bridge with me. As I peered over the side from safety fourteen feet above the water, he strained against my hold, grumbling and letting out little yips in protest, but I knew if he spotted whatever it was in the water, he'd go after it. And there was no way my dog was gonna be shark food, or worse, ripped to shreds by a giant Humboldt squid, on *my* watch!

Before I left the dock in La Paz for this mini-cruise with my pooch, the Cruisers Net scuttlebutt warned of increasing incidents involving giant squid in the Sea of Cortez. Over the past few months, several scuba divers had disappeared—or been found torn to shreds—in suspected attacks.

To make matters worse, one of these attacks had purported witnesses.

Supposedly, in full view of beachgoers near Loreto, a pack of these behemoths attacked several fishing pangas, turning them over and killing seven fishermen. Horrified spectators reported the men's bodies looked like they'd been attacked by giant suction cups and paper shredders. One survivor was "barely identifiable" after being dragged from his boat and "chewed" by the monsters. I'd Googled the incident when I heard about it, but didn't come up with much, so I shrugged it off as urban legend. But, as they say, where there's smoke there's fire, and all of these new incidents gave the story a modicum of credence.

Marine biologists, including my friend, and my best friend Jan's significant other, Dr. Chino, were called to the scene at Loreto and after a few days managed to capture one large squid, a thirty-foot female weighing three hundred and fifty pounds. They speculated that, if this was one of the attackers, the pod was made up of mostly females numbering in the hundreds, and possibly hunting with a gang mentality known to take on prey as large as whales.

Dubbed "*diablos rojas*"—Red Devils—by Mexican fishermen, they are rumored to grow to forty feet and weigh five hundred pounds. Once again, I couldn't find any proof of one this big on the Internet, but the biologists speculated that if these attack reports were true, they might be on the increase due to overfishing in the squid's natural hunting grounds.

Hey, I can relate. I know there are some folks who think of *me* as an overweight red-haired devil, but I prefer to think of myself as a zaftig, titian-tressed sea wench who only turns vicious when really hungry.

Although most of these attacks occurred farther north of the popular cruising grounds close to La Paz, a cautionary notice to take care was released by Port Captains for the entire Sea. They didn't have to warn *me* twice. I grabbed a flare gun from the abandon-ship pack I keep on the bridge.

Bubbles rose and popped on the starboard side, but that was all I could see. Clipping Po Thang's harness to a stainless steel rail, I shushed him so I could listen. Rational thinking told me I was safe so high up on the flying bridge. Or was I? Just how long is the reach of a forty-foot squid's tentacles, anyhow? Hook-laden club tentacles, I might add, that seize a prey with lightening speed, drawing the captive into a squirming nest of eight arms, then chomping chunks of flesh with a massive, powerful, razor-sharp, parrot-like beak. Oh, and if that isn't enough to ruin your whole day, its tongue also sports rings of curved teeth.

Kinda like me attacking a carrot cake.

I shook off that gory image—the squid, not me and a cake—but warning bells were going off as I noticed the garden eels had pulled in, hiding under the sand, and most of the fish had skedaddled from around the boat, fleeing whatever lurked under us.

More bubbles rose and a dark head broke the surface, making me leap backward, away from the railing. I landed on Po Thang's paw, causing us both to yelp. I doubted my bare foot actually hurt him, but the contact gave us both something to yip about. "Sorry, baby," I soothed, petting his soft fur while cautiously peering back over the rail.

I sighed in relief. Backlit in my underwater lights was a common dolphin.

I'd recently learned to identify these dolphins during the summer while working on a dive boat on the Pacific side of the Baja. Our mission was to find what was left of a Manila Galleon that sank there in the late fifteen hundreds, and the expedition leader was Dr. Brigido Comacho Yee, a.k.a. Chino, the aforementioned world-renowned marine biologist, and my best friend Jan's *l'amour du jour*. He and Jan divide their time between his whale camp on the Pacific Coast, and his home on Magdalena Bay just six hours north of La Paz by road.

All boaters find joy in the jumping and chattering antics of dolphin pods traveling with them and playing chicken with the bow wake. The common dolphins are my favorites, as their clowning includes high breaches, somersaults, squeaks, and eye contact.

I'd never seen one alone, nor, like this little guy—if you can call a five-foot critter "little"—lying so still on the surface. Had I not heard what, to my untrained ear, sounded like labored gasps through his blowhole, I might have thought him dead. He slowly raised his head, squeaked at me weakly, then turned and looked behind him.

His tail flukes were wrapped—ensnared, really—in a fishing net, with a huge ball of that net trailing behind. It probably took every bit of his strength to overcome the weight of that mesh trap to get to the surface. I know dolphins cannot breathe underwater, and this one was in dire danger of being pulled under and drowned.

Looking at me again, he seemed to sigh in resignation, then sank beneath the surface. The poor animal was in deep do-do, weighed down by the heavy mesh, and was losing the battle to resurface for air.

It needed help, and needed it pronto.

Boy, oh boy, did that dolphin pick the wrong boat.

# Chapter Two

I had a dolphin in distress that picked my boat for salvation, which already proved this critter had bad judgment. Not that there is any thing wrong with my *boat*.

*Raymond Johnson*, my triple-decked multi-level forty-five-foot trawler, is pretty luxurious and boasts sleeping quarters fore and aft, each with its own head, and a sizeable main cabin with a comfy settee, a high-low coffee table, a dining area with real furniture instead of the usual built-in benches, and a down galley, complete with stainless steel appliances and a breakfast banquette. It is carpeted throughout with a deep plush dark blue marine grade carpet that is luxurious, but a pain in the butt to keep clean. Especially when you have a golden retriever. My next boat will be carpeted in Labrador Gold Dust, or perhaps Yip Yellow?

Back to the problem at hand: the poor dolphin didn't pick the wrong boat, he picked the wrong *crew*.

And speaking of yellow, I, Hetta Coffey, am the original chicken of the sea.

For a gal who lives on the water, I have an uncommon fear of it, and everything that lives in it.

Water is lovely to admire from the safety of some heavy-duty floatation device, like, say, a large yacht. Snorkeling in warm, clear, shallow water is something I enjoy, but there is always a smidgen of trepidation involved, a soupçon of fear of danger messing with my fun. I bolt at the slightest fright, which can be anything from a blowfish getting too close, or even a stingray ten feet away. Even those harmless garden eels give me the creeps, and a real eel? *Fuhgeddaboudit.*

It is definitely *not* in my nature to jump overboard into the sea, at night, alone. I looked over the side at the little guy on the bottom. A couple of bubbles escaped him and tears welled in my eyes. Po Thang gave me a look that said, "Okay, you coward. Let me go and *I'll* go get him."

Okay, maybe I was projecting there, but guilt will do that.

"Oh, hell, dog, you win." We were, after all, in only twelve feet of water and my lights lit the area like a huge aquarium. Still, even though this poor dolphin looked to be asking for help, getting up close and personal with a hunk of wild animal bigger than me just makes no sense.

Lucky for him, I don't have any.

All these thoughts ran through my head as I first launched a woman-overboard ring over the rail. Powerboats rarely sport these devices, but since I had a dog on board, I figured it might come in handy. I threw it upwind so it drifted back to where the dolphin lay on the sand, hoping he'd manage to come up again and use it as a headrest to keep him afloat until I could ...do what?

Opening a locker that used to be a liquor cabinet and wet bar until I'd recently had it remodeled by a carpenter in La Paz, I hauled out my newly acquired dive equipment. While crewing on a dive boat during the summer, I'd gained some confidence with the use of scuba gear, figuring that, with my fear of the sea it might be better if I could breathe while under it.

Shimmying into a light-weight Lycra body suit, I then hiked my wet suit up like a pair of tight jeans, shaking Elizabeth Taylor's "Passion" body powder—a birthday gift that finally came in handy—into the legs as I did so, then managed the arms and all the zipping, tugging and adjusting involved to garner the look of a Jimmy Dean sausage.

Even in the coolish wee hour air, by the time I got into my full regalia I was warming rapidly inside a layer of neoprene, which was probably overkill for the eighty-four degree water temperature, but I considered it extra armor in case this animal didn't take kindly to my rescue attempt.

I had been drilled well over the summer, and easily donned my rebreather—which, thanks to all that training, was repacked and ready to go—but I was sweating bullets inside all that neoprene and Lycra. My dive instructor would have had a cat if he saw me just grabbing everything like that without breaking it all down and repacking and checking valves and tubes and the like, but time was a-wastin'. A dolphin was drowning. I guess. How long a dolphin can last without air I had no idea, but I think I read somewhere it was between five and twenty minutes. If it was five, his clock was running out, pronto.

I started for the swim platform, then went back to the locker and strapped a second scabbard and dive knife to my other leg. I was, after all, about to go into the water with a predator.

Calling a dolphin a predator might get a Flipper fan's panties in a twist, but that is what they are: aquatic fish-eating mammals. And they are at the top of their food chain. It is this predatory behavior that is sometimes their undoing when they raid fishing nets to steal the catch, which might be how this poor thing got himself into such a crappy situation.

Getting chummy with Flipper isn't on par with becoming BFFs with a great white shark, but still....

Sliding into the water, I put on my fins—something I've never quite mastered executing with finesse—then swam along the hull until I was hovering over the dolphin. Donning my mask and mouthpiece, I took a breath and floated away from the boat for a better look. My fears were right on target; this net wasn't one of those light green nylon jobs the Mexican fishermen use, but a heavier, rope-type model one sees decorating beachfront dives the world over. There were even a couple of cork floats still attached, but they were useless. The hemp, or whatever it was made of, was waterlogged, covered with slime, and looked to be heavy enough to entangle me as badly as it had the dolphin.

I flipped back to the swim platform and secured a safety line on both me and the boat, just in case I got literally fouled up and I had to haul myself back to the surface with it.

My first order of business was getting the dolphin to the surface so he could breathe. I figured buddy breathing with him wasn't in the cards. Even if I could hold my mouthpiece over his blowhole, something I considered on par to swapping spit with one of those squid I so feared, he wouldn't know to take a breath, and the whole idea bordered on ridiculous. In for a peso, in for a pound, I grabbed the horseshoe-shaped overboard ring and tried powering it down to the bottom, using my flippers to fight both mine and its buoyancy. It was a losing battle, but my struggles snagged the dolphin's attention.

Using what might have been his last bit of strength, he fought his way to the surface, grabbed a couple of breaths, and sank again. As he went down in defeat, his eyes pleaded for help. Maybe only in my imagination, of course, but it broke my heart to watch his plight. At least now, however, maybe I had another five minutes to free him.

Dive knives are razor sharp, and using one underwater can be tricky. A slip can be disastrous, and if I cut the dolphin he might react violently, causing me to slice myself. Or worse, he'd knock me silly. Some might say he was too late for that one.

Oh, and did I mention that dolphins have teeth?

I decided to try cutting through net trailing a few feet from his tail first, near that clump on the bottom, thus lightening the load so just maybe he could at least rise to the surface and stay there while I got rid of the rest of it.

Hitting a button on my buoyancy regulator, I sank until I was able to stand on the  bottom while hacking the part attached to that heavy, four-foot ball of death. Attacking it without much success, I realized that, ticking clock or no, I had to get a grip. I was tiring rapidly with little result, and my panicky stabbing proved ineffectual. I planted my feet, squared my shoulders, took a few deep breaths and began cutting the heavy line strand by strand, at a maddeningly slow pace.

The dolphin lay still, only once in a while craning his neck as if checking my progress. "Hey, you, human!" he seemed to be saying, "Can you, like, hurry it up a bit? I'm running out of oxygen here."

My concentration on the task at hand was such that, when a dark shape suddenly materialized at my side, I reacted violently. Screaming into my mouthpiece, I kicked away and raised my knife in defense mode, prepared to filet whatever it was like a, well, filet.

When what I thought to be a shark or some other such critter backed off, threw its arms out in a, "Whoa!" move, then gave me two thumbs ups, relief—and something perhaps a bit more liquid—flooded through me. He waggled his own dive knife at me, I finned back to his side, and we attacked the net together.

In no time we severed the last strands holding the clump, but the dolphin didn't rise to the surface. Instead, he'd settled to the sand as if in surrender. My heart sank with him, thinking we were too late, but my new diver friend swam to the dolphin's side, grabbed his dorsal fin and tried swimming him to the surface. It was then I noticed the diver didn't have on tanks or a rebreather, but was free diving.

I pointed at him and gave him the international diver's *ascend* hand sign, then finned to the dolphin. Taking a firm hold on the net still attached to him, I hit my vest's buoyancy regulator button: something I've been warned not to do. Normally this would send me rocketing to the surface, a dangerous move for any diver. However, with a five-foot of dead-weight dolphin in tow, all I did was raise him a couple of feet off the bottom.

The diver returned and swam under the dolphin to push him up, a move I considered dangerous as hell, but between the two of us, we finally hauled the dolphin to the surface, where my companion began slapping the poor creature in the face. I moved away lest a huge hunk of animal woke suddenly and took issue with being whopped in the beak.

Jan's marine biologist boyfriend honey, Chino, an expert on all things living in the sea, told me dolphins cannot breathe underwater, and that the water they appear to blow on rising is actually just the animal clearing water from the area so they didn't ingest it. So, would the dolphin, even though on the surface, know to breathe? Did he have enough oxygen left to blow so he could?

My question was answered shortly when our dolphin blew and breathed. We backed off, giving him plenty of room to swim, but he still had netting impeding his movements and we had to finish the job. I said a little prayer, even though I was fairly certain that particular line of communication had shorted out long ago, but figured if I was requesting divine intervention for the dolphin instead of asking for, say, a new BMW for my backsliding self, it might work.

The dolphin remained where he was, looking at me, then back to his tail again. Hoping this was a sign from on high that if we approached he wouldn't slam-dunk us, we moved in and began removing the rest of the net wrapping his body. In ten minutes he was completely free. My diver friend gave him a pat on the side and away he went.

Back at the swim platform, I pushed my mask onto my head, spit out my regulator and cheered, then turned to thank my new pal. He'd shoved his own mask up into a mass of thick, wet black hair. Morning light revealed a seriously handsome face and dazzling green eyes.

"Well done, Lass," this vision said with a burr reminiscent of Sean Connery.

I love Sean Connery.

Oh, dear.

# Chapter Three

Let me state for the record, right here and now, that I am in love with Jenks Jenkins.

Most of the time.

Like when he's *here*, which is almost never, because he works in Dubai while I live on a boat in Mexico. Just sayin'.

So, when a dripping wet hunk who had just helped me save a dolphin's life praised me and called me, "Lass," I have to admit I had an inappropriate tweak for someone in love with another; a frisson of...okay, lecherousness. Before I could recover sufficiently from this whammy to my system and invite the tweaker aboard for an early morning Scotch or three, he swam away.

Clambering heavily onto the boat like I always do after being weightless for awhile, and gravity revisits, I grabbed my high-powered binoculars to track the Adonic creature back to his boat, but I was too late.

Oh well, it was probably for the best, because I have historically found trouble without actually going after it, so why give myself the opportunity to chase it down? Still, maybe a little dinghy ride through the anchorage later was in order?

Po Thang was going bonkers when I climbed back up on deck, yipping his welcome home yip mixed with groans and growls of supreme miff-dom. Yes, I was back on board, but I'd left him behind. He'd fought his tether and grumped ever since I began suiting up, and he was still at it. My dog loves to dive for pretty stuff on the bottom and is mightily put out when he can't join me. However, having another being to worry about while trying to free a large dolphin with a sharp knife in hand had been out of the question.

Unclipping his vest from the rail, I gave him a hug and a kiss and promised to take him on a swim later. I noticed that oddly sweet odor he exudes when he's stressed, and I stank of a pasty combo of trapped sweat and designer talc gone sour.

Stripping off and washing down the suit, I dragged Po Thang under the outdoor shower head with me. Ignoring my usual penurious water usage rules while cruising, I luxuriated in a long, hot, freshwater-and-suds wash for both of us as a reward for my efforts. I was headed back to port in a couple of days, anyhow. Po Thang, after grumping some, relaxed and enjoyed the shower with me. He always does after his habitual initial attempt to flee. I've never figured out why a water dog like him avoids baths and showers the best he can. Because he's a guy?

The sun had peeked over the surrounding volcanic hills, so I left him on deck to dry while I went below, pulled on clean shorts and a tee shirt, made iced tea, and joined him to let my own short hair dry in the early morning warmth, hoping some vestige of red survived all this salt and sun until I could get a touchup.

Scanning the anchorage for a glimpse of the diver, I thought about that little twinge of lust I experienced earlier, and I wondered if I wasn't just reacting to the ever more rocky road this long-distance relationship with Jenks was traveling.

Maybe I just needed to hear Jenks's voice. Unfortunately, there is no cell service at the island, and my very expensive satellite system went down with a ship I was crewing on during the summer.

I would be more upset about the loss of the sat system if it hadn't been me who sank the damned boat.

I am Hetta Coffey, a single woman of forty—I've gotten over the trauma of saying that "f" word—who lives alone on a boat with a dog.

Okay, so things are not quite as lamentable as that sounds; I only say such things when I'm feeling sorry for myself. I do not garner much sympathy from anyone who knows me because, after all, I live on a yacht in Mexico. Back when I worked as an engineer for large corporations, I traveled the world, stayed in five-star hotels, and ate and drank high on the hog, thanks to a fat expense account. Those days are long gone.

On the upside, I am the CEO, CFO, president, and sole employee of Hetta Coffey, SI, LLC. The SI is my little prank on the phonetic pronunciation of Civil Engineer. An engineer by degree, I specialize in materials management and stay somewhat employed, thanks to a penchant for taking on, shall we say, less than legitimate employ.

On the downside, I remain perpetually single, ten pounds—okay fifteen—overweight, and on the verge of blowing the best relationship I've ever had because I am also bullheaded and, some say, as temperamental as any Texas redhead.

I prefer to think of myself as independent minded. A woman of the world. A bon vivant.

My best friend, Jan, says I'm stubborn, incorrigible, and morally corrupt, which is why she likes me so much.


My pixie cut do dried quickly in the sun and light wind. With a yawn, I realized my night and dive were catching up with me, so I fixed another iced tea, grabbed my Kindle, and moved to a lounge chair under my shaded sundeck.

My body felt like I'd gone a few rounds with Mohammed Ali, the result of muscles tightening during the adrenalin rush while struggling to save the dolphin. I started reading a new book I'd been saving for a special occasion, and I figured being a super hero qualified as such. Po Thang attempted to join me on the narrow cushion, got rebuffed, grumped, then curled up on the other lounge and went to sleep instantly. I tried reading, even making the font larger when the words blurred, but lost that battle and was soon gone myself.

A cold nose nudged me awake. I opened my eyes and realized I had a Kindle on my chest and my reading glasses on my nose. Disoriented by this break in my normal routine, it took me a moment to figure out, from the sun's position, that it was early afternoon. I sat up and looked around, realizing we were the only ones left in the anchorage. This caused a moment's alarm, wondering if the other boaters knew something I didn't. Then reason prevailed. If there were some kind of problem, someone would have alerted me before they left.

Po Thang nudged me again and stared at his empty dish. I realized we had both missed breakfast, so I scrambled eggs with spicy chorizo sausage for two, even though I ran the chance of a snoot full of ferocious dog fart later as a result. And to further make up with him for what he perceived as earlier neglect, I decided, since no one was around to rat us out, to break the stupid no-dogs-on-the-beach rule and take him for a run and a swim.

Jumping into my twenty-two-foot panga, *Se Vende*, we motored to the far north end of the pristine crescent of white sand defining this picture-perfect cove. Inland are boulder-strewn red-brown hills sporting cactus and scrub brush above salt flats—where I envisioned hoards of no-see-ums lurking, waiting for the wind to change so they could ride it straight for my body. But, Lady Luck in the form of that southern breeze was still with us. Hetta One-Bugs Zip.

We walked the length of the deserted beach, me checking for shells on the sand and Po Thang splashing in to dive for shells in the shallows. As he will do, one moment he's bringing me a shell, and the next, the best I can figure, the junction across which a nerve impulse passes from an axon terminal to a neuron—a synapse, by definition—occurs, his doggie brain just plumb shorts out and he loses track of whatever he was doing—not unlike me after one too many glasses of wine. Anyhow, he froze in place, his head whipped around, he stared out to sea, then took off in a run, hit the water and swam across the anchorage, making a beeline for *Raymond Johnson*.

Perhaps he felt the call of Beggin' Strips. Heck, I was in need of a glass of wine myself, and maybe even another nap. I climbed into *Se Vende,* started up the 60-hp Evinrude outboard, and had just put it in gear when, in the middle of the cove right next to where Po Thang smoothly dog paddled, something large splashed.

Po Thang, being the big dufus he is, changed direction and swam toward it.

Opening up that Evinrude, I streaked south, hoping against hope a giant squid or shark hadn't wandered into the cove looking for an afternoon snack. I called for Po Thang to come to me, but, as usual when it suits him, he suffered temporary hearing loss.

"*Some*one," I yelled into that hearing void of his, "is destined for *serious* and hopefully painful doggie boot-camp when we get back to La Paz!"

In the couple of minutes it took me to chase him down, Po Thang had changed direction twice, clearly and stupidly trying to track whatever lurked under him. Half-way back to *Raymond Johnson,* he was in thirty feet of water, so whatever it was in the water could be anything. I'd seen large manta rays, a green six-foot moray eel, dolphin, and all kinds of critters in this cove, and in the near-bottomless waters just offshore, every kind of sea monster lies in wait. At least in my cowardly imagination.

An adrenaline rush hit me hard, causing me to break into a sweat and look around for a weapon of some sort. All I had in the skiff were two wooden paddles, which I vowed to whop Po Thang with when I finally caught up with him.

He started barking and swimming in circles, then, in a heart-stopping moment, went under. There was no yelling for help, for the anchorage was still all ours. I motored to where Po Thang went down and leaned over the gunwale trying to spot him, but in thirty feet of water, the clarity wasn't all that good. Bubbles rose, and I was getting ready to jump in when two heads popped up: one goofy looking retriever, and one dolphin. They were both smiling.

They ignored me and continued to play some game unbeknownst to us humans. Whatever it was involved leaps, squeaks, yips, and a whole lot of splashing. It looked harmless enough, so I relaxed and headed for the boat. And that wine.

On the way, my heart resumed a normal beat, but I wondered whether experiencing two adrenaline blasts and a tweak of lust in one day put me in danger of an impending cardiac arrest.

Did I mention I'm somewhat of a hypochondriac?


My worries over Po Thang gamboling with a large wild animal were quashed when I realized they meant each other no harm. Matter of fact, watching their joy, I realized I was a little jealous of my dog's fickleness with that dolphin, and that was just plain pitiful. I had sunk to a new low.

Taking a sip of wine, I gave myself a mental slap for feeling sorry for myself because my dog had a new friend, and decided to deal with that dastardly net like a grownup.

I'd been too pooped to secure the net that morning, but not wanting it to cause more harm to sea life, or foul someone's anchor or prop, I'd lowered my spare anchor onto it, holding it in place for now.

Leaving the animals to play, I untied the line attached to the anchor I'd lowered on the net to hold it in place on the bottom. I then granny knotted— nautical term for one who cannot tie a decent knot—it to my dinghy lift. Turning on the onboard electric winch designed to lift a dinghy to the top of my sun deck roof, I slowly raised the heavy net onto the swim platform and lashed it down. While cutting into the blob responsible for holding that poor dolphin under the night before, I'd realized it was not just netting, but heavy sisal woven around a metal cage. Some kind of fish trap?

Getting this thing on deck wasn't easy by myself, but using the electric winch and some serious rigging tricks I'd learned from my dad, I finally wrestled it onto the foredeck. I was trying to roll it into an oversized black plastic trash bag when I realized it was encrusted in shellfish which, on further inspection, looked like oysters. I plucked a couple of larger ones from the net, put them into a plastic freezer bag, and added ice and a little sea water. I don't really care for oysters myself, unless they're cleaned, battered and deep fried by someone besides me, but my friend Jan dearly loves them.

Besides, it is against my nature to throw away any form of food.

# Chapter Four

Puppy love?

With a dolphin?

Maybe there was something in the air vents on *Raymond Johnson*?

The next afternoon, after another hour's romp with his new friend—whom I named Bubbles—I decided a little parental counseling was in order.

As I shampooed and dried him off, I offered him a few words of wisdom. "Po Thang, let me give you some advice about love from someone who has been very bad at it, and therefore aware of the pitfalls. I admit to a crappy track record in affairs of the heart, so I've learned a doggone thing or two. I just want you to know that I am not a speciesist, as my mother would probably attest to after meeting a couple of my boyfriends, but the hard truth is, Bubbles is a dolphin. You, on the other hand, are a dawg. Bubbles lives in the water. And not that you don't want to, because you are, after all, a water hound, but the fact is, she's there *all* the time. You are not. Who knows what she does when you're not around? Who she hangs with? Trust me, these inter-species relationships rarely work out. Except for, say, Charles Manson and that creature who married him in prison."

Po Thang yawned and fell asleep, leaving me to wonder if I was talking about his thing with Bubbles, or my own LDR—long distance relationship—with Jenks Jenkins.

As I do when faced with something serious to ponder, I made a spread sheet and did the math.

Jenks and I had started seriously dating over two years ago. During that time—and this took a good part of the rest of the afternoon and a calculator to figure out—we have spent less than two months together, total, which comes to 8.5 percent of the time we've seriously been serious. That is 2.5 days a month! Damned dismal if you ask me.

Yes, we are in almost constant contact, even now, with my ham radio e-mail capabilities, but is that any way to run a romance? Good grief, are both my dog and I in love with geographically, or species, unsuitable others?

And who even knows what could happen if, say, a hunky Scotsman suddenly turned up and dazzled me with an overzealous pursuit of my fair self? That thought sent me into giggles. Overzealous pursuit? Who was I kidding here? The man simply called me, "Lass," and swam away. He probably calls everyone Lass.

*Some*one on this boat has way too much time on her hands and she needs a job! It was obviously time to return to port and dig up some paid employment, since my consulting job at a Baja mine near the town of Santa

Rosalia ran its course when someone up there finally figured out I was milking them like a Jersey cow.

I hate it when that happens.

While I prepared to get underway and head for the marina the next day, I let Po Thang and Bubbles share a farewell early morning romp before raising anchor and heading south. I timed my arrival in La Paz for slack tide and hoped the wind didn't pick up before I was firmly tied to a dock. Entering Marina de la Paz can be a nasty experience even if one of those elements is not favorable, and single-handing in? Even worse. I needed all the breaks I could get.

It was a beautiful day, no wind, not too hot, not too cold, with the kind of glassy water that makes cruising in a power boat a joy. We were in the cut between San Francisco Island and Isla Espiritu Santo when, smack dab in our path, lolled a sailboat that seemed to be adrift. I raised my binoculars to take a closer look and read the boat's name, but I was too far away. No sails up, no sign of an anchor line, no one on deck, and no telltale engine exhaust water. Rats! I've towed more than one boat into port, but I really didn't want to try it without any crew on board my boat to help me snag it.

Sighing, I blasted my horn, hoping to catch their attention, then changed course so I could see the name of the boat and maybe raise them on the radio. It was a fair sized vessel, about thirty-five feet, and obviously a cruiser, judging by the clutter of blue water jugs, yellow diesel jerry cans, and a surf board strapped to the rails. An un-inflated rubber dinghy lay upside down on the foredeck. I tried a couple of times to hail *Carpe Diem*, but there was no response.

Sidling closer, I used my loud speaker to raise someone. Nada.

Crap! Now what?

Spying another sailboat heading north, I called them on the VHF.

"Sailing vessel heading north between Partida and San Francisco, come back to *Raymond Johnson.*"

Almost immediately, *Me Too,* a boat whose crew I knew from Marina de la Paz, responded, listened to what I had to say, and changed course in my direction.

The water was too deep to anchor, so I held my position as *Me Too* approached close enough so we could talk boat to boat. There were three people onboard and, since they trailed a dinghy, one of them volunteered to run over and check out the unresponsive boat.

I sighed again. Valuable daylight was burning, and time and tide wait for no woman.

While I waited to find out if I was going to have to tow the boat into La Paz, I radioed Marina de la Paz and told them I was checking out a sailboat that might be disabled, and would need help once I got into the channel. I also said I'd be late arriving, and they suggested I go to a side tie on the outside dock until the next morning, when conditions would be more favorable for me to dock. Relieved, I relaxed and called Jenks on my cell phone, now that I had a signal.

Left a message.

Called Jan.

Left a message.

Called Mom and Dad.

Left a message.

Gave up.

Jill, the woman from *Me Too,* returned to tell me there was no one on board the drifter, so I called Marina de la Paz again, told them the name of the boat, and that I would be towing her in. They said they'd report the problem to the Port Captain and asked me to monitor Channel 16 so I could be contacted, maybe by the Mexican Navy. Anyhow, someone would meet me near the channel entrance and take over the tow.

Unable to bring my heavy fiberglass panga, *Se Vende,* on board my boat, and not wanting *two* boats trailing behind me, I asked the four sailors to help me side-tie *Carpe Diem* to *Raymond Johnson* for an easy tow in the slight seas and light wind.

I chugged slowly for port hoping against hope conditions did not change before the handoff. As it was, should trouble arise, I could easily cut *Carpe Diem* loose and let someone else come and get her.

Boats from all over the area had evidently followed my radio conversations, and a few called to let me know they were available to help when I neared the channel if need be. I thanked them all, then told them I couldn't chat because I had to monitor 16. Nevertheless, inquisitiveness being in my genes, I set my radio on scan and listened in. Speculation was all over the charts, from *Carpe Diem* slipping anchor while the owner was in the water, to whether yet another diver had fallen victim to a giant squid attack.

The idea that the owner might be stranded on one of the islands sounded better to me than his being dragged overboard, shredded like pulled pork and eaten by a monstrous Red Devil.

My grandmother always said nosiness should be my middle name, and who am I to argue with a sweet old lady? About thirty minutes into the slow tow, Grandma proved right, and curiosity got the best of me.

Since *Carpe Diem* was side-tied to my boat, boarding her wasn't all that hard. I put *Raymond Johnson* in neutral, let her idle, and dropped down onto the sailboat's deck. I'd hitched Po Thang's harness to a stanchion so he couldn't follow, since one nosy critter on an abandoned boat is enough. I did, however, have to listen to his bellyaching as I prowled around looking for clues.

The first thing I noticed was what looked like blood smears in the cockpit, but that is not all that unusual on cruising boats, and given the three fishing poles hanging off the back, this sailor liked to fish. He might have snagged one and not cleaned up. But still.

The hatch leading down into the main boat was wide open, so I went down for a look. Everything seemed orderly so I made my way to the navigation station, hoping the boater, like most of us, kept a packet of all his paperwork handy in case of an emergency abandon ship drill, or even for checking into a marina.

Sure enough, a clear plastic bag was nestled next to the radio, along with a few other folders. The pouch contained a Passport issued to Frederick P. Clark, a Mexican tourist visa, a ten-year Mexican boat import permit, US coast guard documentation certificate, insurance info, fishing license, Mexican *Parque Nacional* permits, and anything needed by a legit boater in Mexico. Many try to cut corners, but not this guy; he had it all.

I grabbed a piece of paper from his printer and jotted down all the information someone might need in order to contact family, friends, or the US Coast Guard, because Mexican officialdom works in slow-mo and I wanted to give his family and US officials a head's up. I pocketed his California drivers license, two credit cards, and a thousand pesos because I didn't want them going walkabout during this initial investigation. I left two hundred pesos so no one would think this guy went AWOL on purpose. Even if he did.

Po Thang's "someone is coming" barks caught my attention, and when I stuck my head out, I spotted a boat in the distance that seemed to be making a beeline for us. I hurried back to where I could heft myself onto *Raymond Johnson*, but my foot slipped and I almost dislocated a shoulder when I caught myself on my boat's rail.

Looking down, I saw a glob of something icky where my foot slid. Fish parts? Left over bait? God, I hoped so.

Climbing painfully onto my own deck, I slipped off my boat shoes, rushed inside, grabbed the camera and got a zoom shot of the stuff on *Carpe Diem's* deck.

I soon identified the oncoming craft as a small Mexican Navy boat and let out a groan. I had hoped one of the marinas had responded, because the way things work in Mexico, I had little hope the handover was going to go quickly.

And I was right. The naval officer in charge, as friendly as he was, was nonetheless mired by the swamp of Mexican officialdom, which comes with reams of paper, rubber stamping and the promise of my first born, in order to finally get rid of *Carpe Diem* and head for port.

No good deed goes unpunished.

The sun was hovering on the horizon when I pulled alongside the marina and basically jammed my boat in between two megayachts.

The tide had turned and was ripping out: a bad thing. The wind, however, was on my beam and would push me sideways into the dock. With no one on board to throw a line from my bow to the marina personnel standing by on the dock, my game plan was simple: loop a bow line several times over a rail on the side away from the now side-tied *Se Vende*, hope like hell my end didn't fall into the water before someone was able to grab it, and then ram the dock as far forward as the space between those two monster yachts allowed.

A gathering awaited my return, to help with lines, watch what was sure to be a less than elegant docking exercise, and to get the lowdown from me on *Carpe Diem*. In addition to marina personnel and some cruisers I know, several nervous-looking crew from the multimillion dollar beauties awaited. Who needs television when you have docking boats to watch? A man I recognized as the captain of the hundred-footer I was aiming for looked prepared to jump, throwing his body in between his yacht's swim platform and my bow.

I made a pass, went to neutral to judge the wind and tide, pulled a hard U-turn, aimed for the dock and powered into the oncoming tide with way more speed than normal.

Not for the first time I thought, *Why, oh, why don't boats have brakes?*

No boats were harmed during this crash landing into the dock, but I scattered the crowd when, after a brave soul latched onto my bow line and rapidly secured it to a cleat, I put the boat into reverse, threw the wheel over and gave the engines full throttle for a few seconds, swinging the aft into the dock with a satisfying whack of my fenders.

In the end, I received a smattering of applause and hoots, which I acknowledged with a bow before my shaky legs powered me to the head below.

# Chapter Five

Bubbles, blowing burbles against the hull, woke us at five the next morning.

Po Thang was off the bed and up the steps before I could grab him, but I'd locked the doggie door the night before, as I do at the dock. And, as always, Po Thang crashed into the locked door a few times and howled in frustration before getting the message that he was no longer free to roam at will.

With the arrival of his BFF, he paced and grumbled, looking for an alternate escape route, but I had the boat buttoned up tight. Pulling on my jeans—speaking of tight—I gave him a sympathy pat. "Sorry, Romeo, no Juliet stuff today. She shouldn't even be here. I've never seen a dolphin in the marina."

I'd seen them swimming in the bay, but never inside the marina itself, so I made a management decision; I was wide awake, there was no wind or current to speak of, and it was getting light enough for me to maneuver my way to my dock. Better yet, I could see that the other half of my two-boat slip was empty, so all I had to do was aim and I'd get in without much damage. Just kidding. I really can dock a boat, but it is sooo much easier when there isn't a half-million dollars worth of fiberglass sharing the slip.

I started the engines, which roused a crewmember from one of the mega-yachts. He hustled to handle my lines, probably eager to get us gone, since Po Thang, held prisoner inside the cabin, was raising all Billy Hell.

If you are going to single-hand a boat, you come up with clever plans when docking and anchoring. My docking procedure was the lasso theory. I rigged a breast line on a center cleat of *Raymond Johnson* and after getting into a slip, I'd stop the boat the best I could, wait until I bumped the dock, and was able to lasso the dock cleat from the flying bridge. Without another boat to worry about next to me, all I had to do was cinch us in, then, even with a tricky tide or wind, at least the center of the boat was snugged in securely. Getting the bow and aft lines was then a piece of cake .

And, since I had no neighbor, I had the leisure of finding a place for *Se Vende* later in the day, since the pesky sucker increased the width of my boat by a good five feet.

After shutting the engines down and patting myself on the back for a job well done, I downed a celebratory cup of coffee and hooked up to power, water, and Internet: all those blessedly convenient luxuries you learn to either do without or conserve while anchored out.

As an appeasement to my very disgruntled dog—as I hoped, Bubbles had not followed us in—I took him for a long walk into town.

The *malecon*, or bay front walkway, stretches for five kilometers from Marina de la Paz all the way to the other end of town and is our favorite morning walk. The bronze artworks alone, some of them eleven feet high and depicting sea life and historical characters, are worth the trip. Since we were early, the daily clean up crews were out sweeping into piles whatever went on the night before. The *malecon* is a popular spot for discothèques (yes, they still have them), bars, restaurants and draws young people who hang out all night, drinking and dancing. The aftermath often resembles a war zone early on in the day, but by seven a.m. everything is usually spic-and-span.

Even though meeting and greeting other walkers and dogs is a great way to start the day, my patience level is soon tested. I'm only good for about a mile each way because being dragged much farther by a badly leash-trained dog soon becomes a test upon our relationship. Like, I want to kill him. Nary a palm tree escapes a sniff and a leg lift, every dog must be nose-greeted—and some are not all that friendly—and if I'm not vigilant, someone's breakfast is raided. If we were to stay in port, *some*one needed training! Probably me.

A skater whizzed by being pulled by a panting yellow lab, which struck me as a great idea until I realized I'd have to skate and would probably get yanked off the wall and into the surf by my dog.

We paused at one of my favorite art pieces, a huge chrome plated pearl in a bronze shell. Po Thang whined longingly at the sculpture of a mermaid playing with a dolphin. Young love is a bitch.

Returning to the boat in time to hear the eight a.m. cruisers VHF radio net, I was surprised to see a beautiful sailboat had somehow managed to squeeze into the other half of my slip despite *Se Vende* only allowing a couple of feet between us. Crap! I was also amazed the marina management folks, nice as they are, weren't already demanding I move my panga.

The net was abuzz with news of *Carpe Diem*. Turns out the owner, Freddie, had been anchored in La Paz harbor for a couple of weeks before, when he headed north. He was a diver and a single-hander, and as I read between the lines of some comments, on a tight budget and a bit of a loner. I'd get the real scoop later, at the daily Club Cruceros clubhouse coffee klatch in the marina.

Minutes after the net closed, I was making toast and eggs for us when I heard the unmistakable sound of bagpipe music. Drawn out on deck, I recognized trouble in the form of a pec-hugging black tee shirt and a kilt.

Playing *Amazing Grace*.

He winked.

I choked on my toast.


"Jan," I screeched into my cell phone minutes after realizing that the diver from my San Francisco Island dolphin rescue and this piece of Scottish beefcake were one and the same, and we were living a mere four feet apart, "you have to come down here. *Now*."

"Can I brush my teeth first?"

"No."

"What's the big hurry? Are you back at the dock? I got your message yesterday, but it was really late, so I thought I'd call you this morning. What's going on?"

"I need you here, now."

"Why?"

"I might need moral support."

"You don't have any morals."

"I rest my case."

After Jan and I talked, I called Jenks. I really, really, needed some reassuring words from that man. You know, like, reassuring me I am everything in a woman he could possibly desire, and he loved me more than bologna.

"Hey there, Honey," his deep, soothing voice said. "I got your message. You back in port?"

"I love you," I blurted.

"Are you all right?"

"Of course I am. I just...well, I love you. That's all."

"Who're you trying to convince, me or yourself?" he joked. Little did he know how close to the truth he was.

"When can you come for a visit? I'm lonely, and I miss you." Oh, boy, did that sound needy, so I added, "And I have bologna." One of the things Jenks says he loves about me is my bullheaded independence. Okay, maybe not the bullheaded part so much.

"You're worrying me, Hetta. What's wrong? Are you sick? Po Thang okay? You need bail money again?"

I laughed, relieved that I could. "Nope, not sick and not in jail. But I do have a lovesick hound on my hands," I said, hoping to change direction, lighten the chat before I said something like, "And there is this handsome Scot next to me at the marina who plays bagpipes and calls me Lass, and you're not here and I'm so lonely I'm tempted to jump his haggis."

During the rest of our twenty minute call, I recounted the story of Bubbles, me finding a sailboat adrift, and the Navy meeting me to take the boat off my hands. I skipped admitting to my iffy docking technique—no harm no foul, right? By the time I hung up, I felt much, much better.

And, there was icing on the cake; my call to Jan set in motion a diversionary tactic to keep me away from any possible hanky-panky. She'd be on my boat by late afternoon, all five-foot eleven inches of blonde haired, blue-eyed, man-killer.

If anyone can put a tilt in a Scotsman's kilt, it is she.

Jan arrived in time for cocktail hour, which in the past was a precursor to way too much alcohol over *several* hours. We had, however, come to the conclusion that we should try using adult beverages, like, say, adults. Hey, it could happen.

We took our drinks out on deck and she asked, "So, what's the big deal that had me driving six hours to get here?"

"Uh, oysters."

"Say what?"

"I got you oysters and you gotta eat 'em, because I took them out of the water and put them in the fridge yesterday."

She narrowed her eyes. "And this you consider an emergency?"

"You like them, I found them, and now both you and they are here."

She looked doubtful, but asked, "Hookay, then. What kind are they?"

"Ones with shells?"

"One would hope. Okay, let's see these treasures you dragged my butt down two-hundred miles of Baja One to eat."

I went into the galley and took a bowl from the fridge. I'd read on the Internet to cover fresh oysters with wet paper towels and refrigerate at a temperature of forty degrees or so. "The Net said not to keep them more than a couple of days like this, and if they opened up to throw 'em out. They aren't open."

Jan picked one up and sniffed it. "Seems okay, but they sure are small."

"Yeah, I thought so, too. Not like the ones you dove for on the Pacific side."

"I've never seen any like these before. Maybe they aren't even oysters. Gimme a knife."

I fetched my knife from the dive locker and she expertly pried open one of the shells, inspected what I consider the ick factor inside, gave it a sniff, and decided they were indeed oysters and might be okay to eat. Just to be on the safe side though, she decided to steam and re-chill them.

With her oysters back on ice and our main course heating, we moved out on deck for another cocktail. In honor of our newly turned over leaf, it was only our second drink.

What a concept.


The oysters had popped open on steaming, so Jan snagged some Tabasco sauce and tackled one. It was so small it was barely a good bite and she gingerly tested it with her front teeth.

"What do your think?"

"Tough as shoe leather. Sorry, Hetta. You went to a ton of trouble for nothing."

"Oh, well, Po Thang'll eat it. Here boy," I called, offering the, to me, nasty looking critter.

Po Thang, always polite, sniffed it, took it between his front teeth as Jan had done, bit down, and spit it out.

Jan hooted. "A dawg of discriminating taste. Must take after his Auntie Jan."

I frowned at the blob on my carpet and went for a paper towel. Swooping it up, I felt a lump and inspected it. "Jan! Look at this!"

"Wha—Oh. My. God. A pearl!"

Forgetting all about our rapidly cooling stroganoff, we washed the pearl—Jan insisted we do so in salt water—and inspected our find. It had an incredible luster, an iridescence not unlike that of the inside of an abalone shell, but darker. Black actually.

Jan went online and identified my find as Pteria Rainbow lipped pearl oysters, and declared I had hit the pearl jackpot. Especially if this one turned out to be natural and not cultured.

We finally reheated dinner and speculated about what we had over a bottle of wine. So much for leaf turning.

After dinner we inspected the rest of the oysters, and found two more pearls, smaller and not as round. Jan said they were baroques, but were probably still valuable.

"Hetta, what did you do with that net?"

"I threw it in the garbage bin behind the yacht club."

And that is how, in full view of amused cruisers, Jan and I dumpster dove. Dived?

Into a Mexican dumpster.

Our mission was accomplished, but at great loss of dignity.

We lugged the large black garbage bag containing a severely reeking net back to the boat, triple bagged it and dropped it into *Se Vende*, which had been given a one day reprieve at my side until it found a new home. By now we were fairly odiferous ourselves and decided to let reeking nets lie for the night and took badly needed showers.

All this hard work called for a second bottle of wine.

Sipping the last of it on deck, Jan reminded me we were supposed to go shopping for my mom's birthday present, which she would carry north with her in a few weeks. Her own mother was having foot surgery and Jan was needed to help out for a few days.

"You could come with me, ya know," she said.

"I could, I guess. But I really don't want to spend the money right now. Maybe the Trob can come up with something that'll pay the bills."

The Trob is Fidel Wontrobski, the guy who keeps me one bare step ahead of bankruptcy. His father was a Polish communist, thus the name. He's an engineering genius with less than stellar people skills, but a big cheese at the mega-firm, Baxter Brothers, in San Francisco. I once graced their personnel roster, but fell into disgrace because I wasn't, in their estimation, a team player, just because I ratted them out to a client for price gouging. Despite that little fall from grace, the Trob and I have remained friends and he feeds me clients the B brothers don't feel like gouging. That's *my* job.

"Good. You need to stay busy, ya know." She waved her almost empty wine glass and gave me a look. "So, are you ready to tell me why you *really* wanted me here in such a big ole hurry?"

"I told you. Oysters."

"Not buying it. Known you way too long."

I shrugged.

"Okay, so don't tell me. Since you are totally incapable of keeping a secret, I'll find out soon enough."

Out of the corner of my eye I spotted the kilted wonder standing on his back deck. "Yep, you surely will. Very soon. Like, in five, four, three, two...."

The skirl of a bagpipe wailing "The Yellow Rose of Texas" from the boat next to us made Jan swivel in her chair, and Po Thang cover his ears with his paws. Spotting all that plaid-clad hunkiness, Jan's mouth dropped open and she looked at me, then back again. And when said hunk pointed at me and said, between breaths, "This is for you, Hetta Lass," she swiveled back.

"Oh, hell, Hetta. What have you done now?"

Being serenaded called for a wee bit more wine.

# Chapter Six

"Ya know, Hetta," Jan whispered as we carbo-loaded *huevos a la Mexicana*, refried beans, tortillas, and salsa at the Dock Café in preparation for a day of crime, "it isn't like you harvested those oysters on purpose. You just found a net and it had oyster pearls in it. And since it looks like a carefully built net for oyster farming, it must have broken loose."

"I do know that. But I sure as hell don't want to have to explain that to anyone in authority who knows it's been against the law since 1939 to dive for pearl oysters. You know how things work down here. We'll need a fence."

Jan raised an eyebrow. "What you mean is we *still* need a fence."

Over the past summer we had "liberated" a stash of Spanish silver coins minted in Mexico in the early fifteen hundreds that, if the Mexican government found out we had them, would be confiscated. My safe was brimming with contraband in need of a buyer, but first we had to find someone who could fence the goods. Someone in low places.

"Boy, do we," I agreed.

Jan buttered a tortilla, which is what we Texans do, just in case our cholesterol is a little low that day. "What do you think the pearls are worth?"

"According to the Internet, the one perfectly round pearl, if it's cultured, sells for a hundred or so. And if it is cultured, we won't have a problem selling it. On the other hand, should it be natural? Katy bar the door."

"Who can tell us? We can't just walk into the pearl farm up in Guaymas and say, "We found this oyster on the beach and there was this pearl in it. Or can we?"

"Still checking that out. I did see there is a pearl place here in La Paz, so tomorrow let's drop in and grill 'em for info. And, maybe buy your mom some earrings for her birthday."

We plowed back into our food, then Jan said, "We probably should have invited that Scottish hunk over after all the playing he did for you."

"Better to let those bagpipes lie. Besides I'm fresh out of haggis."

"Betcha don't even know what that is."

"Sure I do."

"Okay, what is it?"

"Chitlins and grits?"

"You're asking me?"

"Anyhow, I'm trying to stay out of trouble, not invite it over for a drink."

"Since when?"

"Since I'm feeling lonely. Tired of being alone."

"I'm here, and you have Po Thang."

"You know what I mean."

"I sure do. Gotta admit, he does seem to have a thing for you. Time was you'd a already played his bagpipes by now."

"I'm a reformed woman."

Jan almost spit out her refrieds.

After breakfast we loaded up Po Thang, drinking water, sunscreen, dive knives, a cooler of beer and sandwiches, even more plastic bags, and snorkeling gear into *Se Vende* for a run to the other side of El Magote, a barrier peninsula protecting La Paz harbor.

This seven-mile long spit between the harbor and the open water of the Sea of Cortez has some sandy beaches on the sea side, and when the north wind isn't blowing, can be a great place to hang out. We had hopes of swimming with a whale shark, but their season for hanging out near La Paz is early winter to late spring, so chances of finding one were slim. There are some condos and a golf course on one end of the spit side wide open to hurricanes—why on earth did someone think this was a good place to build? Just sayin'—and is only readily accessible to the public via a small water taxi that runs every half hour. It can be driven, but the road is the pits and takes for-ever.

I knew of a stretch of beach remote enough that prying eyes can't witness the shucking of booty, and where Po Thang can run freely. Letting him loose is an iffy proposition where temptations are afoot, because he suffers from DAWGS: Doggie Auditory Willful Guile Syndrome, a condition that prevents him from hearing me yelling, from fifteen feet away, "COME HERE YOU LITTLE TURD!" On the other hand, opening a candy wrapper at a hundred yards has him by my side in record time.

While Po Thang ran and sniffed and splashed after fish—hopefully not a stingray—in the shallows, Jan and I dragged the reeking black plastic bag onto the beach and cut it open.

"Ack," Jan complained, "we should have brought your rebreather."

"Hold your breath. We'll take turns. You go first."

"Why do I have to go first?"

"Because I have to go throw up now."

Po Thang rushed us, grabbed the net and started pulling it toward the water, so we had to throw ourselves onto the mess to hold it. Thinking this was a great game, he jumped on top of us. In the ensuing dustup Jan, Po Thang, and I got slimed, but we finally managed to shove the dog out of the way and tie the net to my panga.

Undaunted, Po Thang lunged into the net again, and came up with an oyster. As is his habit, he trotted to my feet, deposited it, and went for another. We popped a beer and let him do the dirty work.

"That dawg is really growing on me, Jan."

"You do realize he's gonna stink for days, don't you?"

"Nope, because I'm going to make him swim home."

"Slave driver."

Po Thang brought another five oysters to the pile before lying down on the job. It was time for us humans to check them for pearls, but the dog now took proprietary custody, sitting on the pile and growling when we tried picking out an oyster up. I was headed for his leash when he froze in mid-growl, yipped happily, and rushed into the water.

Bubbles was back.

When we headed back to port, she followed for awhile, swimming alongside Po Thang, but as we made the turn around the end tip of the Magote and headed for the marina, she fell off, gave one last leap and was gone.

Po Thang, back in *Se Vende,* peered longingly over the transom, but Jan held him so he couldn't jump back into the water. She hugged and cooed to him while he whined and howled.

Love's a bitch.

# Chapter Seven

As we parked *Se Vende* behind *Raymond Johnson*, I was feeling a little down, since this was my last trip in my much loved twenty-two-foot panga. I'd already found a buyer for her, and my new custom-built, nine-foot panga would be finished soon, and cradled on the roof of the sundeck, thanks to my handy dandy lifting system. I loved that old seaworthy, but cumbersome, *Se Vende*, but the new, smaller, dink would be a much smarter addition for cruising back up the coast to California.

And another bummer: I couldn't help but notice, with what I'll admit was a little disappointment, that my man in plaid and his boat were gone. Rats, I hadn't even caught his name, but I knew his boat's name, so perhaps a little snoopery might be in order down the line. Not that I care, mind you, but he did call me Lass.

After some rigorous scrubbing—not the pearls, those we rubbed with a towel and table salt to remove oyster gunk and bacteria, just like the Internet (that blessed new knower of all things) told us to—and shampooing, Jan, Po Thang, and I smelled civilized enough to enter the Dock Café for hamburgers. Po Thang dearly loves the Café, because the outdoor section is dog friendly and gives him an opportunity to hone his, "So, you gonna eat all of that?" eye-beg.

"I guess you noticed that Scottish hunk's boat's gone," Jan said with just a smidgen of malice. She so likes messing with me.

"Really? No, I didn't notice."

"Like hell."

I waited until she raised her burger to her lips and took a big bite before saying, "Besides, who gives a damn about that Highlander look-alike. I mean, who names his boat *Full Kilt Boogie,* anyhow?"

Jan's eyes went wide and her hand boggled. She almost dropped her burger as she choked on laughter. Po Thang took notice and went on alert, just in case a treat was in order, but Jan managed to catch both her burger and her breath.

"You set me up," she yelped.

"Yep, he is the reason you are here, my dear. Not that it matters now, but your job was to put a full tilt in his kilt, thereby keeping *me* out of trouble."


We were still cackling when my cell phone rang.

It was the Trob.

"Yo, Wontrobski, what's the haps?" I asked, trying to stifle a giggle.

"What are you celebrating?"

"How do you know I'm celebrating anything?"

"You sound happy."

"Don't I usually?"

"No."

Golly gee, I guess I'd better brush up on my telephone skills. I'm normally a phone deceiver of the highest order. "Jan and I are celebrating...Wednesday."

"Okay."

"Did you call for a reason?"

"Yes."

I rolled my eyes at Jan, who enjoys watching me struggle to converse with the mostly monosyllabic Trob. I love the guy, but mundane stuff like small talk falls far below his stratospheric intellectual capabilities. He is an engineering genius at one of the largest Engineering and Construction companies in the world, but his people skills seriously suck.

"Would you perhaps like to share with me what that might be?"

"E-mail."

"Roger. I'll get right back to you, soon as I finish this beer."

"Who is Roger?"

"Hanging up."

"Bye."

Jan took a swig of Tecate and said, "Gosh, Hetta, that was a pretty long conversation for the Trob."

"My guess is he has a job for me and has sent me an e-mail about it."

"How do you always know what he means?"

"I speak fluent shorthand."

"Dating yourself there."

"Saw it in an old movie."

Po Thang whined that he needed a walk. I also speak dawg.

Jan took Po Thang for a stroll while I checked my e-mail for Trob's big news.

I read it twice, then again. What the hell? I called him back.

"Wontrobski, are you telling me someone wants to hire me to captain their boat, or that someone wants to hire me *and* my boat?"

"Your call."

"To do what? Not that I really care if the price is right. My bank account is in dire straits."

"You name it."

"You're kidding me," I said, although I know my mentor never kids anyone.

"No."

"Oh, never mind. Who is my new boss and what should I charge him or her?"

"Don't know."

I sighed. "Just give me a contact number and I'll sort it out. One question, is this in any way connected to my skill set as an engineer?"

"Maybe."

I gritted my teeth. "The number, please."

"E-mail only."

While I waited for his e-mail with my contact's e-mail address, I mulled over this new turn of events. I am in no way legally allowed to charter my boat in Mexico, so if I got caught *Raymond Johnson* could be confiscated. On the other hand, whoever wants my services came through the Trob, so the potential client must know who I am, and where I am. I trust the Trob, so whoever it is must be able to pay in US dollars to a San Francisco bank account as we require, and on the up and up. Or at least out on parole.

58

Jan, Po Thang, and the e-mail arrived at the boat about the same time, so I quickly clued her in on this mysterious twist of fortune.

"Lemme get this straight. Some shady character wants to hire you and your boat to do...what?"

"Dunno. And who says they're shady?"

"Excuse me? Want to re-read that e-mail?"

I read it aloud.

*" 'Subject: Contact.*

*Need exclusive e-mail address for our correspondence only. Use this e-mail address only one time to reply with this information. Name price for thirty days of services, plus expenses, for Hetta Coffey LLC and vessel,* Raymond Johnson. *Will require meals for one person, full time, for at least one month. This person will require a cabin. Must have reply next four hours.' "*

"You don't find this all a little...odd?"

"Nah. I find this an opportunity to expand my coffers. "

"Or your coffin? And what do you mean when you say you're broke? Hell, you've had some pretty cushy contracts since we left the Bay Area."

"I've also had a lot of expenses. This boat is a money pit, docks are expensive, and I had to buy another vehicle after mine went over a cliff."

"At least you weren't in it. Okay, I *am* a CPA, ya know. Let's run some numbers."

We went month by month, listing all of my income and outgo, what funds I had left, and what I needed to survive until I got me, and my boat, back to the States.

"You're right, Hetta. You're broke."

"Told you."

"Hell, I haven't been paid but a mere pittance for working at the fish camp all this time, and I'm still better off than you are."

"You don't have boat payments, car payments, dock payments, and a dog that could eat Australia."

"But you have hidden assets."

"Very hidden. Between the gold bullion I liberated from the Japanese goons last summer, the coins we skimmed off the Galleon find, and now the pearls, we probably have over a million bucks in the boat safe. Unfortunately, we have no way of selling any of that loot."

"And when we do, we might get a quarter of what that booty would be if legit."

Jan seized the remote, did a quick search, and punched a key. Garth Brooks loudly singing, "I've got friends in low places" blared from the ship's speakers.

She used the remote as a fake mic, so I laughed and jumped in with our practiced moves to one of our favorite songs. We needed some of Garth's friends about now.

When the song ended, I said, "We need this job, Jan."

"We?" Jan put her arms around Po Thang's neck and said into his ear, "And your mommy is a moron who is gonna reply to an anonymous e-mail, demand a small fortune, and let some stranger on board for who knows what purposes."

Po Thang shook his ear and snorted.

"Exactly."

"You are putting words in my dog's mouth. Think about it. What have *you* got planned for the next month that entails a bunch of money?"

"Well, I...Oh, what the heck. Add another two—no, make that three—hundred a day for the gourmet chef."

We high-fived, already celebrating a new and profitable adventure.

Putting our heads and calculators together, we made a spread sheet. Jan, as a CPA, is even better than I am at padding a bill. She always thinks of stuff I overlook, and I've spent my entire career estimating costs for large projects so I know how to stick it to a client. We make a great team. Jenks says we'll look good in prison stripes some day.

Jan did a fingernail drum roll next to her keyboard. "Let's start with the basics. What does it cost to operate a boat like this for a month?"

"Depends whether I'm at a dock, or at anchor, or on the move."

"And we don't know what this person wants us to do, right?"

"Right."

"So we nail him for all three. Dock fee, fuel, and all. How much will that be?"

"Dock is easy. About a grand."

"Highway robbery. How can they get away charging these prices in Mexico?"

"Supply and demand. I pay for a fifty-foot slip, a parking space for the pickup, and a liveaboard fee when I'm here. If there are three of us staying aboard, that'll triple."

"Okay." She typed 1200.00 into the spread sheet, hesitated, deleted it and added another five hundred. "CPA fee. Now, Fuel?"

"Lemme think. The fuel tank capacity is four hundred and fifty gallons, and we don't know how much we'll use, so just to be safe, let's gouge...uh, charge for full tanks up front, then if we need more, the guest can pay at the pump. Sooo, with diesel running about four bucks a gallon down here...."

"I'll round that up to two grand. Holy crap, Hetta, I don't think you can afford this tub."

"You're telling me? Okay what else?"

"I'm going online to see what a boat like this rents for from a charter company, you put together a list of other stuff you can think of."

And so it went, until we came up with a grand total of, gulp, thirty thousand bucks! For a thousand dollars a day, I didn't care if our mystery guest was Jack the Ripper.

I created a new e-mail account, pothangcruises@yahoo.com, and sent the estimate to Mr. or Mrs. or Ms. Mystery within the four hour deadline, and thirty minutes later the Trob called to say he had a deposit of forty thou for me, as well as his probably exorbitant fee, solidly in the bank.

"Forty?" I raised my fist into the air and gave it a pump.

"I padded it by an extra ten, even though I am sure you already did some creative math on your own."

"Did you trace the depositor yet?" There is nothing the Trob cannot hack into.

"It was through a third or fourth party, so it will take longer than usual. I'll let you know."

"Okay, transfer...?" I looked at Jan for input. She's the CPA, after all. She flashed all ten fingers twice. "Twenty into my Hetta Coffey LLC account. I'd like to keep the rest off the IRS radar."

After I hung up, Jan shook her finger at me. "Ya know, one of these days the IRS is gonna bust you all the way into Club Fed."

"And I suppose you're gonna report that nine thousand you're gonna pocket this month?"

"Of course not. I ain't a CPA for nuthin'."

We nicknamed our mystery client Señor Deep Pockets, even though we were not sure it was a mister. I mean, it could be Oprah Winfrey for all we knew, but we figured *Raymond Johnson* wasn't the kind of yacht she'd charter. Nope, this was a guy, for sure. He hadn't demanded the owner's cabin, a dead giveaway.

Jan and I skipped dinner after that huge, late hamburger lunch. We did celebrate our successful day on the beach searching that stinky net for more pay dirt. I broke out the best wine we had on board and we toasted to our newly found good fortunes, but after one glass each our day caught up with us, and we were both yawning.

"It's only six. Too early to crash. Wanna watch a movie?" I suggested.

"Got any new ones?"

"Yep, checked out a couple from the Club Cruseros lending library." I found the DVDs, we picked a rom-com—our favorite genre—and were settling in to watch a flick with a totally predictable ending when, moments after Po Thang growled and jumped off the settee, there was a sharp rap on the hull.

"Dang," I grumbled, and put the movie on PAUSE.

"I'll get it," Jan volunteered, while I tried muzzling a perturbed Po Thang. He hates hull rappers. "It's okay, we'll get back to the movie. Here's a hint, she gets the guy."

Jan went out on deck and returned with an amused expression on her face. "Oooh, men! Even better, men in uniform."

"Oh, dear, do they have a warrant?"

# Chapter Eight

In preparation for greeting men in uniform, I tied the gnarling Po Thang to a dining room table leg, asked Jan to turn on the charm to soften up our visitors, and made a pot of coffee for the entourage of officialdom assembled on my GO AWAY, THIS MEANS YOU! dock mat.

While Jan ushered the men inside and got them settled into the settee and a chair or two, I unearthed a bag of chocolate cookies for us humans and a box of Hush Puppies for my dog. After Po Thang quit his grousing, the Port Captain, a naval officer of some kind, and the chief of police visibly relaxed.

They'd stationed heavily armed bodyguards out on the dock. The guards naturally grabbed the attention of other boaters, and I got radio calls asking if everything was okay. I reassured them all was well and hoped like hell I was right, but it was nice to know cruisers were on the ball lest I had a problem and was forced to go nuts on a bunch of guys with guns.

That crazy *gringa* thing is only to be used as a last resort; Mexicans just naturally hate it when some nutso foreigner of the female type throws a hissy fit, but it usually gets the job done. Guys? Not so much, as many a male cruiser who has tried going macho on the most macho dudes in the world have learned the hard way.

First off, the men thanked me for receiving them without notice—like I had a choice?—and for towing *Carpe Diem* into port. Then the questions started. Where had I been when I came upon *Carpe Diem*? For how long? I noted the Port Captain nodded slightly at my answers, so he must have checked his records for when I notified the powers that be I was leaving port for a few days.

They didn't take notes, so I figured I'd have to do this all again, which prompted me to carefully tell the truth, something I'm not very good at. At least this time veracity didn't require my usual creative embellishments. They seemed fascinated that I, a woman, had taken *Raymond Johnson* out to the islands solo, and I suspected after awhile that they were fishing for any hint I'd rendezvoused with *Carpe Diem* at some point. The next question proved me right.

"Did you know Mr. Clark?" The head cop asked.

"I do not recall meeting him, but we could have both attended a cruiser event at some point," I answered, sounding for all the world like some poor soul being grilled by a bunch of self-serving congresspersons.

The cop cut his eyes at Navy Dude.

Never one to let events take their course, I asked, "Why do you ask?"

Navy Dude looked a little uncomfortable and said, "We, uh, found your card on his boat."

"Really? That's interesting. Cruisers dole them out like Christmas candy." To make my point I reached into my pocket, pulled out a few cards, and gave them to my visitors. "He had one of these?"

They all nodded. My boat cards, unlike my business cards with Hetta Coffey LLC on them, were new ones I'd recently had made with a photo of me, Jenks, and Po Thang onboard *Raymond Johnson*. I had another cruiser climb up on a hill and snap us sitting on the swim platform. With a cactus and rocks in the foreground, and the boat resting in the turquoise water of Agua Verde, the photo epitomized the contrast of cruising where the desert meets the sea.

On the card were printed my name, boat name, e-mail address and Ham callsign.

How Freddie came by my boat card, I had no idea, but I had a desk drawer full of similar cards from cruisers I never even remembered meeting. The only other place I'd seen cards given out with such abandon was when I worked in Japan; my *meishi* was in English on one side and Japanese on the other. I always suspected the Japanese side, written in kanji, said something like, "Don't mess with this *Gaijin* nut case."

Jan had been listening carefully, probably on the alert for any signs of entrapment. We both know that in Mexico people are reluctant to get involved with anything that puts them on official's radar. It is for this reason that a car crash in downtown Mexico City during rush hour has no witnesses. We *gringos* are not that smart, and Jan had already chided me for even getting involved with *Carpe Diem*. And now, with the direction this chit chat was going—from casual to something of an interrogation—she butted in and asked, in flawless Spanish, "So, have you found him?"

Three heads swung in tandem as the dumbfounded men realized that that this blonde *gringa* with the long legs and big blue eyes had just nailed them. I love it when that happens.

Not one to be left on the sidelines, I threw in, "And, since you are here asking me questions, I assume he is dead."

Navy Dude recovered first. "Not...officially."

Rather than ask what the hell this meant, at this point I probably should have said something like, "I want a lawyer," but this is Mexico, where lawyers make politicians look like our Lady of Guadalupe.

"Yeah," Jan asked, "so you haven't found him then?"

"No. But we fear the worst. The Red Devils...."


After the men left, we grabbed what was left of our dinner wine, and the few cookies still on the plate and headed up on deck.

"Well, I guess you're off the suspect list, Hetta, unless you're somehow able to morph into a giant monster with murderous tentacles. Oh, wait, there are those who think you quite capable of such."

I shot her the finger.

On a roll, she added, "You oughta send that nasty assed squid a thank you note for leaving a piece of her tentacle behind."

"Yep. About that?"

"What?"

"While I am overjoyed at being off the suspect list, don't you think that clue was just a little too convenient?"

"Hetta Coffey, do not go there. Do *not* get any further involved. The dude is most likely dead, case closed. Leave it alone. I mean it."

"Okay, okay. Jeez, but what a way to go. It's hard to believe this poor guy was turned into hamburger meat by marauding calamari."

"Chino says that's exactly what supposedly happened off Loreto last year."

"Those were open fishing pangas, but *Carpe Diem* has at least four feet of freeboard. The whole thing reminds me of "The Creature from the Black Lagoon," except at least the creature was somewhat likeable."

"The Mexican Tourist bureau is gonna have a serious PR problem on its hands."

"*If* the story gets out, you mean."

"We promised to keep our mouths shut in return for the details, Hetta. No blabbing."

"And we just let another cruiser become Hamburger Helper? No way."

"So, how you gonna let anyone know? The port captain strongly hinted he'd impound your boat and have us deported if we talk about this with anyone."

"Yeah, no more Mr. Nice Guy there. I'm taking him off my Christmas card list."

"Or, maybe he *knew* we'd spill the beans, and that way *he* won't have to piss off the almighty tourist bureau?"

"Yeah, well, I'm not betting my boat on it. But we gotta do something. We can't just let cruisers wander around out there without a warning of some kind. Maybe we should tell your Doctor Chino so he can let the cat out of the bag somehow?"

"No way. He won't let me go on our mystery cruise."

"Like you ever do what he says?" Like I can talk? Jenks says he thinks he'll start asking me *not* to do what he *wants* me to do so I'll *do* it.

"Well, no, but why go looking for a showdown? Besides, Hetta, you'll think of something. You always do. Something stupid, of course, but something."

"Thanks, I think. Anyhow, until we do we gotta somehow get a head's up alert out to the cruising world, but mainly we have to concentrate on getting this tub ready for said mystery cruise.

We clinked glasses, toasting the possibilities of a lucrative month ahead, one with the titillating element of mystery and adventure thrown in.

However, later that night, as I was drifting off in my big old comfy bed with my big old furry buddy, it did cross my mind that maybe Jan and I might consider a *modus vivendi* assessment.

# Chapter Nine

An e-mail arrived the next morning, giving us more instructions for what our client needed on board, and a schedule. A very tight schedule, considering all we had to do.

One thing we learned was our deep pockets passenger did not want to stay at the dock, but neither did he give a clue as to where he wanted to go. I say "he" because we now were pretty sure this was a guy due to his grocery list: hamburger meat, steaks, bacon, and beer. Call me a sexist, but that sounds like dude food to me.

Jan and I decided a run to Costco in Cabo San Lucas was in order, mainly because we wanted to expand our wine cellar with our vict...uh, client's moola.

I hired a singlehander/anchorout/sailor on *Casual Water*, Dick Atkinson, who was perpetually short on cash, but had a reputation for being reliable, to dog-and-boat sit for the day because I didn't want to haul Po Thang with us.

As I drove, we went over the cruise schedule and shopping lists, Jan making notes on the clipboard as we came up with stuff we didn't want to forget. Or goodies we normally couldn't afford. By the time we got to Costco, she was on page two.

Luckily I had two chest freezers on board, one in the engine room and one on deck. The deck freezer was for fish only, where we kept bait and catches. Whether living on a boat away from a dock, or keeping food on the table in a remote whale research camp, provisioning for a month is no easy task, but both Jan and I have become master provisioners.

Jan's menu plan for the month included serving seafood as often as possible, but we couldn't always count on it due to weather and our historical bad luck as anglers. We'd even tried our hand at netting our own shrimp, but the barter system is so much easier and successful. During bad weather we were usually holed up in the same anchorage with shrimp boats, their crew eager to trade shrimp and fish for chicken, SPAM, hot dogs, and a couple of magazines from the *Playboy* stash I keep on board for just this purpose. Someone gave my father a subscription and he saves them for me. After reading all the articles, of course.

Fresh veggies are always a major problem— we'd be down to cabbage and carrots after a month—so we stocked canned beets and frozen peas, broccoli, cauliflower and the like so once the fresh stuff was gone, we'd have side dishes. Mexican boxed milk has the shelf life of nuclear waste, and since their eggs are not refrigerated, a few flats last well over a month if kept in a cool, dark space.

I'd borrowed ice chests from just about every boat on our dock, filled my entire truck bed with them, and we left by seven in the morning.

"Dang, Hetta, I'm plumb wore out and we ain't even halfway to Cabo."

"Tell me about it. Let's grab breakfast and coffee in Todo Santos to revive ourselves. I think, this early in the morning, we can get through town without being spotted."

"Ha! One can hope. Last time through we were lured by the Shopping Goddess, led astray by colorful gauze and bangles, which led to a need to show off our new attire to the bar staff and patrons at the Hotel California. Too bad we're probably unwelcome there, like, forever."

"Betcha the bartender still loves us. Don't you just wonder, though, whether that admirer of yours was a real bullfighter?"

"My admirer? It wasn't *me* he was waving his big old, uh, cape at."

"That's only because, Miz Jan, you were way too engaged in stomping all Billy hell out of a tabletop. Not a bad flamenco, I have to admit."

"Ah, to be young again."

"That was three months ago, Chica."

"Yabbut, we are reformed women."

We shared a yuk, and threw the hotel a kiss as we rolled by.


We didn't get back to the boat until almost four, and it looked as though Santa had arrived early this year. The decks were piled with cardboard boxes and canvas bags. And, atop my mast, was a contraption that looked somewhat like my old satellite system, only sleeker and smaller.

Dick and Po Thang were watching *Animal Planet* and eating popcorn when we arrived. I do not have television service on my boat, nor popcorn.

Po Thang seemed somewhat glad to see us, but other than a half-hearted tail thump, he was reluctant to leave his bowl of popcorn to greet us properly. Flighty, my fur child.

I waved my arms around. "What the hell happened here? Po Thang get on the Internet and order out Amazon?"

Dick turned off *The Dog Whisperer* and shrugged. "Guys just started coming up to the boat and unloading stuff, then these techie types showed. They gave me a work order, with your name on it, to install the Satellite system. Sure wish you'd' a let me know about that."

"Sure wish *I'd* a known about that. Do you have a copy of the paperwork?"

He went to the dining table, riffled through a stack of paper that wasn't there when I left that morning, and handed me a sheaf of crumpled sheets and brochures for both a satellite marine television, and Internet and telephone system. A purchase order made out to, and approved by one Hetta Coffey, Captain, was stapled to a brochure, along with an invoice for more than ten thousand bucks. I almost fainted until I noticed a small stamp: PAID IN FULL.

Once able to breathe again, I slumped down onto the settee, and Po Thang wiggled his way between me and that coveted bowl of popcorn. "You think I'd eat any of that after you've had your slobbery snout in there?" I asked him. He smelled like Redenbacher Carmel Corn. My favorite.

"Well, maybe," I teased, as I reached for Po Thang's bowl, "I could find one little slobberless piece?" My dog shoved my hand away with his nose and planted his head over the bowl.

Dick laughed. "I'll make more," he volunteered, heading for the galley.

"I suppose this abundance of popcorn is accounted for on one of," I waved the stack of receipts at him, "these?"

"Yep. Came with all these other boxes. Two full cases of Orville, just about every flavor they make! If I had a microwave on *Casual Water*, I'd ask for a few to take home."

Jan and I gave each other a high five. "There is a God!"

By midnight we had all of our Costco treasures stowed, and had even managed to get into some of the more promising boxes piled on my decks. Actually, we suspended the stowing duties when we spotted a Bacardi label and discovered it was a full case of Ron Zacapa Centenario 23. To ensure it was delivered safely, we opened it to inspect for breakage. Finding none, we broke out a bottle to test for taste. One cannot be too cautious, ya know.

At fifty bucks a liter, this was no rum to mix with Coke.

So we didn't.

Toasting our benefactor—whom we now dubbed VDP for Very Deep Pockets—for his good taste in rum, popcorn, boats, technical devices and, after a few shots of his Guatemalan nectar, his superb taste in women. Namely, us.

To our credit, we only had a few small glasses each of this stellar stuff while playing our Guess the Guest game. What we knew so far was: he had a fat wallet, he drank good rum, loved popcorn, wanted to leave the dock and go somewhere, and, judging from the expensive fishing poles, gold plated reels, and one electric reel that also showed up that day, he wanted to fish. And for big game, because that power driven job—which I'd heard is illegal in Mexico—was capable of landing a small whale.

I checked for e-mail just before going off to Ron Zacapa-induced night-night and learned we were to depart La Paz in two days, and that Daddy Big Bucks would rendezvous with us at Caleta Partida, a little over twenty miles to the north. Also, had I not already done so, I was to leave *Se Vende*, my old panga, behind, as "her services would not be required for the duration of the voyage."

Striking what I considered an aristocratic pose, I read that last line to Jan with the accent and bearing of someone straight out of *Downton Abbey*, our new favorite television series.

Jan hooted. "Ya think he's a Brit?"

"Maybe. I mean, who even uses prose like that these days?" I printed out all the e-mails so we could peruse them later for clues, then hit the sheets, as we had much to do during the next couple of days.

The next day was a blur of activity, which started very early with making last minute lists over huge mugs of Nescafe Classico. With so much to do, I put the cruiser's net on the ship's speakers so we could catch the weather forecast and the latest news. We'd listened to the Sonrisa Net weather on ham radio earlier, so we knew we were in for a few days of benign weather, but then Santa Ana winds were expected in California, and they were usually a sure sign of some nasty northers to follow in the Sea of Cortez.

Jan and I cheered when a cruiser relayed a report that he'd heard from a guy who knew a guy in the

Mexican navy who told him that Freddie Clark was most likely killed by one of those Red Devils, and the Net Control operator lost total control of the net as hysteria rose.

I did a fist pump on hearing that report. I know, we shouldn't have been so happy at the bad news, or the fear it caused, but at least now I wouldn't be accused of being the blabberer and thereby land on the Port Captain's bad-girl list. The last thing I needed was for him to impound *Raymond Johnson* before my cash cow arrived.

Just to be safe, however, I didn't tell the marina office we were leaving until right at closing time on Saturday, and we sneaked out at first light on Sunday morning, thereby ensuring the *Capitania del Puerto* didn't get wind of our slipping out of port until at least Monday morning.

As required by law, I called the *Capitania* to report our departure as we left La Paz Bay, but nobody answered.

Maybe if I'd been on the correct channel and turned up the power? Oh, well.

# Chapter Ten

The destination for our mysterious rendezvous was the Caleta Partida anchorage. Reputed to be what's left of an extinct volcano crater sandwiched between the Islands of Espiritu Santo and Partida, this protected anchorage was a wise choice. The islands were once one, until the volcano blew, leaving us boaters one of the most secure moorages in the Sea of Cortez. It is also the only one in the islands north of La Paz that I really trust, because I'd ridden out southerly, westerly and northerly winds there safely.

My favored spot is near the entrance, snugged up next to a fish camp where no sailboat with more than a three-foot draft dares go. Anchored in only twelve feet of water, one is safe from everything but the rare strong easterly, and even then there would not be much fetch—nautical speak for not enough distance for the wind to whip up the water—and thereby no large wave action. It was an ideal spot to wait for Deep Pockets.

Jan was jazzed, as this part of the Sea was all new to her. I was more than happy to share it with her and play tour guide. I was, after all, the expert on board; I'd been there. And, of course, I never pass up a chance to be a know-it-all.

Since we stole away so early, we anchored at Balandra, just twelve nautical miles north of La Paz, for breakfast. This beautiful place, with its famous *El Hongo de Piedra*, or mushroom rock, along with turquoise water and sugary sand beaches, is a summertime favorite for the locals. I hadn't been there in awhile because getting blown out by Coromuels during their season is a good possibility.

"Okay, what's a Coromuel?" Jan wanted know.

"Depends on who you talk to. It's a south, southwest wind that blows in spring and summer. Cools La Paz down, but plays hell with the anchorages. Anyhow, I've heard tell that the name, Coromuel, is the Hispanicization of Cromwell. Some say he was a pirate who used the predictable wind to raid Manila Galleons. I doubt it, though, because as we know, those ships stopped at Cabo, not here."

Jan pointed to the narrow-necked mushroom-shaped rock. "Jeez, how does it survive hurricanes?"

"It doesn't. Didn't. It collapsed under its own weight several years ago, and the nice folks from the Bercovich Boat Works—I pointed their yard out to you as we went by—and some typical Mexican ingenuity for fixing stuff by heavy lifting, drilling, and a lot of marine epoxy, managed to put Humpty Dumpty back together again. Don't you just love the way Mexicans can repair almost anything? In the States, we just throw things away and buy new ones, but the Mexicans fix 'em. We've learned a lot down here."

Jan took a sip of coffee and cocked an eyebrow. "Sure have. We've honed our deceitful ways to a new pinnacle. Progress of sorts, I guess."

"Whaddya mean?"

"Might I remind you, Miz Hetta, we've left a perfectly safe dock for a rendezvous with an unknown someone, all for the purpose of what could possibly be ill-gained lucre. And in doing so we are thereby jeopardizing relationships with two of the best men we ever met."

"Oh, come on, that *dinero* ain't ill-gotten. We're earning it fair and square, no matter where it originated."

"I'm more worried about the origina*tor*."

"Phooey. All we're doing is renting out the boat for a month. I mean, what can go wrong?"

I endured her guffawing with grace.


After breakfast we slowly motored north using only one engine at a time to save fuel. Skirting Isla Ispiritu Santo, we were entranced by a rising sun painting volcanic rocks and striated cliffs tones of light pink to dark red. Verdant cactus seemed to defy gravity, clinging to what were once molten rock bluffs resembling honeycomb toffee. Pelican's wet undersides reflected turquoise water, painting them light green.

I pointed to sandstone cliffs worn smooth by wind and water of the ages. "It still takes my breath away. With all my travels around the world, I've never seen anything to top the Sea of Cortez for sheer dramatic beauty."

"A lot more drama since you arrived, I'd bet."

"What's with you? Having second thoughts about being chief cook and bottle washer on our mystery cruise?"

"Nah, I can deal with whatever being the galley slave part brings. I guess I'm just a little antsy about this squid thing. Where have most of those incidents taken place?"

"Not around these parts. Or at least, I don't think so. *Carpe Diem* probably drifted down from up north on the tide after poor Freddie was killed. Best I can figure, and according to the coconut telegraph, the attack might have taken place somewhere between San Jose Island and Loreto. Which is close enough for me, thank you."

"When Chino told me about that attack in Loreto last year, he said he was not convinced the story was true, and still thinks it was some kind of hoax."

"I thought he went to investigate."

"He did. He went to find the squid and tried to figure out what really happened. He told me he never met anyone who actually saw the attack, and suspected the one picture was Photoshopped."

"But they caught the squid, right?"

"They caught *a* squid, but it took him and his team over a week to find one, and even then he says there is no evidence the poor thing had anything to do with the alleged attack."

"Why on earth would someone fabricate a story like that?"

Jan shook her head. "Dunno. Maybe we should Snopes it."

"I will, soon as we get anchored. Sure is gonna be great having total communication on board for the next month."

"And security. If one of those oversized calamari slimes his way onto *Raymond Johnson's* decks, we'll know."

"Knowing and doing something about it are two different things. I sooo miss my guns."

She patted my hand. "Poor Hetta. So many bad guys, so little ammo."

We turned in early, anticipating our guest would arrive by lunchtime the next day. I checked my e-mail to see if we had an update from him, but no such luck.

Googling, *squid attack Loreto*, I came upon the actual article in something called the Weekly World News, with a banner claiming it to be, "The world's only reliable news." The article featured a photo of panga fishermen being thrown into turbulent water, allegedly into the maws of Red Devils. Snopes, however, called the whole thing a hoax.

Evidently someone out there has *way* too much time on their hands.

Like me. I LIKED the Weekly World News on Facebook.

We'd also e-mailed Jenks and Chino, a sticky wicket at best. We had not informed our men of this trip yet, feeling it is easier to ask for forgiveness than permission. Of course, in our case, that permission thing didn't exactly fly anyway, but for the moment we were off the hook because they would figure as long as we were able to e-mail and Skype, we were still at the dock. Oh, the tangled web.

With a full-blown satellite system on board, we could also fire up the security alarm system, a big plus when we did have to fess up to what we were up to.

Well, Jan would be the one to confess because Chino had all kinds of contacts in La Paz. Or, even drop in himself. Jenks was so far away I could keep him in the dark for a month, but Chino was a totally different problem.

After a day of cruising, I thought I'd drop off immediately but, to paraphrase Shakespeare's King Henry, uneasy lies the head that wears the captain's hat, and there was much to consider. Weather, mystery men, not being straight with Jenks, and leaving port without a dinghy. Where we were, we could practically walk to shore if something went terribly wrong, and I also had a survival raft strapped to the top deck, but it still bothered me. Who? What? Where? When? and Why? played pinball in my wide-awake brain, resulting in a major headache.

*Who* was coming?

*What* were we going to be doing for the next month?

And *where*?

*When* would this dude arrive?

And *why* didn't I just get married at twenty-one, and have a white picket fence, and a divorce, like so many of my friends?

# Chapter Eleven

Without any idea of when our Mr. Mysterious would arrive, we went about our daily routine under the assumption there would be one more for lunch or dinner. Jan always cooks for six anyway, because we adore leftovers—*if* we can fight Po Thang off long enough to get them into the freezer.

After breakfast and performing the myriad basic necessary chores when anchoring out, we decided to go snorkeling. The water was still seventy-eight and by late morning the air temp was balmy enough to go bobbing for lobsters in a hole I knew of not all that far from the boat.

Without a dinghy we'd have to swim for it, but it would give Po Thang a workout. Mexican law forbade us to take lobster, but I had a sneaky method that didn't require a spear gun, so we loaded up our dive bags with drinking water, an old mop handle, bait, beer, and pantyhose.

One of my least favorite things about lobster is they hang out in holes and keep bad company. Where lobster lurk, so do morays, as moray eels prize a lobster dinner as much as we do. Unfortunately, morays also consider these lobster lairs within their property lines and do not take kindly to poachers.

Finding a flat offshore rock to perch upon, I pulled out the pantyhose, shoved Po Thang away from the bait bag, stuffed some old stinky fish guts I'd thawed out into a leg, tied the ends, and attached them to the mop handle.

I swam to an underwater ledge, inspected it carefully for large toothy eels with bad attitudes, and located a promising crevice. Jamming the mop handle down into the crack, panty leg end first, I made sure it was secure, then paddled back out to the rock for a beer.

While we knew the odds of snagging a spiny lobster for dinner were not all that good, it gave us an excuse to sit on a warm sunny rock and sip a cool one. Po Thang, miffed at not getting to go after our baited mop handle, groused a little but then settled down for a nap.

From our vantage point at the entrance to the anchorage, we'd be able to spot new traffic coming or going, and could be back at the boat in twenty minutes if need be. Of course, we had no idea what time our guy would arrive, or how, but my guess was a panga bigger and newer than my old *Se Vende* if he planned to use those snazzy deep sea fishing rods he'd sent to *Raymond Johnson.* My boat is a cruiser, not a high speed fish killer.

We gave the lobster an hour and I went back for the mop handle. Giving it a tug, it felt like maybe I had a bug, so I called for Jan to come with a dive bag.

While these guys do not have claws, their spines make them hard to handle, so it's easier to pull the stubborn little devils out of their happy homes when you have two people working at it. Her job was to bag the lobster and fend off Po Thang, who thinks anything that moves underwater is fair game.

The hole was about four feet down and we were only wearing snorkels and masks, making the aquatic creatures far better adapted to escape than us landlubbers are at chasing them. Mother Nature, however, didn't count on sharp spines getting tangled in pantyhose. Must be an evolutionary thing.

We had a tug of war on our hands, but after ten minutes of working in shifts, Jan jerked a foot-long lobster from it's lair and I bagged it, pantyhose and all.

Back on our rock we took a breather, put the lobster into a canvas bag instead of our net one. I'd learned the year before not to trail a net bag with lobster and bait behind me when a huge moray shadowed me back to the boat. Well, not *all* the way back because I shoved the whole danged shebang at the eel and swam for my life. Cowardice runs right strong in these veins.

Halfway back to *Raymond Johnson* I heard the unmistakable rumble of a fast moving boat. Jan, also immediately on the alert, herded Po Thang closer to shore and I followed. There have been way too many instances of swimmers run over in the Sea of Cortez; when these pangas are running fast, they aren't always on a plane, and the driver can't see anyone in front of them. And, because we were hugging shore for the most part, we didn't bring the "diver down" red and white float flag with us. Dumb and Dumber strike again.

Sure enough, a large fancy panga with a center cockpit and bimini shade roared by, streaking into the anchorage at a speed absolutely guaranteed to piss off every boater there.

"Get ready for a wake!" I yelled at Jan. She grabbed Po Thang's harness and hauled him away from the nearby rocks, while I paddled for dear life in the same direction. A three foot wake hit us smack in the face, but at least we weren't whacked into a rock. Spluttering curses, we swam for the boat, only to get buffeted again as the A-hole streaked back out to sea.

Masts rocked wildly, and even *Raymond Johnson,* as heavy and stable as she is, rolled in the mess created by the jerk. I never got a good look at the driver, but the panga was light blue, an unusual color, and if I saw it again, I'd recognize it, for sure.

Back on the boat—we had to tread water until the swim platform settled down enough so we could safely board—we used the outdoor shower for ourselves and Po Thang, then settled down with sandwiches on the flying bridge while listening in on radio conversations, a cruiser pastime. The chatter in the anchorage was light, mostly people complaining about things that fell over when the wake hit them. On a boat, if it *can* move, it *will* move, something I always try to remember.

We were playing a game of Baja Rummy when I heard another motor, and saw a panga streaking for the entrance. "Oh, hell, here we go again. What's with these guys?"

"Jerks. Hey, at least this one is slowing down, and it isn't the idiot who came through before. This panga isn't blue."

As we watched, a white panga slowed and headed straight for us. "Looks like we might have company, Jan me girl," I said as I gathered the cards. I was losing, so the arrival of what I hoped was our guest was timely. Jan waggled the score sheet at me. "We'll finish this later. No way are you gonna weasel out."

Rats. Oh, well, at least now maybe our man of mystery would be revealed.

Po Thang went on point, staring intently at the fancy white super panga headed our way. As a rule, he dislikes the high-end tenders and pangas, favoring rubber dinghies and old skiffs bearing what he perceived as other boaters and, thereby, dog-friendly. Mexicans, he has learned, are wary of him, and he plays that to the hilt, getting his macho in. Now he looked uncertain. He had a momentary tail wag of recognition, then tucked that tail and headed below. Great guard dog, that.

The glare on the boat's windscreen prevented us from identifying the driver, but from Po Thang's reaction, I was on the alert. I could tell there was only one person in the open panga, and that this was no regular fishing panga; this sucker was state of the art, at least twenty-five feet long, and was equipped with huge twin outboards on the transom. From their deep thrum, I told Jan I thought they were diesels.

"Diesel outboards? I've never seen one," she said.

"There's a reason for that. They cost a bundle. And he's got two. God only knows how fast that sucker can go. I sure hope it is ours...I want to drive it."

Jan and I moved to the swim platform, put out two large fenders and readied ourselves to catch his line. The driver, wearing a baseball cap and dark glasses, threw Jan the bow line and smartly maneuvered the panga alongside. I grabbed the aft rail and snugged him in.

"*Gracias, quierda.* Have you missed me?"

Jan and I chorused, "Nacho?"

# Chapter Twelve

Nacho.

Of all the people in the world I would expect to charter my boat, Nacho would be the last. He was more likely to steal it.

What can I say? During our acquaintanceship, for lack of a better word, I've known him as a drug punk, kidnapper, murderer, and a man of mystery who makes things happen. Bad things.

His phone number, the one I have burned into my memory in case I need a bad guy, is 1-800-gotbadzz, and his motto: We get what's bugging you.

It used to be 1-800-gotbads? until I reminded him there is no question mark on the phone. He said it didn't matter because I was never, ever, to call him again.

Which is kind of a shame, since he has used some of his questionable skills to get me out of a couple of jams, and that murder I mentioned? He killed a guy who was gonna kill me, so I can hardly hold *that* against him. The fact that he has strongly hinted he'd prefer I hold something else of mine against him—and I gotta admit the temptation's tantalizing—is flattering. And, to his credit, he *has* forgiven me for stealing his off-road vehicle, credit cards and flattening one of his gang rides.

Jan and I think he is both handsome and charming, in a criminal sort of way. Tantalized by his dark secret life, we've spent untold hours speculating on who he works for, but we simply don't know.

But one thing I *did* know *now*: We work for him.

As we waited for him on deck while he shut down the boat, Jan whispered, "Oh, crap, Jenks isn't gonna like this."

Boy was she right. Until I turned over a new leaf and fell for Jenks, Nacho was just the kind of man I was attracted to: untrustworthy, uncontrollable, unpredictable, handsome, charming and certainly no one you could take home to meet the folks.

Jenks is infinitely trustworthy and lets me think I am in control. He's also solid and handsome in a Nordic way, and his charm is genuine, which is why my Mom and I love him. He is also the most self-confident man I know, and he sort of trusts me, but where Nacho is concerned, he was not going to like the idea of us cohabitating, so to speak, on my boat for an entire month.

"What Jenks doesn't know won't hurt him," I said between my teeth.

"Chino ain't gonna be thrilled, either, even if Nacho did sort of save his grandmother from drug dealers once."

"You gonna tell him?"

"Not no, but hell no."

"So, what *are* we going to tell Jenks and Chino? They're already gonna have a cat that we left the dock, much less for a month."

"You'll figure it out, like always. You are hands down the best liar I know."

"Thanks. I think."

While Nacho settled into his cabin, Jan and I speculated as to why he chartered us. Me. We whispered while putting together a tasty array of hors d'oeuvres. Smoked marlin, a mound of boiled Sea of Cortez blue shrimp, some lobster chunks, melted butter with garlic, and a fresh baked baguette did the job.

"I don't get it," Jan murmured. "Why would he choose you, instead of another real charter? I mean, he *knows* you are freakin' nuts."

"While you, on the other hand, are the very epitome of sanity?"

"He didn't even know I was involved. Or did he? Anyhow, he's never seen *me* run someone down in the street like a dog."

"I see your point. But, he knows when folks just need killin'."

"Ya think he wants us to kill someone?" She sounded a little too excited about this possibility.

"Why would he want us to off anyone at all? I mean, he's the killer for hire."

"I can heeear you," Nacho whispered in my ear.

I jumped about a foot, shrieked, and almost cut off a finger with the bread knife. "Dammit, Nacho," I yelled, waving the knife at him, "don't you know better than to sneak up on a woman who has a sharp instrument in her hand?"

When I yelped, Po Thang, who had made a habit of inhabiting any deck Nacho didn't, ran growling and snapping into the galley. One look at Nacho and he turned tail again.

Nacho shrugged. "We will reach our peace. He is very friendly when you are not around."

Jan laughed. "Isn't everyone?"

I poked her in the ribs, but she ignored me and told Nacho, "Just slip him some smoked marlin, he'll be your new best friend. Trust me. Now, who wants to choose the white wine?"

We moved out on deck where we sipped a crisp white Nacho had paid big bucks for, noshed, and made small talk, which was somewhat difficult. There was that nine-hundred pound gorilla at the table. I was doing my very best to keep a civil tongue because I was in possession of a bunch of Nacho's money and wasn't inclined to give it back. But what did he want for it?

I took a ladylike slug of wine and asked, "Okay, Buster, what do you want?"

Jan cut her eyes at me, Po Thang looked up at my sharp tone, and Nacho didn't even blink. "I want to fish."

This was not what I expected. "Is that spelled with a Ph, or an F?"

He looked confused. "Excuse me?"

"Are you after fish, as in F-I-S-H, or are you P-H-I-S-H-I-N-G?"

"I do not know what phishing means."

"Snooping around for information to be used for nefarious purposes," Jan explained. "Hetta's just being a pill. I mean, what on earth could we know that you want to find out about?"

Not to be put off by Jan's attempt at peacemaking, I said, "I want a straight answer, Nacho. What are you doing here, and why for an entire month?"

Nacho sighed and handed my dog a large piece of smoked marlin. Po Thang vacuumed it down and gave his new BFF an adoring look. Fickle little dung dropper.

"I'm waiting. It is not too late to put you back in that fancy panga and send you packing."

"I am being truthful. I want to go fishing for some very large fish, and I could think of no one more perfect to do it with than you, and your boat. Jan? She is an unexpected, but delightful bonus. At least we will eat well."

Jan gave *her* new BFF a dazzling smile and batted her eyelashes. Fickleness was out of control on my boat. "For dinner we're having *Steak au poivre vert*, *pommes dauphinoise*, and *salade* with my homemade vinaigrette. Chocolate soufflé for dessert."

"Fabulous. I brought a bottle of el Presidente brandy that will be perfect with the soufflé."

"Why don't you two get a room, and take my dog with you," I snarled.

"So touchy," Nacho said.

"And, *amigo*, are you sure you wouldn't rather have the little woman here whip up some refried beans and a *cerveza*? She slaps a mean tortilla these days, what with her culinary studies at the fish camp."

"Bravo, Café, you have outdone yourself. You managed to insult both of us *and* work in a racial slur. I see your impertinence has not been abated by achieving middle age."

Ouch! Does this guy know how to get even or what? And with such a big word, to boot!

All three of us broke into raucous laughter while Po Thang used our inattention to dash in and finish off the marlin.

# Chapter Thirteen

Our shared inappropriate senses of humor broke the ice, which is what happens when three people, all of whom live lives outside the norm, crack themselves up over their ability to be impolitic together.

An unspoken truce was reached, and we enjoyed Jan's fabulous dinner of steak with a green peppercorn sauce accompanied by tasty mashed potatoes fried into savory bites. I had to admit Nacho was right, and having Jan aboard was going to make this little voyage a culinary delight, and what the hell, sooner or later Nacho would have to let us know why we were *really* hired.

After our soufflé, we took our brandy and retired to the deck again. Lights from several other boats twinkled in the anchorage, but for now we were the largest vessel. Mellowed by good food and wine, I decided to let the big question rest until morning, and we managed to find neutral topics to talk about. Not easy when our history together is rife with turbulence, but I figured recounting our adventures the past summer diving for the remains of a Manila Galleon was fairly safe ground.

"So, you both did a lot of diving?" Nacho asked.

"Oh, yes," Jan told him. "We learned to use rebreathers and helped with the discovery dives. No really deep stuff for us, because I'm just about as much a chicken as Hetta is. And Po Thang got really good at retrieving—"

I kicked her under the table before she could blab that we did a little extracurricular treasure hunting, and Po Thang was masterful at retrieving Spanish *reales* that didn't have a chance in hell of finding their way into the dive ship's discovery records.

"Uh, shells," I said. "He dives for shells. Doggone good at it."

"And did you find the treasures you sought?"

"Nothing earth shattering. As you know, Chino wanted to dig up, literally, some family history. We raised a few cannon and coins before Hetta went and sank his ship."

Nacho smiled. "I heard something of that."

"Hey, I didn't do it on purpose. Those Japanese guys were gonna take us out to sea and feed us to the fish, so I had to do something. How was I to know the ship would get all lopsided and sink?"

"So much gold is indeed heavy." Nacho said this in a matter-of-fact tone.

Rats, he knew about the bullion we'd found in the wreckage of a Japanese WWII freighter loaded with loot meant for the purchase of Mexico. After Japan won the war, which they really believed they would, I guess they figured they'd need to secure their borders from warmongers like themselves, so they made some kind of deal to buy Mexico. Anyway, it was interesting that Nacho knew so much about what we did on our summer vacation. How does he do that?

My uncharacteristic silence snagged Nacho's attention. "And what a shame you had to legally give *all* those Spanish *reales* you recovered from the galleon to the Mexican government." Sarcasm, when not used by me, is annoying.

Jan and I, once again surprised by his implied knowledge of our alleged crime, tried to look innocent, but Po Thang hung his head. It was he, after all, who found those Spanish coins. I could see us in court, pointing and saying, "The dog did it!"

"Of course, if you had, by chance, ended up with a few coins, you'd have a problem finding somewhere to sell them, no?"

We innocents bobbed our heads in unison.

"Unless," he sipped his el Presidente Mexican brandy—which to me tastes a little crude, but he evidently loves, considering he had us buy two cases and then brought a bottle—"you knew someone with connections who could find a market for such things as stolen Mexican archeological treasures, and booty left over from ill-gotten and ill-intended Japanese gold? Not to mention pearls?"

I felt my stomach take a dive, and then my blood pressure soar. "Hold that thought," I told him. I reached over and hit a couple of buttons on my remote, and the Garth Brooks song, "Friends in Low Places" blared from the outdoor speakers.

Jan yeehawed and sprang to her feet. We grabbed our microphones—in this case a couple of empty beer bottles—and sang the opening lines. Nacho looked confused, but when we pointed at him while singing the chorus, "I've got friends in low places," he had the good grace to shake his head and smile at our antics.

When the song ended he raised his snifter. "Bravo!"

We took exaggerated bows.

"So, Nacho," Jan said when we caught our breath, "you wanna be our fence? That is, if we had something to move, which we do not."

His smile widened. "I came to fish, however you may spell it. It seems I may have gotten lucky already." He yawned, stood and stretched. "But for now, I need sleep. Tomorrow we will plan a real fishing expedition."

As he walked away, Disloyal Dawg dogged his heels.

"Sumamabee! He's here for our stash? How in the hell does he know about...well, any of it?" Jan hissed. "I guess that's why they call him The Shadow?"

I snorted into my brandy. "He gave himself that name. His California Drivers license gives his name as Lamont Cranston, a.k.a. the Shadow. I know that because I stole it."

"Old history. He got it back. You think he went to all this trouble to get his hands on our nest egg?"

"Maybe. But why spend forty grand to do so? Nope, he's after something else, and I want to know what. Looks like you're gonna have to sleep with him."

Jan raised an eyebrow. "That's your solution? Why me? It's you he likes."

"Likes? Good grief, I wonder how he treats people *he doesn't* like." I leaned in close and whispered. "Why the hell didn't we put that loot from last summer in a bank safe deposit box instead of in the boat safe?"

"I told you, the Mexican bank wouldn't give us one. We don't have a Mexican account, and I sure as hell couldn't put it in Chino's box cuz then he'd know we stole it."

"Stole is such a harsh word. We...appropriated...our fair share. Of the coins, anyhow. And the gold was legal plunder, in my opinion."

"Chino might not see it quite that way. But you did the right thing for once in your life by giving him the bullion bars you legally plundered, except that one. I mean, it was the least you could do after scuttling his dive ship."

"I did not scuttle...oh, never mind. The Japanese government, or whoever was responsible for stashing the gold on Chino's dive boat, and then stealing said ship, are responsible. I'm sure they've recovered their bullion by now. Almost all of it anyhow." We exchanged conspiratorial grins and clinked glasses.

"Nacho for sure had some kind of connection to those Japanese goons, so he probably knew the gold existed, and they were looking for it. And that they found it."

"Then *you* found it. And since Nacho is familiar with your larcenous proclivities, he figured you couldn't possibly have *not* glommed on to some."

I ignored her insult as to my questionable ethics when dealing with men with no ethics at all. "I think he was either working with them, or against them. How *would* he know for sure we cadged a little booty for ourselves?"

"Well, duh, I think we just told him."

"Crap. We gotta cut back on the booze for the duration of this voyage. Okay, so we kinda gave up the ghost, but why would he be suspicious in the first place?"

"Uh, Hetta, he, like, knows you?"

We cleaned up the galley, which brought Po Thang nosing around to see if there was garbage in need of disposing.

He looked slightly remorseful for his disloyalties, but I wasn't letting him off the hook. "What? Your new best buddy run out of handouts? And you think we're gonna reward that type of perfidy?"

He sat, raised a paw and gave us his best hang dawg look. It worked like it always does.

Since we were now bunking together for the duration of the voyage, Jan and I had to share my queen bed, which was mostly taken up by Po Thang. We kicked him off a couple of times but the minute we dozed off, he crept back up.

We finally gave up trying to keep him in his own bed and I was just dozing off on my tiny sliver of mattress when Jan whispered, "On the bright side, it looks like we finally got us a fence. I was wondering what we were gonna do. No way, Jose, was I going to try and take a bullion bar across the US border."

I yawned. "Amen. We figure our stash is worth over a million if we could legally unload it, half to a quarter of that on the blackmarket, *if* we could even find a shady buyer. Let's say Nacho wants his cut, what do you figure is the normal percentage for a fence's take these days?"

"I dunno. Maybe we can Google it?"

For some reason this struck us as hilarious. Or maybe it was the ridiculousness of the entire situation.

Catching my breath, I gasped, "How many of our friends do you figure are on a yacht in Mexico, with a known criminal type, and a million bucks in gold coins, pearls and bullion they can't get rid of? "

"I dunno, let's Google it."

# Chapter Fourteen

I gave up fighting for my part of the bed during the wee hours, and moved to the main cabin to sleep on the settee. Of course, Po Thang followed me and attempted to horn in on that space, as well, but by now I was completely out of patience with him and let him know it. He settled for sleeping with his chin on my feet.

In a deep sleep, I cursed when the coffee maker burbled and woke me. Nacho was rustling around in the galley. I squinted at the ship's clock: 5:00 a.m. Crap! Nacho is an early riser? Who'd 'a thunk it?

We both got a cup and moved to the back deck to enjoy the sunrise. I wrapped myself in a snuggle blanket Jan gave me that has a bikini-clad woman's body printed on the front. Although one side of his lips twitched when he saw me, Nacho—probably a keen self-preservationist—refrained from commenting. He was dressed in sharp khaki cargo shorts and a Ralph

Lauren Polo shirt, and even though I'd donned sunglasses on the way outside to at least hide puffy eyes, I knew I looked like I'd slept on my head.

Po Thang made his way to the foredeck and used the pee pad, but only after whining for a boat ride to shore. When he returned he made a beeline for Nacho, who praised him and scratched his back right in front of his tail, sending my dog into an ecstasy of wiggles. Faithless furface.

"How would you like to go to shore, my friend?" Nacho asked Fickle.

It is said that dogs laugh with their tails, and if that's true my dog was in hysterics. "Uh-oh you used the G-word. Now you've got him all excited for nothing. Of course he'd love to, but no dogs allowed on the island."

"I can run him over to the mainland beach," he said, pointing toward the distant shore with his coffee cup. "How far is it?"

"Maybe ten miles. You'll make a friend for life," I said, begrudging his generosity because being grateful to him for anything tended to piss me off. I hate it when bad guys do good things that lead me to think they aren't all that bad when I know they are, and then I end up with said bad guy who proves me right in the first place when he jilts me and runs away with my money....

"Hetta? Are you all right?" Nacho stood and reached over to touch my hand.

I snatched my arm inside my blankie. "What? Why?"

"Because you looked so...sad."

I took a sip of now-cold coffee. "Well, I'm not."

"Good. So, are you ready?"

"For what?"

"To go to the beach, *mi Corazón.*"

Hoping he didn't realize the discombobulating emotions he sets off when he calls me that, I sprang up and headed for my cabin. "I'll go get Jan."

Why does "my heart" sound so incredibly sexy in Spanish? Or is it just the way Nacho says it?

Jan and I packed a picnic basket of goodies and a cooler with beer and soft drinks while Nacho rigged fishing poles with hopes of snagging our dinner. Po Thang impatiently whined for us all to get a move on.

Finally, everyone was in the boat and we set off, trolling at a leisurely six knots in a boat capable of doing almost forty. We'd heard reports that dorado—mahi-mahi—were still being caught in the warmer than usual water, so Nacho had rigged for one, using a "lucky" lure he'd made himself using a treble hook and a shredded Mylar balloon. Not sure what the Sierra Club would have to say about that, but it worked and only one fish was harmed. He hooked the thirty pounder halfway to shore, and landed it despite a frenetic dog on board.

We drifted in a light breeze while Nacho cleaned our dinner. The fish fight served as an icebreaker, soothing the tension between me and Nacho for the time being. Our only point of contention was how the fish was to be cooked; Nacho wanted it fried, Mexican style. Jan said nope, it should be wrapped in foil with garlic and lime slices and thrown on the grill. I thought sautéed in garlic/butter/tequila would be grand.

Nacho was leaning over the side, rinsing a filet, when out of nowhere Bubbles swooped in and stole it. Po Thang, delighted to see his friend, jumped overboard, rocking the boat and almost launching

Nacho headlong into the water. When he recovered his balance, he reached into a small cuddy cabin built under the steering wheel and pulled out a Springfield 9mm XDM identical to mine back in Arizona, evidently intending to plug the fish thief.

I had a moment of gun envy before Jan and I executed a perfect double team tackle on him, taking him down onto the boat's floorboards, knocking the gun from his grip. Jan sat on him, pushing his face into an overturned bait bucket of squid parts.

I fondled the gun.


Things were a lit-tle tense at the dinner table.

As a consolation prize for getting roughed up by a couple of women, we cooked what was left of the fish filets the way Nacho wanted them: Deep fried in a *capeador* coating. *Capeador* comes in a powder form and is made with flour, masa flour, MSG, and enough bi-carb to make it fizz when I add the dark beer. Chilled for ten minutes in the freezer, the batter adheres to the cold filets and they puff up when they hit the hot oil. I had to agree with Nacho that it didn't get any better than this. Jan said we were rednecks.

"So, this dolphin, she is yours?" he asked while washing down the last bite of mahi-mahi dinner with a good crisp Domaine des Préauds Pouilly-Fuissé he probably didn't realize set him back fifty bucks. Jan and I are so fond of shopping with OPM. We also enjoy drinking good wine on Other People's Money.

"Not really. I guess she's Po Thang's, if she has to be labeled as anyone's. They are best buds."

It was obvious the wine had a mellowing effect, because he gave me a wide grin and a slight leer. "And you approve of this mixed race thing?"

"We are an equal opportunity boat," I sniffed, annoyed that his question somehow suggested...something.

Jan laughed. "Oh, yeah, we don't discriminate. In fact, Hetta is one of the least discriminating people I know."

"Hey! You two cut it out. Besides, I've had a serious talk with Po Thang about the inter-species thing," I said this with an air of exaggerated solemnity.

Nacho threw back his head and howled with laughter. This set off Jan and me, ending in a tummy hurting guffaw fest. When we finally settled down and started trading laugh lines about our day, tears rolled as we tried to one-up the other with juvenile one-liners like, "What do you get when you cross a dog and a dolphin."

"I do...not...know," hiccuped Nacho.

"A porposeful relationship."

Jan threw her hands in a stop motion, but then said, "Maybe Po Thang thinks Bubbles is a catfish and that's why he chases her?"

"Okay that's it! Everyone just stop!" I turned away so I couldn't see them and we managed to calm down.

Nacho went for a fresh bottle of wine and when he came back I said, "Oh, Nacho, the look on your face when Bubbles snatched that filet out of your hand was priceless. I thought big bad men like you couldn't be rattled, but that Bubbles did the job."

He tried to look indignant, but failed. "She took me by surprise. And by the way, what are you going to do about her?"

"What do you mean?"

"To me this dolphin seems in danger of becoming too friendly with humans, and dogs. Not all of us are kind, you know."

"What are you, then, human or dog?"

"Hetta!" Jan spluttered. "How rude. You must have heard somewhere that old age is charming in the elderly."

"*Downton Abbey*!" Nacho said.

We stared at him, waiting for an explanation. He shrugged. "The dowager countess. Someone said something like that to her in *Downton Abbey*, and I thought it very clever."

"You watch *Downton Abbey*?" Jan asked, clearly surprised.

"Doesn't everyone?" Nacho stood, gave us a regal bow and headed for his cabin, leaving us with our mouths hanging open.

"Nacho's gay?" Jan asked, cracking us up again.

"I doubt it. But Jenks and Chino wouldn't be caught dead watching *Downton Abbey*."

"Even if they did, they danged sure wouldn't admit it."

Hmmmm. That Nacho is surely an enigma.

# Chapter Fifteen

"Why so uncommonly quiet this morning?" Jan asked me while we had coffee on deck.

Nacho had left early in his panga, intimating he preferred to fish without interference from dogs, dolphins, and daffy dames. Po Thang was still pouting at the abandonment.

"Do you ever wonder if there is any such thing as the perfect man out there?"

"I thought we had them."

"They wouldn't like *Downton Abbey*."

Jan sighed. "Who would have thought Nacho was in touch with his feminine side?"

"Wonders never cease. But what I really wonder is why he's here? Other than to rob us blind?"

"I'm fairly certain that's not it. He's up to something, for sure. But why does he need us?"

"Cover? Hiding in plain sight?"

We lapsed into thoughtful silence, until a ringing phone broke in. Rushing down into the cabin, I saw the caller was Jenks. "Hi, Honey! How're things in beautiful downtown Dubai?"

"Where are you, Hetta?"

"Uh, on the boat."

"And where is the boat?"

"In the Sea of Cortez?"

"You know what I mean. Chino called. Evidently a friend of his stopped by to see you and Jan late yesterday afternoon and guess what? Your slip is empty. What's up?"

Jan and I made faces at each other. "Fishing."

"Fishing?"

"Yep, we got bored and went fishing. Caught one, too."

"So, you're back in La Paz now?"

"Uh, not exactly. We sort of decided to go hang out at Partida for awhile. You know how safe it is, what with all the cruisers here. And this time of year, no serious weather is even in sight."

Silence.

Not one to let silence linger I asked, "Have you watched *Downton Abbey* yet? Oops, gotta go. Fish on!"

"Well, Hetta, that was pretty lame."

"What was I supposed to say? He had me dead to rights. I promised to stay put, and I didn't."

"But, *Downton Abbey*?"

"You're right. We're gonna have to tell the guys we're chartered for a month. They won't be happy, but it has to be done. We're caught."

"You first."

I reluctantly called Jenks back and told him about the one month charter. That he was not pleased is putting it mildly. "You what?"

"Oh, calm down. I doubt we'll even leave Partida. Guy just wants to fish and he has his own panga. Besides, I need the dough, and it was the Trob who set it up."

"Wontrobski? Well, that's some consolation. Can't you at least get another crew member to help out?"

"Hey! Jan and I are perfectly capable of handling whatever comes up. This isn't our first rodeo, you know."

"This guy who chartered you. Is he a competent sailor? He could be a problem if he's a greenhorn."

"He seems very capable and familiar with his boat. We'll be fine. I'll report in every day if it will make you feel better." I sounded testy.

"You don't have to report to me, and you know it."

I wasn't sure I liked the way that sounded. Too detached? I wanted him attached without telling me what to do. Now who was being difficult? Get a grip, here, Hetta. "You worry too much," I said softly.

"Hetta, someone has to. By the way, what was that about some Abbey?"

Chino was no happier than Jenks about our latest venture, but reluctantly admitted we were probably fine, considering the time of year and where we were.

He hadn't seen *Downton Abbey*, either.

"Well, that's a load off," Jan admitted while I helped her peel apples for a pie. "We also managed not to mention *who* we had on board."

"Which brings us full circle. Why is Nacho here, and what does he really want?"

"I dunno. Let's toss his cabin."

"Ya think Nacho saw this coming?" Jan drawled after we spent twenty minutes searching his cabin.

I held up the third note we found, this one from under his mattress, each one with the same written message: "Is this any way to treat a paying guest, Hetta?"

"He's got your number."

"Obviously we are wasting our time here. Can we bug his boat?"

"I've got a couple of handy devices with me. Girl can't leave home without a few electronic gadgets, you know."

I wrote something rude on the note and stuffed it back under the mattress before slamming his door shut.

Jan headed for what we call our spy locker and unearthed a bag of goodies we had leftover from a previous caper. "Where we gonna plant these? They're designed to plug into a computer's serial port. And he takes his computer with him on the boat, doesn't he?"

"He has an iPad, and it wasn't in his cabin, so I'd say that's a yes. Paranoid so-and-so probably thinks we'll try to hack him."

"Which we would. Problem is, he's sure to notice a thumb drive sticking out of his computer anyhow, doncha think?"

"Okay, then, I have these." She held up what looked like a ball point pen, and a tiny device about the size of a paperclip. "Voice activated. I'll plant 'em on his boat when he gets back."

"Better than nothing, I guess. However, I think we need to get our bugging guru on the phone."

Rosario Pardo now lives in San Jose, California, with his sig-other, Doctor Devine, a.k.a. Doctor Diane

Powell. She's a marine biologist, and they met at the whale camp when she was hired as Chino's assistant, much to the chagrin, at first, of Jan. First time I ever saw her jealous.

I met Rosario when he stole my Velveeta cheese, a hanging crime in my book. He was on the lam and hiding on my boat while I was away, but Jan and I trapped and hawg tied him, then learned he thought at least one of the people I was working with at the mine conspired to try and kill him. Which, considering the dearth of Velveeta in central Baja, I felt like doing myself. Rosario turned out to be a computer whiz with a bent toward cyber fraud. It is a trait I can admire when used properly. Jan and I learned a few things from him.

When we reached him at his home office, Jan explained our dilemma. He told her an iPad didn't take the devices we had, then asked who we were trying to hack. "Are you completely nuts? You're going to bug Nacho? *The* Nacho who is either a very bad guy, or a very bad guy who kills bad guys?"

"That would be him. He's, uh, sorta living with us."

Since we had him on Skype we enjoyed his expression, which was somewhere between disbelief and horror. "I will not be a part of this."

"You've suddenly developed scruples? You had no problem bugging *us*, if I recall," I shot back at him.

"You would not kill me for it."

"You underestimate me. Come on, Rosario, you owe us."

He sighed. "An iPad?"

We nodded.

He shook his head. "If I had this iPad, I could do something, but otherwise, no way."

"Crappola. Oh, well, is Doc Delish around? I need to talk to her."

He left and came back with Di in tow. Even though still drop dead gorgeous in the centerfold vein, Jan's streak of jealousy was water under the whale now that the doctor was with Rosario. In another country.

"Hey, you two, what's up?" she asked, those enviable green eyes full of curiosity.

"Bubbles."

Hearing mention of his friend, Po Thang jumped to his feet and tore out on deck.

"Huh?" asked Doc Dish.

"Bubbles is a common dolphin I cut out of a nasty net and now she's adopted Po Thang, or vice versa. Anyhow, she follows the boat around, and she and der hund have a thing going. What's up with that?"

"She's alone?"

"Yes."

"Simple. She's lonely. Dolphins are basically social animals."

"The Sea of Cortez is chock full of dolphins. What is she, some kind of porpoise pariah?"

"Nice piece of alliteration. It's not all that normal but on occasion they do travel alone. We suspect these loners reconnect with pods at some point. Why don't you ask Chino about her?"

"Uh, well, uh..."

"Oh, crap. Are you two on the outs again?"

"No, of course not. I'm working with Hetta on a charter."

In the background Rosario said, "With Nacho. "

Diane's eyes grew wide. "Let me guess. Jenks and Chino don't know this?"

"Not exactly."

"You two need keepers."

"Are we the only ones who don't think we're nuts?"

"I think *you're* nuts," Jan said. She sipped her iced tea and put it down on the deck next to her lounge chair. "Evidently I am considered guilty by association."

"Po Thang, how about you? Are we bonkers?"

"Woof."

"See, he doesn't think so."

"Matter of interpretation."

An idea sprang to mind. "Oh, oh, I've got it! Agent double-oh-D!"

Both Jan and Po Thang cocked their heads, Jan in question, and the dog maybe thinking my excitement involved food, or a walk, or something other than the boredom of hanging around on the boat with a couple of chatting chicas.

"Double-Oh-Dawg. Critter cam, and chip."

"Genius! Po Thang, how would you like to go for nice long boat ride with your Uncle Nacho *mañana*?"

"Woof."

Po Thang has the distinction of not only belonging to *moi,* he is also imbedded with a state-of-the-art GPS tracker invented by his Uncle Craig, veterinarian *extraordinaire*. These gizmos are normally implanted in large farm animals so ranchers riding souped up ATVs can run 'em to ground. However, when Po Thang exhibited a propensity for straying like a free range dogie—which I suspect is how he ended up stranded on the lonely mountainside on Baja's Mex 1 where we found and rescued him—we chipped his wayward rear end.

I'd tried a collar unit, but it didn't have the range and wasn't completely waterproof, so when he went to the beach I had to remove it. Po Thang, after all, is a water-lovin' dog. Now, with his embedded chip, and if he's within ten miles, I can find him with my handy dandy tracker unit.

And, when he took to diving for gold coins during our summer expedition/treasure hunt with Chino last summer, we also fitted him with a critter cam, just in case he tried to skim off the top.

And now he had a new mission: Agent Double O Dawg.

# Chapter Sixteen

"*¡No, absolutamente no!*" Tio Nacho declared.

"Aw come on, Nacho. Po Thang likes you, and he's stuck on the boat because he can't go ashore, which, after all is your doing because you want us to anchor here. Before you start fishing, you can run him over to the coast or another island and let him run on the beach for awhile. He won't be any trouble."

"And besides," Jan whined, "we're stuck here all day, cooking and cleaning, while you go off for a fun day of fishing."

"You sound like my first wife. Nag, nag, nag."

Jan and I exchanged a look. Nacho was married at some point? What about now? "First? How many wives have there been?"

"None of your business. *¡Jesus y Maria!* help me, I feel like I have two of them *now*."

"Poor baby. Let me fetch your slippers, pipe, and a nice drink of something tasty. Say, arsenic?"

Nacho stomped off to his cabin. We heard the galumph of the shower's water pump, the length of time he showered grating on my nerves. Water conservation on a boat is important. I flipped off the water pump at the master, thereby ensuring his uber shower didn't last more than three more gallons.

When he emerged ten minutes later, thick black hair water-sparkled, I expected to get an earful, but instead a wide smile revealed extra-white teeth against that beautiful café au lait complexion of his. Either he had hatched a shortened shower-inspired plot to tie me to the anchor and pitch me overboard, or his mood had altered. He shook the note he'd left under his mattress for me to find. "I can see you got my message. You never disappoint."

Rats, he'd booby-trapped his *billet-doux* so if it moved he'd know it. I handed him a glass of water. "Hemlock?"

"I think I prefer a mojito, which I shall make myself so as to control the contents. Anyone else care to join me?"

While suspicious with his turn of temper, I also love mojitos so agreed it was a grand idea. He took his time conjuring up a large pitcher full, carefully bruising mint leaves in blue agave syrup, then adding dark rum and fresh squeezed lime juice.

We moved to the back deck, where he added ice to glasses, and poured us each a drink, garnishing them with mint leaves.

I took a delicate belt and, never one to back down from an unsettled issue, I first complimented his prowess as a *muy macho* mojito maker, then followed up with a, "So?"

"So, what?"

"You gonna take our poor pitiful pup on a boat ride tomorrow? Po Thang, look pitiful."

It had taken me two days, several pounds of chicken, and a ton of patience on the dog's part for me to train him to stretch out his front legs and bow, letting his head droop to his paws, then look up with those begging eyes. Okay, I didn't teach him the beg bit, and in his doggie mind he was probably begging for chicken, but the act was comical. And almost always worked.

"No. And if you don't stop this alliteration thing, I may take you, instead. On a one-way ride."

"Please do," Jan said.

"Alliteration, Nacho? How very...educated, for a drug dealer. But forget me. It isn't Po Thang's fault that you stick us here on the boat all day, every day, with no damned dinghy for shore trips." I jerked my head at Po Thang and used my "pitiful" hand sign. "Just look at the poor, pitiful—"

"Stop! I give up. I'll take him with me tomorrow. But just this once."

"It's all I ask."

Jan and I blew up an inflatable kayak Jenks bought me that had never until that day seen a breath of air. I hate kayaks. Then we launched the paddleboard he figured I'd need. I also hate paddle-boarding. Jan agreed to paddle the kayak and drag me ashore on the paddleboard so we could go for that hike.

Before they left, we outfitted Po Thang in his life vest, complete with hidden critter cam, and tested the GPS chip. We could get minute by minute updates for the GPS locations from the handheld gizmo Craig gave me, but once the Critter Cam left wi-fi range, which was two minutes after the panga sped off, we'd have to wait for video downloads until they returned. Jan had planted the pen and recorder in the panga, but we weren't sure they would work over the outboard noise, since they were sound activated.

The camera lens in Po Thang's collar was almost undetectable if you weren't looking for it, and Nacho had no reason to look. By tonight, we'd at least know where Nacho and Po Thang went today.

Jan packed up food and water and I loaded up notebooks, pens, and the like to record the track of their trip as long as we could.

The minute they left, Jan paddled us for shore, and we raced up the highest hill to get a better handle, and maybe even a visual on our quarry. Luckily Nacho took his time leaving the anchorage, putting along baiting fishing lines and feeding them out.

We, on the other hand, almost broke our necks scrambling up the treacherous volcanic rubble pathway. By the time we reached the top, Nacho was out of sight, but we immediately picked up a GPS reading and Jan marked her chart. Twenty boring minutes later, the boat stopped for a brief ten minutes, then took off like a bat out of hell. So much for Po Thang's long romp on some beach.

Another hour went by. "Hetta, he's running a grid. Look here."

She'd connected the X's she'd made on the chart. "He started here," she pointed to a place on the chart marked as a *bajo*, or underwater sea mount, "and is running a pattern from there. What do you figure he's got on the bottom of that boat besides a depth sounder?"

"Magnetometer? Who knows? He takes his iPad with him, maybe he has something that connects to it."

"I think that's to keep our grubby paws off it."

"There's that. Betcha a peso he's taking underwater videos."

"We'll know more tonight."

By the time Nacho sidled his panga alongside the swim platform late that afternoon, we were back on board anxiously awaiting the results of 00Dawg's first day as an unwitting undercover operative. Po Thang scrambled up onto the main deck and sat, waiting for the mandatory desalting wash down before going further. While Jan concocted his dinner of chicken meat and Kibble, I carefully removed his life vest, rinsed it, and him, and pocketed the camera out of sight of Nacho.

Leaving both the vest and tired dog out in the sun to dry, Jan and I feigned fatigue ourselves, and told Nacho we were going to my room for a pre-cocktail hour shower and nap. He headed for his own cabin to do the same.

Craig, my vet friend in Arizona, had upgraded my critter cam to last five hours on batteries, and Jan and I had integrated the camera into his life jacket so it was barely visible. We knew we had five hours of data to run through, but with a fast scan, we got maybe halfway through in less than an hour, but most of it was useless. There was that brief romp on the beach, then we started tracing their trip by landmarks and the GPS marks on the chart, but really there was nothing but water, water, and more water.

Po Thang's habit of doing his Titanic-nose-point in the bow of the panga was useful until he got bored and curled up for a nap. The only thing we learned from the camera is that he has a propensity to lick his nether parts a lot. He did catch one interesting shot of Nacho taking a whiz overboard—no close up of Nacho's nether parts, much to our dismay—and later landing a fish for dinner.

"We need more," I said, shutting down the video.

"We certainly do. I've always wondered what Mr. Macho had in those shorts."

"That is not what I meant. Besides, I don't care what he has in his drawers."

"Liar."

"Just stop it. What I meant about *more*, is we have to talk Nacho into taking Po Thang with him again tomorrow. Whatever he's looking for didn't get found today. Po Thang looked at him a lot, and even though I couldn't hear Nacho over the engine and water noise, I could tell he baby talked Po Thang. Wish I could read lips. I've gotta get those voice recorders you planted on his boat. Maybe while Nacho makes drinks? Anyhow, since der dawg behaved himself, maybe Nacho actually liked having the company."

Jan was studying the chart we'd marked up. "This *bajo*," she tapped the paper at the underwater sea mount location, "was his focus today. If he goes somewhere else tomorrow, and runs another grid, we'll know he's on a search for sure. But for what, and why so secretive? Seems to me he'd ask us to help."

"I'd say he don't want no stinkin' help."

"One thing we do know."

"What?"

"We're gonna have some seriously buff legs from running up and down that damned hill every day to track him."

"Yeah. Let's carbo-load."

# Chapter Seventeen

We gathered on deck for cocktails at five, Nacho having volunteered once again to concoct something exotic: Mango daiquiris, with his secret ingredient, a dash of cayenne pepper. *¡Fabulosa!*

Sipping and chatting while keeping an eye out for fish, diving birds, all the usual animal life that being on a boat in the Sea of Cortez offers up each and every day, I noticed a dinghy coming our way from the direction of a group of boats at the other end of the anchorage. As they neared, I recognized Karen, Kevin and Puddles the Poodle from the sailboat, *Raisin' Cain.*

Po Thang went all wiggly at spying one of his dock buddies, and I waved to them, hoping maybe they were going somewhere else. No such luck. "Follow my lead," I said to Jan under my breath.

"Hetta!" Karen yelled. "Nice to see you out here." They sidled up next to us and the dogs whined at each other and the large standard poodle reared up and put his paws on the rub rail. Po Thang leaned out for a nose touch.

"You guys going out for a cocktail cruise?" I asked, hoping it was so. I wasn't really up for company, or explaining Nacho.

"Yeah. I see you traded up," Kevin teased, nodding at Nacho's super panga. "Or did *Se Vende* get an extreme makeover?"

"*Se Vende* is history, but the new dinghy I'm having built at the panga factory isn't finished yet. This is a...loaner."

While we were talking the dogs continued yipping at each other and our visitors craned their necks at Jan and Nacho, waiting for an intro.

Crap. "Uh, this is my best friend, Jan, and our—"

Nacho stood, rushed over and reached his hand down. "Jenks Jenkins. Nice to meet you."

The couple exchanged a look, then Kevin recovered and shook his hand. "Well, gosh, Jenks, Hetta has told us so much about you. It's nice to finally meet you. How do you like living in Dubai?"

Nacho didn't miss a beat. "Hot."

The couple chuckled at Nacho's ever-so-clever response, and Kevin said they needed to move on.

"Sure you don't have time to come aboard for a drink?" Nacho asked. Drink came out as dr-INK when I stomped his bare foot.

"Maybe another time. We're heading for the beach around the corner to let Puddles puddle, and take an illegal run. The park patrol hardly ever come out this late."

"Great," I said, a little too gleefully. "Y'all have fun."

"You want us to take Po Thang?"

"Not today. He's already had a run, and we just got him cleaned up, but he'd love a rain check."

Po Thang gave me a dirty look.

Kevin started his outboard and gave us a wave. "Later." They sped away, and over the engine noise we heard Karen say, "Funny, he doesn't *look* Scandinavian. Maybe he's some kind of Norwegian gypsy?"

Jan howled and I scowled at both her and Nacho, the latter of whom was trying to look innocent.

"What the hell were you thinking?" I demanded. Po Thang, hearing the threat in my voice, sidled over, leaned up against Jan and looked as culpable as the real culprit should have.

Nacho shrugged. "It just seemed the easy thing to say."

"Yeah, you're probably right. I was going to introduce you as our boat boy."

His eyes narrowed. "I think there is a racial insult in there."

"Yep."

Dinner was broiled snapper, polenta with garlic and sundried tomatoes, and julienned carrots. The atmosphere was a tad strained after Nacho introducing himself as Jenks, but since that *faux pas* had Nacho on the defensive, I used it to my advantage and dove in for the kill while we dug into Jan's famous flourless dark chocolate cake.

"Jan this is fabulous. Too bad we can't continue to eat like this every day."

Nacho's head jerked my way. "What do you mean?"

"Taking that hike today reminded us we needed more exercise, but Po Thang is a problem. Jan and I can get to shore, but leaving him on the boat is just inhumane, if you know what I mean. Besides, he'll disturb the entire anchorage, howling to beat the band."

As if to confirm this, Po Thang let out a little arf.

"Bottom line? We're gonna have to cut the calories on this ship. It'll have to be salad from here on out," I declared, cashing in on the old adage, the way to a man's heart is through his stomach.

"Salad?" Nacho squeaked.

"Yep, rabbit food. Veggies. Low carb veggies, at that. No starchy stuff like Jan's excellent polenta here. Maybe we'll celebrate every day or so with a strawberry or two."

"What? I hired this boat and with it, meals and crew."

"Well, of course you did. But we didn't provide a menu, did we? Or, who would do the cooking. I think I'll step in and take over the kitchen to make sure we don't all pork up from lack of exercise. Okay by you, Jan?"

She bobbed her head.

*Do we know how to nail a guy where it hurts, or what?*

Nacho certainly looked to be in pain. "Perhaps," he said, "I should take Po Thang with me again tomorrow. You two take a hike," he looked like that might be a double entendre, "and then Jan will cook?"

*Hook, line, and sinker.*

Boat boys can be so gullible.


Day two of Deputy Dawg's surveillance garnered more of the same boring run. Nacho ran another grid pattern, boosting our suspicion that he was on the search for more than fish.

Before dinner—which Nacho would be vastly relieved to see was much more than rabbit food—we downloaded the critter cam video and finally something new popped up.

Almost halfway through the day's cam results, I was roused from an almost comatose state while watching the same water world—and the boat's floorboards every time Po Thang got bored and took a nap—when the picture boggled as my spook jumped to his feet.

Another panga came into camera range and headed straight for Nacho's boat, and our Po-parazzi's critter cam. I couldn't hear his barks, but from the way the camera jerked, he was giving someone an earful. I called Jan over to watch with me.

"That panga look familiar to you?"

She gave me a thumbs-up. "Absolutely. Not many powder blue super pangas around here, and this one is a dead ringer for the one that charged around rocking the anchorage and pissing everyone off right before Nacho showed up."

"Yep, that's what I thought."

As we watched, the blue panga came alongside Nacho's boat. Po Thang scrambled to that side of the boat and was, from the earthquake of movement, raising a ruckus.

"We gotta get a critter cam with sound," Jan grumbled.

I paused the video. "Have you downloaded both our sound recorders yet?"

"Yes, but everything is really muffled. Almost useless. I'll try to tweak it later."

I resumed the video. Po Thang was suddenly jerked back and sat, probably still rumbling but not enough to shake the camera that much. Nacho's hand came into view as he threw out a fender, then caught a line from the guy in the blue panga.

The driver was Hispanic, thick hair cut short, dressed like a yachtie in a tee shirt reading I HEART BAJA, cargo shorts, and a baseball cap. Dark glasses covered his eyes, but even if they hadn't, I knew he was no one I recognized.

Po Thang's head swayed back and forth, following a brief conversation we couldn't hear, and capturing the handoff of what looked like a waterproof bag, and a large red snapper. Po Thang forgot about the interloper long enough to follow that snapper, trying to grab it before Nacho put it on ice and slammed the cooler lid, almost whacking the nosy dog in the snout. We didn't see where Nacho put the bag, because our agent lost interest and went back to terrorizing the panga's driver.

Nacho untied the blue panga and it sped away, and we didn't catch the name because Po Thang was bouncing off the gunwales, showing Nacho what a great guard dog he was now that the threat was gone. We could, however, just make out "La Paz" painted near the stern.

I turned off the video. "Curiouser and curiouser. I'd kill to know what's in that bag. Did you notice Nacho bringing it on board when he and Po Thang got back?"

"Naw, I was being mauled by a large wet dog," Jan said, "but I did notice he had his backpack in hand. Betcha it's stashed inside."

"Most likely. So, we'll have to distract Nacho long enough to search his cabin. We won't need more than a few minutes. You got any ideas?"

"Lemme think." She gazed into space, tapped her cheek a few times and gave me what I knew to be a deceptively sweet smile. "Yes."

Jan has an admirably positive outlook toward problem solving; one could only hope no boat boys would be seriously maimed.

Nacho, freshly showered and dressed in clean shorts and a bush shirt, was cutting limes when Jan and I arrived in the galley later that day. A tantalizing waft of coconut-and-lime scented air drifted our way. Either Nacho had on a new aftershave, or he was mixing some delectable cocktails.

"Ooooh, what's your concoction of the night, bartender?" Jan asked.

"Cocos Locos." We watched as he mixed coconut cream, lime juice, spiced rum, simple sugar syrup—which Jan made in large batches using raw sugar and water, boiled down to a thick syrup—and added club soda.

"Yumsters."

Giving the mix a stir, he asked Jan, "What are we having for dinner tonight? The snapper I caught?"

Jan snorted, subtlety not being one of her major attributes. "Even though we *really* appreciate that fish *you* caught today, I thought we'd have something besides fish for a change. I made a meatloaf, and macaroni and cheese."

By his wide grin, I surmised our Nacho was a comfort food aficionado. And that both Jan's derision and the sarcasm dripping from her "caught" remark went right over his head. He finished his mixing, loaded the pitcher onto a tray with some cheese and crackers

I'd thrown together and we all adjourned to the aft deck, Po Thang leading the way.

After we'd had two drinks each, Nacho asked if we wanted more, a rhetorical question on my boat. As he stood, Jan gave me a wink, then yelled, "Hey! Did you see that?" pointing behind the boat.

Nacho, who was in the process of standing, spun around to check out what Jan had seen. "No, what?"

"Something jumped out of the water! I think it landed in your panga!" Jan rushed down the steps to the back deck, and Nacho, pitcher still in hand, followed.

As planned, I moved near the cabin door.

Jan is both agile and strong, but the way she managed to knock him over the rail and into the water was something to behold. It involved a stumble, a leg wrap, a push, a pull, and a splash. Just to make it look really good, she fell into the drink with him. And, never one to be left out of a good time, Po Thang dove in on top of them.

"Oh, gosh, is everyone all right?" I yelled as Nacho came up spluttering trilingual obscenities in English, Spanish, and Spanglish. Someone's mother, as well as several saints' ears, must have been on fire.

Jan, treading water well out of Nacho's threatening reach, laughed and yelled, "We're okay, Hetta. Come on in, the water's fine."

"I'll pass. I'll be right back with towels."

Racing into the main cabin, and Nacho's quarters, I found his backpack and quickly located and removed a pouch we saw the blue panga dude give him. Inside was a thumb drive, so I raced to my computer, quickly downloaded the contents into my computer, and had everything back where it belonged just as I heard them pulling themselves up the swim ladder, onto the dive platform.

Grabbing a stack of towels, I hotfooted it back on deck to find all three of them on the swim platform, dripping dry. Jan and Nacho were laughing, a good sign that he wasn't going to kill her. Po Thang waited until I got within range to give a mighty shake, making sure I got drenched, as well.

After we all showered and were in clean, dry clothes again, I found another pitcher to replace the one lost overboard, and Nacho threw together another batch of Cocos Locos.

Returning to the back deck where our eventful Happy Hour adventure began, Jan took a gulp of her drink and said, "So good. Nacho, sorry about that unscheduled dip. I can be so clumsy sometimes. But you gotta admit it was kinda fun."

He grinned. "Yes, but please, let us not make it a habit. I forgive you, but only because you made macaroni and cheese."

"My pleasure. Hetta'll go down and get that pitcher off the bottom tomorrow morning before you take off, right Hetta?" She gave me a meaningful look, the meaning of which escaped me.

"Hey," I protested, "why do I have to—"

Her head tilt, raised eyebrow, and wide eyes reminded me of part two and three of our plot.

"Oh. Sure. No problemo. What time are you going fishing tomorrow, Nacho?"

"Actually, I must make a run into La Paz for fuel and a few other things. I thought to go tomorrow. I will fish on the way in, and back."

"Cool," Jan said. "We need to get more fresh veggies, booze and a bunch of other stuff. What time shall we leave?"

"Well, uh, I didn't..." he shrugged in defeat. "Nine okay with you?"

"Sure thing. Hetta, you comin' with us?"

"Nope. Po Thang and I'll have a spa day. Maybe I'll do our nails."

Po Thang looked up at the mention of his name and gave me a tail thump.

Little did he know he might be in for a Harlot Red pedi.

# Chapter Eighteen

It took two dives to retrieve my Waterford Crystal pitcher which, while totally impractical on a boat, is still my favorite. It was resting on the sand in twelve feet of water, and was none the worse for wear after being dropped by Nacho on his unscheduled dunking the evening before.

More importantly, as part *deux* of our hatched scheme, I also got a gander at the bottom of Nacho's boat while I was down there, and underwater shots of some equipment that was definitely not like anything attached to *my* boat's hull. I'd been on a dive boat most of the previous summer, and from what I could tell Nacho's boat was equipped with sonar and underwater cameras.

Jan and I ran and re-ran the contents of the thumb drive I lifted—and hacked—from Nacho's backpack the night before, but were left more baffled than ever.

Not that being in a state of confusion is all that unusual in my case, but even with all our snooping, we were no closer to discovering what Nacho was up to on those daily forays of grid-running. One thing for sure, it was *not* fishing.

The minute Jan and Nacho shoved off for La Paz, I turned on a wonderful toy we'd gotten the year before from Rosario, our sometime partner in crime, hacker nonpareil, and techie-snooping genius: a tiny GPS tracking receiver we found in our bag of tricks. I picked up an immediate readout from the other end of the GPS device, the one in Jan's jacket pocket, but would soon find a home in some well-concealed compartment on Nacho's boat before they returned.

We'd decided to plant the GPS sending unit in case Deputy Dawg wore out his welcome on Nacho's daily trips. The new gadget had a twenty-five-mile range and I checked it repeatedly until I lost the signal in less than an hour. So much for Nacho fishing on the way into town; not many fish are going to hit a hook being dragged at thirty-five miles an hour.

Once I lost the signal, I moved my laptop to the sundeck table, planning on enjoying the solitude while rechecking that thumb drive's contents I'd downloaded the night before, just in case we'd suffered a Coco Loco induced attention deficit attack. After running through it again, I saw we hadn't missed a thing, but by the coordinates we knew it was a combined Google Earth printout, and an aerial video of the same area of the site where Nacho had been running that search of his.

Jan and I guessed he was using his own underwater cameras, GPS coordinated, along with Google Earth and video to find something. But what?

Jan called me on my satellite phone mid-afternoon. "Having a good time without me?"

"Actually, yes. I have newly red hair, and Po Thang and I both have Harlot Red nails. He's not too happy about it, but I think the nails complement his coat. How was your run into La Paz besides fast?"

"Smooth as a baby's butt. We made it pronto."

"I figured as much. I lost the GPS signal pretty soon after you guys took off, but all systems are a go. Have you planted your end yet?"

"Not yet. My end is planted on a barstool at the Dock Café right now. Nacho just left for parts unknown in town, and I'm still trying to decide where on his boat is the best place to put the tracking device."

"Hide it well, Sherlock. What time you getting back? Want me to put something in the oven for dinner?"

"That's why I'm callin'. When we got into the marina this morning they had a message for you. Your new pangita can be delivered tomorrow if you want us to wait for it."

"Super. You've made my day. First, I'll get an entire evening of peace and quiet, and we'll have wheels of our own when Nacho takes off every day. Where are y'all gonna stay tonight?"

"Nacho says he has a friend in town he'll stay with. When I spring my Jeep from the parking garage, I'll get my emergency overnight bag I always keep in it, then check into that little hotel right by the marina. I'll shop for groceries later today, so let me know if you think of anything else we need. The hotel has a fridge and freezer to stash everything in until we pack up to come back to the boat tomorrow. The panga factory guy says they'll deliver your dinghy around ten, and then we'll head back, but we gotta take time to refuel."

"Call me on the radio when you get within range and I'll check our tracking."

"Roger that. Have you figured out what you want to name your new dink? I can pick up some vinyl stick-on letters at the chandlery."

"Not really. I'll miss the old *Se Vende*. Maybe I'll keep the name. I'm glad I went ahead and bought that new fifteen horse Evinrude before we left, but I've only got two five gallon jerry jugs of gas. How about picking up another jug and fill it while you guys are at the fuel dock."

"You've got it, Chica. *Hasta mañana*."

"*Hasta*."

After I hung up with Jan, I contemplated what to do with the rest of my glorious folks-free day. Without a dinghy, I was pretty stuck on the boat, and with my newly tinted locks, I wasn't tempted to take a color-stripping salt water dunk. I knew I could call Karen and Kevin, who were still in the anchorage, and beg a ride, but didn't relish giving up my day alone.

As will happen when faced with a major decision, I took a nap.

When I woke, I was momentarily disoriented. It was dark, and I was on a sundeck lounge chair, wrapped in my bikini print blankie. Po Thang's low growl accompanied the distinctive ka-chunk sound of anchor chain links clanking out of a windlass chock.

"Hush, Thang. It's just a sailboat dropping anchor."

I unwrapped myself and went to the flying bridge. The sailboat's running lights were still on, as was his anchor light. Po Thang, on point, rumbled unhappily at this interloper who had the nerve to anchor near his boat. Matter of fact, I let out a little growl myself when I realized the boat was much closer to us than I like, and in an area a little too shallow for the average sailboater's comfort zone.

"Must be a charter," I told Po Thang. "Let's just hope the wind doesn't come up and he drags down on us."

I realized my own boat was completely dark and flipped on the deck lights, lest the new arrival hadn't seen us. However, when I looked up at my own anchor light, a solar powered job, it glowed brightly. Okay, so they saw us and anchored too close anyway. Charter for sure.

Not willing to re-anchor to get away from this annoying boat, I went into the galley to find us dinner. I opened the fridge and spotted the snapper filets from Nacho's "catch" the day before. "Some catch, huh? He caught it when that blue panga dude handed it to him. But, hey never look a gift fish in the mouth. How would you like your fish prepared this evening, sir? Sautéed wiz zee *buerre d'ail*? Or perhaps béarnaise sauce?"

Po Thang didn't seem to care, so rather than go to the trouble of making béarnaise, I smooshed garlic cloves with the flat of a large knife, added the garlic to butter and olive oil in my great-grandmother's iron skillet, and put it over low heat to gunch—culinary technical term—before turning up the heat and adding the fish. I popped some of the leftover mac and cheese into the microwave, which reminded me to check my battery levels after dinner, what with the microwave being the arch enemy of batteries. I rarely ran it unless the generator was running, but I felt like living dangerously.

By some miracle I found half a bottle of Pouilly-Fume in the fridge, right next to the container of mac and cheese. The odds of these two things surviving intact overnight on *Raymond Johnson* made me wish I'd bought a lottery ticket.

I gave Po Thang some dried dog food with sautéed snapper mixed in, but he gave me a glower that said he knew I was eating mac and cheese, and not sharing.

"Okay, here's the deal," I told him, "finish the dried stuff and, even though I know better, I promise to save you a large spoonful of mac and cheese for dessert. I wonder if there is such a thing as doggie Beano? I'll have to ask your Uncle Craig."

He stared at my plate.

"Eat. Your. Dinner."

Glare with woof.

"I mean it."

Whiney growl.

I turned away and protected my food with my arms. "I'm not looking at you," I singsonged.

Yip.

"You're driving me nuts here. Oh, what the hell, stop your grousing." I spooned mac and cheese into his bowl. Dog discipline is not my strong suit. Good thing I never had children.

Finally left to eat my meal in peace before it got cold, I shoveled down the mac and cheese first. Out of sight, out of doggy mind, right?

I finished my dinner, making sure, just for spite, that there was not even a tiny piece of anything left, and put my plate down for him to clean.

Pushing into my seatback, I took a sip of the perfectly chilled crisp white wine, then sat up straight, my head swiveling toward a sound. Was that bagpipe music? Coming from the sailboat anchored right next to me?

Great Scot!

# Chapter Nineteen

The bagpipes gave a last gasp, as only bagpipes can, and about two minutes later I heard Sean Connery's voice on my VHF radio. "*Raymond Johnson, Raymond Johnson, Full Kilt Boogie.*"

"Po Thang," I told my dog, "I really should not answer this, right?," even as I reached for the mic.

His tail wagged in agreement. Either that, or he thought I said "You want an entire T-bone steak?"

"*Full Kilt Boogie*, this is *Raymond Johnson*, switch to 88." I chose eighty-eight because most boaters don't have that channel on autotune. Why have everyone in the anchorage reading my mail?

I switched from channel sixteen to eighty-eight and waited. A minute later, Sean called and I answered. "Hetta here. That you next to me?" Like I didn't know.

"Aye. We keep bumping up against each other, so I thought it time we actually met."

*Or bumped up against each other for real?*
*Bad Hetta!*

"Uh, sure. Want to come over for coffee in the morning?"

"I thought to bring you a bottle of wine tonight."
Oh, well, I tried. Right?


I had time to brush on blush and pouf my hair before his dinghy bumped—that word again!—against my swim platform, and Po Thang banged up against the locked doggie door trying to get out of the cabin.

Releasing the hound, I followed to find a hunk of Scot—unfortunately, no kilt, just shorts and a tee shirt—already on my back deck, petting the formerly furious dog, who was chewing on an oversized dog treat. My dog has a keen affinity for palm greasing. Kinda like me.

Accepting my own kind of treat—a bottle of wine—from his large hand, I stuck out my own paw. "Hetta Coffey."

He bowed and kissed my hand, which sent an electric shock through my body. Looking up into my eyes with his green ones, he said, "Artherrrr MacKenzie Gra-ham. Mac to my friends." Putting his other hand over mine, he held on until Po Thang, thinking there might be another treat involved, nosed our hands apart.

Rattled, I stammered, "Uh, welcome aboard?"

"It is my pleasure. Nice dug."

"Huh?"

He patted Po Thang's head. "Yer dug."

Po Thang gave him a lick. Fickly dug, in my book.

"Wine!" I yipped.

"Aye."

It seemed we were inventing a new language here.

A glass of good burgundy goes a long way toward breaking down language barriers. I thanked him for his help with the rescue of Bubbles two weeks before, he praised my bravery for tackling the job by myself. A mutual admiration society.

Although I'd told myself I wouldn't have a second glass of wine, I did.

We talked about where we came from (Stornoway, Isle of Lewis/Austin, Kingdom of Texas) why we were in the Sea (stop on the way to the South Pacific and around the world/I wish I knew), careers (Corporate Sales/Engineering consultant), and the like.

The bottle was soon empty, and I made a grownup decision not to open another. Then, as wine will do, it changed my mind. I stood to get another bottle when my Satfone rang.

Does Jenks have a sixth sense about such things? Here I was, on the brink of getting drunk with a hunk, when up pops Jenks on Skype. I told him to stand by, went out to tell Mac I had to take the call, and he got the hint and left.

"Sorry about that. A neighbor stopped by and I was just saying goodnight."

"You still at Partida?"

"Yep. The water is still a swimmable temperature, and no northers yet this year. Matter of fact, I went for a swim this morning. And guess what? The new dinghy is ready. Jan's picking it up tomorrow morning." The minute I said this, I feared I'd opened a can of worms.

"Jan's in La Paz?"

"Uh, yes. Our charter folk," I thought this sounded better than charter dude, "had to go in for fuel for the fishing boat, so she caught a ride. We're running through our fresh fruit and veggies. One thing we have plenty of is fresh fish."

"Wish I was there. I'm getting real tired of hotel food. So you've got the boat to yourself, huh? I know you don't like people on the boat that much. Maybe this charter will cure you of wanting to do any more of them. Are the guests nice?"

"We're getting along just fine." I was a little wine-fogged, and was trying desperately to remember what I'd told him so far about the "folk" we had on board. A good liar, I am a less than stellar remember-er. I always remember what others have to say, but me? I sometimes mess up. Maybe someday I'll just start telling the truth?

A pig flew by.

After talking with Jenks, I buttoned up the boat and went to bed with my Kindle and dug. I read a few minutes, heard a splash outside, got up and rechecked my locks, went back to my book, heard another splash, looked out again, and was back in bed when I realized Po Thang hadn't even twitched an ear. I trust his instincts and keen ears, so I read until I drifted off into a deep sleep.

Which ended at six a.m. with the arrival of Bubbles.

Po Thang was ecstatic, and spent a good two hours in the water with his aquatic buddy while I gave the boat a good cleaning, inside and out. We'd rinsed the boat with fresh water and squeegeed the windows when we'd arrived, but it was time for some boat soap and elbow grease. I consider it my boat aerobics.

What I've never figured out is why, when you're floating in the water, miles from the nearest road, and there has been no wind, I get dirt all over the boat. I keep a fresh-water foot bath for dipping off sand and salt water when boarding, and a no-shoes rule past the entryway from the swim platform. Po Thang gets a wash down every time he goes in the water or on shore. And yet I found myself scrubbing, then rinsing, brownish tinted water all the way down from the flying bridge.

Jan's radio call let me know they were on their way with an ETA around 11:30, so I wrapped up my boat chores, threw together a tuna noodle casserole, and popped it into the oven.

Back on deck as I was hanging wipe-down rags over the rails to dry, the unique harmonic of a bagpipe gave me an emotional charge. I've always had a drippy response to the pipes, maybe leftover from hearing the incomparable version of the "Amazing Grace" melody played against that low drone, or something. Whatever, it gives me goose bumps, and sometimes makes me tear up. Mac and his pipes were becoming serious mind messer-uppers.

Not everyone shared my fascination with Mac's pipes, for as soon as the bagpipe wailed, Bubbles performed a couple of high leaps and took off like a shot, out to sea, leaving Po Thang paddling in confused circles. He couldn't see her wake like I could from the boat, so he dog paddled around a bit, waiting, before giving up and launching himself onto the swim platform. He whined while I washed and rough dried him, then sat on his towel in the sun, gazing longingly out to sea. Love can be so cruel.

"I know, Honey. Been there. There was this ski instructor—"

Po Thang barked and thumped his tail, then Nacho's low rumbling engines preceded his entry into the anchorage. My new dinghy trailed behind him.

Yippee. Wheels!

Jan embraced my exuberant, but still damp dog while Nacho and I maneuvered my new dink alongside *Raymond Johnson*, and tied her off where I'd already deployed fenders.

"Hetta, look at the transom," Jan told me.

I walked aft where I could see the back of the pangita. In large black letters, I saw, *Po Boy*. I laughed and Jan asked, "So, you like the name?"

"Yes, I do."

"Oh, good. I wanted to surprise you."

"What if I didn't like it?"

"We'll peel it off. It's only electrical tape, but I bought that vinyl lettering kit for the permanent name."

Bagpipes piped and Jan spun around. "You are kidding me. I leave for one lousy night!"

Nacho had also turned to listen. "Who is that?"

"Hetta's boyfriend," Jan said.

"Not so."

"So."

"Hetta has a boyfriend? I mean besides Jenks. And me?"

I threw up my hands and stormed to the galley to check on the casserole. Jan followed, still laughing. "Jeez, Hetta, we were just kidding you. Why so touchy?"

Letting out a long breath, I admitted, "I honestly do not know. Bagpipe music makes me cry, and he keeps on playing the damned thing."

"He just quit, so you can dry those crocodile tears."

I gave her shoulder a backhanded tap. "Oh, shut up. Let's put away the groceries and have lunch."

Nacho made several trips to his boat and hauled in goodies for Jan and me to stow. We probably had enough on board now to provision the *QEII* for a transatlantic voyage.

We'd just finished putting everything away when the timer dinged. "Let's eat! I'll bring the casserole, Jan you grab the salad. Nacho, get the plates, napkins, and silverware. Everyone get what you want to drink."

"Aye, aye, *capitán*," Nacho said as he grabbed four plates. "Oh, I invited Mac to join us. Hope you don't mind."

I was the last up on deck, carrying the heavy, still bubbling, Le Creuset casserole dish with both hot-pad covered hands. I'd tucked an ice cold Tecate under my arm and when Mac saw me coming, he rushed over and removed the beer from my freezing arm pit. His knuckles brushed my boob in the process.

My cheeks flamed and I almost dropped our lunch.

Jan, who was watching the whole thing with a smirk, asked, "Hetta. That new blush you're wearing?"

"Hot dish!" I declared.

"I couldn't agree more," she drawled.

I plopped the casserole on a trivet in the middle of the table and tromped on Jan's bare toes under the table.

"Ouch! Watch it, Hetta."

"Oops, sorry," I crooned, looking down. "Hey, is that a new nail polish color? It's really good at covering up that fungus."

Nacho intervened by pushing a chair seat into my knee backs, forcing me to sit. He threw a napkin in my lap and popped my beer tab. "Glass for *madame*?" he asked.

I shook my head and took a long pull directly from the can.

Nacho, still in his maitre d' mode, asked Mac what he wanted to drink.

"Did we finish that great bottle of Burgundy last night, Hetta? If not, I"ll take a glass."

Jan lowered her sunglasses and waggled her eyebrows at me.

Nacho's mouth fell open.

Mac waited for an answer.

I chugged my beer.

# Chapter Twenty

After an awkward silence when Mac spilled the beans about us sharing some wine the night before, the conversation became stilted and the meal was quickly over. Mac returned to *Full Kilt Boogie* and Nacho decided to knock the saltwater off *his* boat, and also volunteered to mount the motor on my new dink, *Po Boy*.

"Awkward! Your Scot sure has a way of dumping cold water on polite conversation," Jan drawled as we washed the dishes. "But on the bright side, your casserole was a winner. Fresh tuna always makes the diff."

"You didn't help matters, putting him on the spot like that. Whether he has a significant other is none of our bidness."

"Maybe not, but he sidestepped the question and changed the subject in a hurry, didn't he? I'm just looking out for you."

"I told you, nothing happened!"

"I don't doubt it for a moment. I mean, you, alone with a handsome hunk who obviously has the hots for you? What on earth could possibly have happened?"

I whacked her with the dish towel. "We shared a bottle of wine and talked. Then Jenks called on Skype, so I sent Mac packing."

"Sounds like Jenks has excellent timing."

"Oh, come on. Give me a little credit."

"Surely you jest. I have known your ways for far too long. But, hey, anything you say." Then she giggled. "Did you see the look on Nacho's face when Mac brought up your little wine fest last night?"

"Nope."

"Bull. I think he's jealous."

"Well, maybe that'll teach him to invite people for lunch."

"Hello? He *is* the paying guest. I think that gives him some privileges."

"I guess, but first he tells people I know from the dock that he's Jenks, and then invites Mac for lunch. I may have to cut those privileges. This is *my* boat."

Jan snagged a piece of tuna from a plate and offered it to Po Thang. He took it, but not with his usual enthusiasm. "What's with him?"

"He's pouting. Bubbles showed up today and they played for awhile, but then she took off like a shot when she heard Mac's bagpipe."

"Interesting."

"What's interesting?"

"Out at the whale camp Chino and I have noticed that dolphins and whales are actually drawn to music, not scared off by it."

"Do you ever play bagpipe recordings? Maybe they don't like it for some reason."

"They love those best of all. Maybe Bubbles just doesn't like your new boyfriend."

"He's not...oh, never mind. Mac helped me save her life, how could she not like him?"

"You're asking me? She's your dolphin."

"*My* dolphin. *My* boyfriend. Cut it out."

"Okay, okay." Then she grinned. "I have gossip, by the way."

"Oooh, dish!"

"Word has it there was another giant squid attack."

"Crap, just when we thought it was safe to go back into the water. Where?"

"East of here. Out in the Sea, and...wait for it. Wait for it. Wait—"

I threatened her with my Grandma's iron skillet held high over my head.

"Close to where Nacho has been running his grid. Coincidence? You be the judge."

"Holy crap, that is way too close. No more swimming for you, Po Thang, that's for sure." Then a wash of dread made my stomach drop. "Do squid eat dolphins?"

"Chino told me only sharks and Orcas feed on dolphins as a rule, but a giant Humboldt, especially a huge one almost the size of this boat? Any danged thing it can catch and shred."

"Gee, thanks for that mental picture. I didn't need to sleep tonight anyhow. Who did the squid get this time?"

"That's not clear. It was all over the radio that another diver had died, but no info on whether it was a *gringo* or a Mexican."

"But it was near where Nacho goes almost every day? Could he possibly be looking for Humboldts? And if so, why? What did Nacho say about the attack?"

"He's skeptical, but that's about it. He really didn't want to discuss it. Did you figure out what was on that thumb drive you copied from his room?"

"Not really. Looks like an aerial shot. Not from a satellite, but maybe a small plane. With the coordinates, I know about where it was located, but all I can see is water, so who knows? One thing for sure, though. Nacho is getting an outside assist from someone in his search for whatever it is."

She glanced out the hatch. "He's still washing his boat. Let's take a look at those photos."

Down in my cabin, I locked the door and brought up what Nacho had on the thumb drive: a series of still shots of water, water and more water. No land identifiers, nada.

Jan pointed to a spot of lighter blue. "Can you zoom in?"

I did, but the only obvious clue was that the water was shallower in that spot. "Could be a reef," I speculated, "or a *bajo*; we know there's more than one sea mount out there, so that's what it is."

"Are all the pictures like this?"

"Pretty much. The last five look a little different." I fast forwarded through the photos until I hit one that was not like the first ten.

"Those are underwater shots, so obviously not taken from a plane. I'll bet these were from Nacho's boat and he planned to use them as an overlay or something. Interesting, I guess, but—" I was rudely side-butted out of my chair by Jan.

She grabbed the mouse, enlarged the picture in one spot, and whispered, "Bingo."

"Bingo? What do you see?"

Pointing to the screen, she drew some imaginary lines with her finger.

I leaned in, and now that she said it, there did seem to be a brownish area with rectangular patterns not found in nature. "You're right. An anomaly. Just what Chino taught us to look for last summer when we were searching for that wreck site."

"Field trip?"

"For sure."

Nacho had mounted the fifteen horsepower outboard on *Po Boy*, so I hooked it up to a red five-gallon gas container I'd filled back in La Paz before we left for Partida. My new nine-foot pangita was made from a mold originally designed by Malcolm Schroyer, a *gringo* credited with making the first fiberglass pangas in the Baja. I'd heard talk of this small panga, which was no longer in production. Not one to be put off when I want something badly enough, I tracked down the mold in a warehouse in La Paz and had a local panga factory make one just for me. And I wonder why I'm always broke?

I took my new snazzy dink for a test run, then returned for Jan and a very annoyed dog who, like me, hates being left behind.

After stowing a heavy duty fishing pole, my tackle box, a handheld radio in case we ran into trouble, and our life jackets aboard, we slowly motored out of the anchorage and then I opened *Po Boy* up. We were up on a plane on the smooth sea and whizzing along at a good thirty in no time. My new rig performed seamlessly. We reached the *bajo* using my handheld

GPS coordinates and slowed to look for those anomalies we'd spotted on the photos.

One thing for sure, we were not going into the water to look for them when there were reports of murderous Red Devils—not that a nine-foot panga was much protection against a thirty-foot monster—but I wanted to get a feel for the area. And Jan had a plan for snagging one of whatever those brown things were down there.

Jan dug a huge treble hook out of my tackle box, and lowered it until it touched bottom, then reeled in. It came up clean.

"Rats. Try again," I said, "but look at that wind line out there." I pointed out to sea at the white ripples that had suddenly raised on the surface. "We'd better not stay out here long."

She gave the treble hook two more tries as I kept an eye on the seas, but no luck.

A gust hit us. "We gotta make tracks, Chica, here comes the wind. Matter of fact, we're gonna have to take the shortcut from the east side of the island. Hang on, team!"

Heading south with the wind and building seas at our back, my new pangita rode the chop like a champ, but we passengers got plenty wet. In no time we rounded into the cut and were completely, thankfully, protected from both wind and spray. The afternoon sun beat down on us and we quickly warmed up.

I'd traveled through the shallow, winding channel that cut between the two islands several times, but only at high tide, and I was riding with someone in a rubber inflatable at the time. Even then, there was no more than three feet of water in the deep spots.

The tide was going out fast and even though my new pangita had only a foot and a half draft, that was when unloaded. We were forced to get out of the boat and push and pull *Po Boy* through the cut.

Po Thang, Parque Nacional rules notwithstanding, ran freely back and forth on the sand, splashing across the shallow, narrow pass in front and behind us as Jan and I, shuffling our feet in hopes of not stepping on a stingray, pulled the heavy dinghy with two lines. I cringed every time Po Thang splashed into the water, hoping he didn't get nailed with a barb. It had happened twice before, and the time it takes to get to the boat and heat a pot of very hot water for his paw— thereby stopping his pain—is nerve-wracking for both of us. I was going to have to write a letter to the Reef Runner manufacturers about maybe making doggie versions.

Jan and I loudly hummed "The Song of the Volga Boatmen" and interspersed the only words we knew—"Yo, heave ho! Yo, heave ho!"—like the Russian barge haulers of bygone days. We also broke out into a lively version of "Chain Gang."

With a bare six inches or so of water under her hull, *Po Boy* occasionally grounded on a lump of sand and we'd have to rock the gunwales to break her free.

"I need a break," Jan declared. That sun didn't feel so grand anymore, and we were both fairly winded from slogging in the soft, wet sand bottom, pulling a barely afloat hundred and twenty-five pound dingy with a sixty-five pound outboard motor and thirty-five pounds of gasoline. "Can't we hook the danged dawg up and make *him* drag the boat?"

"He's a retriever, not a huskie. Besides, we're almost there. Put yer back into it me matey! Heave ho!"

"Yeah, well heave—hey, where's Nacho going, and why's he towing *Full Kilt Boogie*?

153

We watched as Nacho's boat, with Mac's sailboat in tow, slowly motored out of the anchorage and turned northward.

"Gee, Hetta, was it something you said?"

"Very funny. Wonder where they're off to? Not that I care, but neither one of them mentioned leaving. This is weird." I reached into the dinghy, pulled out a waterproof pouch and removed my handheld VHF radio. "*Nacho, Nacho, Po Boy.*"

We waited. No reply.

"*Full Kilt Boogie, Po Boy.*"

Nada.

"Okay, let's get this puppy into deeper water and go after them,"

Jan had her hands on her hips and was staring back at my dinghy. "Not unless you've got a shovel, Vladimir."

*Po Boy* was sitting in a pool of water, but her bow chine was wedged in the sand in less than six inches of water. And, the tide definitely outgoing.

"I'll remove the gas tank while you unload anything else that'll come out easily. We may have to dismount the outboard, as well. Gimme your earrings."

"What? These earrings?" She fingered one of the bangles. "Chino gave me these. What do you want them for?"

"Cuz I don't wear earrings?" I held out my hand and she reluctantly handed over the big shiny gold hoops. "Po Thang! Here boy!"

Po Thang loped up to us and skidded to a halt with his tongue hanging out the side of his mouth and a silly grin on his face. He shared his coating of seawater laden sand with us and sat panting, waiting to see what was in the works.

"Hold his collar, Auntie Jan."

"Got him."

I dangled the earrings in front of his nose, just out of lunge distance. He almost pulled Jan off her feet, but she recovered and dug her heels in while I scooped a hole in the sand barrier entrapping our pangita, then buried the shiny treasures in it.

"Hey! I see what you're up to, and you better hope it works, or you're gonna be digging out here until you find 'em again."

"Never fear. Let the beast go."

Po Thang pounced on the earring burial ground and began an excavation surely to end up in China. He quickly unearthed one earring and tried to run with it, but Jan was ready for him. She snagged his collar and buried her heels again, commanding him to "Sit! And leave it." He gingerly deposited the earring on the sand, Jan jammed it into her pocket, and he went back for the other one. Several repeats of the retrieval game, and he'd cut a channel just deep enough so we could pull the boat forward.

"Such a good dog!" we told him, and rewarded him with hugs.

Finally afloat in the anchorage, we loaded our gear and ourselves back into *Po Boy*, but had lost at least three-quarters of an hour since we watched Nacho and Mac leave.

"Think we can catch them?" Jan asked.

"I don't even want to try. It's too choppy now to go north into it, and with a new boat and motor, I just don't think it's a good idea. And on top of that, it's getting late, the motor is new, I don't know its range and don't want to guess us into a dangerous situation. Let's just go back to *Raymond Johnson*. Maybe Nacho left us a note."

"He doesn't have to report his comings and goings to us, ya know."

"Maybe not technically, but if he wants another decent meal on this cruise, he'd better start."

I washed Po Thang down while Jan went inside to check for a note. "Nope. Nothing!" she yelled.

Toweling off my dog, I yelled back, "Okay, turn on the radar. I'll be right in."

By now, the boats were no longer painting— nautical speak for showing blobs—on the radar screen, as we were blocked by a hill right in the wrong place. I fiddled with the radar, hoping to get something while Jan went for our new espionage tool, the GPS locater she'd planted on Nacho's panga. Getting a strong signal, she plotted his position on our master chart. "Looks like they're abreast of Los Islotes."

"Islotes is eight miles or so north of here. Maybe they decided to go for a dive with the sea lions. But why take both boats? And why when the wind is up."

"Call 'em again."

No luck.

"Gee, I'm still sure it was something you said, Hetta."

"And that's still not funny. They're on the move, but not very fast. Wonder where they're going? Not that I really care, but neither one of them mentioned leaving before we took off in *Po Boy.*"

Po Thang looked up expectantly and we both laughed. "Maybe naming the new pangita you-know-what wasn't such a bright idea. Your poor dog is going to be in a constant state of confusion."

"Then we'll be equals. Dammit, I know you think I'm a stone-cold control freak, but Nacho taking off without a word pisses me off."

"I remind you, he doesn't answer to you."

"True, but he'd better turn that boat around pretty soon. I mean, who's gonna mix the drink of the day?" I asked as we secured my new dinghy for the night, and replaced the gas tank with a full one. Now we were ready for another run if need be.

We also took the time to remove the name, *Po Boy*, from the transom, and replace it with the vinyl letter set Jan brought. *DawgHouse* seemed appropriate.

Later, in the galley, Jan pulled toothsome tidbits from the fridge while trying to lighten our worries about Nacho by singing, "Got along without 'em before we met 'em!" an old tune we both loved.

"What's for chow? I mean, customer on board or not, we gotta eat?"

"I've got it all planned out, but first, we both need a shower. Po Thang smells better than we do after that slog through the cut. Then I'm gonna make canapés. If Nacho doesn't get back for dinner, it's his loss, 'cause I'm gonna cook up that yellowtail we snagged on the way in from La Paz this morning."

"More for us," I said flippantly, but I felt less than flippant. This control freak had no control over a worrisome situation, which is never a good thing.

By the time Jan made her famous guacamole and I put together a batch of Margaritas from a mix, light was fading fast. Checking the GPS locator again, I saw that Nacho's boat was headed east now, out to sea. "Okay," I said, "I never thought I'd hear myself say this, but I'm getting a little worried about Nacho."

"Oh, come on, admit it. You have a teensy weensy crush on him."

"Do not."

"Do too."

Arguing this subject with Jan was a waste of time, so I asked, "And you're gonna tell me *you* aren't in the least bit intrigued with our bad boy?"

"Nope."

"Liar."

She stuck her tongue out at me, and I did the same to her. Maturity might not be our strong suit.

"What I don't understand, and don't take this wrong," she said, "is that both Mac and Nacho have the hots for *you*. What am I, chopped liver?"

"I don't care, because if you're jealous of me, my day is made. My month. My year. My—"

"Am *not* jealous. It's just that…"

"It's just that for twenty years you've been the man-magnet and I've been Cinderella, *way* before the slipper thing."

"That is not what I meant, at all. I can certainly understand why Nacho's enchanted with a woman who threatened him with death by flare gun, blew up his buddy's truck, stole *his* fancy off-road rig, and tried, on several occasions, to kill him. You're his kind of chick. But Mac? I dunno, it kinda seems too…convenient."

"Okay, I'm taking this the wrong way. Want another Margarita?"

"Is there a cow in Texas?"

While we finished our second pitcher, Jan grilled the yellowtail filets and whipped up a lime, butter, tequila and diced *habañero* chile sauce. I made a salad.

As we did almost every night, we took our grub and a bottle of wine to the sundeck. We'd just finished eating when I spotted a set of running lights coming into the harbor, and from the looks of it, they could belong to a super panga. And despite my protestations of not worrying about Nacho, I felt a wave of relief.

# Chapter Twenty-One

"Jan! Incoming navigation lights! Looks like a super panga to me. Maybe Nacho's coming back?"

Po Thang rumbled. Nope, not Nacho. Dang.

But the boat was definitely headed our way, and the regular pangas from the fish camp behind us didn't even have running lights. If they used any illumination at all, it was a flashlight or a propane lantern, which, coupled with their habitually leaky gasoline containers, was a serious hazard to health.

I flipped on the outdoor spots aimed behind the boat, which was Po Thang's cue to rush onto the swim platform and snap at leaping fish. Any thoughts he had of an approaching panga were no longer anywhere in that space between his ears. Then, as though a switch turned on, he remembered and barked a warning as the panga entered the circle of light.

"Well, well," Jan said. "The mysterious blue panga."

Since Nacho's boat was gone, the driver sidled alongside the swim platform and waved, then threw out fenders, making it obvious he planned to tie up to us.

"What do you think, Hetta? Fiend or friend?"

Po Thang, whose back hair was up as he stood his ground on the dive platform, vociferously voted, FIEND! I called him back to the sundeck, and miracle of miracles, he loped up the steps. I think he was looking for an excuse to back off without seeming like a sissy.

"Good dog! Jan," I whispered, although the motor on the panga would blanket my words, "get the flare gun while I talk to this dude. We know he, or someone else in this blue panga, met Nacho out at the *bajo* and handed over the aerial shots, which doesn't necessarily make him a villain. But, better safe than sorry. Boy, do I miss my guns!"

"Not any more."

"What do you mean?"

"I sorta lifted Nacho's piece from his panga, and hid it in our groceries. It's behind the cereal in the pantry."

"What? Why didn't you tell me?" I was elated for a second, then a thought hit me. "Oh, hell! What if Nacho needs it right now?" Then reality set in and I slapped myself. "What am I saying? Jan, I have never been prouder. Get that puppy."

Jan was right back with Nacho's big handgun in a plastic bag. Stepping up to an outdoor light I peered in and saw it was chambered. Had I known it was ready to blast away at the touch of a trigger, I would have fetched it myself, but luckily Jan's carrying it in a bag precluded any chance of an accidental discharge.

However, I vowed she and I were going to spend some time familiarizing her with how not to handle a gun.

With my back to our incoming visitor, even though I knew he couldn't see me past the glare of the spotlights trained on him, I released the magazine and cleared the chamber. There were nineteen bullets in the clip, which I slammed back in place. Racking one into the chamber, I slipped the ejected shell into a pocket, and the big heavy handgun into the other. It weighed that side of my shorts down, so I pulled on a windbreaker to cover up the obvious bulge.

Now armed with eighteen chances to wipe out any threat, I twitched my lip a la Clint Eastwood.

Jan cracked, "I see I've made your day. Is that a pistol in your pocket, Chica, or are you just glad we have company?"

"Let's just say we're geared up to entertain in style."

Our visitor sidled alongside and I recognized him as the same guy on the critter cam. "*¡Hola!* I am look *por* Señor Ignacio."

"Aren't we all?"

"*¿Mande?*" Which means something between, "What?" and, "Excuse me?"

"Why are you looking for him?"

"I 'ave," he dangled a pouch similar to the one we found in Nacho's cabin containing the thumb drive we "borrowed" and downloaded, "uh, *mesaje*."

"A message," Jan said.

I held out my hand. "You can give it to me."

He shook his head, stuffed the pouch deep into a cargo pocket in his shorts and zipped it closed. "*No es posible. Solament el Senor Ignacio. ¿A donde es?*"

"Wouldn't we like to know? *Aya,*" I waved my hand toward the northeast. "*Posible el bajo.*"

He made a show of looking confused, as though he had no idea where the *bajo* was. So, not willing to give him a clue we'd *seen* him there, with Nacho, I threw him a bone. "Maybe fishing."

"*En la noche? Porque?*"

That was a strange question from someone who looked to be trying to pass himself off as a an upscale Mexican fisherman; they generally fish at night. But, oh well, the charade must go on. "Why at night? I don't know. *No se.* Jan, take over here. I've just about run out of Spanish."

"Let's invite him up for a beer, and grill him like that yellowtail we just ate."


Our visitor, Javier, was fairly lubricated by his fourth beer. A handsome young man, muscular and probably in his twenties, he was a good boat handler and I suspected from a fishing family like so many others youths in the Sea. Now, however, he was working as a courier, and as such had been sent out with an urgent message requiring hand delivery. Urgent enough, he confided with a note of pride, for them to send him out at night.

He was to hand off the pouch to *el señor* Ignacio only, anchor, sleep in his boat, then return to La Paz at first light with something Nacho was supposed to give him. What, he didn't know. He was upset at failing to do what he was sent to do, and hoped *el señor* would return before morning.

No amount of beer, or even a generous serving of mac and cheese—something he said he had never eaten, but loved—made him give up that pouch. Nor did Jan's mile-long legs and blonde hair manage to entice him to stay on our boat for the night, or even tie up to us while he slept on his own boat.

Jan suggested that if Nacho didn't return, we all go out in Javier's panga the next morning and search for him. This, Javier agreed to, albeit reluctantly.

"Maybe he'd like to call his boss and explain the situation?" I suggested to Jan with a hidden wink in her direction..

He seemed uncertain about the idea, but another beer convinced him he would be better off letting whoever was jerking his chain back in La Paz—or wherever—know that *el señor* Ignacio, and his boat, were amongst the missing.

And when he did make that call, *we* would then have the phone number in our duplicitous little hands.

"Jan, give Javier another beer. I'll go down and turn on the satellite system. I'll yell when he can call his *jefe*."

She nodded, knowing full well I was on my way to set up the phone to record every word on both ends. Poor unsuspecting Javier went along like a lamb to slaughter. Evidently Mexican women are more trustworthy than *gringas*. Especially *these gringas*.

I'm not sure how Mexican women operate, but many southern women never argue with their men, but somehow get their way. I was about fourteen, and already butting heads with my dad, when Mom gave up the secret: Let them think they are in control.

Of course, she didn't say it like that, because the word, *control*, wasn't popular yet. Nope, but I watched her in action over the years, and sure enough, by the time she brought up something that might seem in the least bit contentious, he was already on her side, and yep, he thought it was his idea in the first place.

Unfortunately I missed inheriting that grace gene, but have instead developed some serious deviousness skills.

Which is probably one of many reasons I am still single at forty.

While Javier was making that call I raised and wiggled my eyebrows at Jan, and tilted my head. "Yoy know, Janster, if anyone could get her hands into that guy's pants, it would be you."

"I ain't no pickpocket."

"Dang. I want that pouch."

"Then get it yourself. You want me to rope and hawg-tie him for you?"

I knew she was serious. She'd spent considerable time in the rodeo circuit in high school, and even college. "Naw. I want him to trust us."

We both howled at that idea, because we'd given Javier a false sense of privacy by leaving him to make his call. Hopefully, what with the beer and being alone in the cabin, he'd say something to his boss he might not have otherwise.

He wasn't on the phone but a few minutes, and then he thanked us for his beer and grub and boarded his panga to go anchor out for the night. Before he left, I nudged Jan to pose the question we thought might possibly change his mind about staying on board *Raymond Johnson* for the night. "Javier, Honey," Jan's voice fairly dripped with sincerity and concern, "aren't you worried about the Red Devils? Your boat is so open."

"*No, señorita.*"

"Why? People have been dying, we hear."

He shrugged. "*Mala suerte*." Bad luck. He crossed himself and jumped in his boat, evidently content to let God take over.

We waved and Jan yelled, "*¡Que le vaya bien!*" which is something like "May you travel well," but in this case I translated as, "Good freakin' luck when a ten-foot, sucker-laden tentacle grabs you, and stuffs you into a hellacious beak that chews you into steak tartar!"

It's the thought that counts.

# Chapter Twenty-two

Javier, thankfully un-chewed by my imagined slimy devils, was waiting for us at first light, sitting quietly in his panga he'd silently tied—totally unnoticed by anyone onboard *Raymond Johnson*—to my swim platform.

I was going to have to dock my guard dog's salary.

Jan whipped up a hearty breakfast for four while I surreptitiously checked my secret GPS tracker. Nacho's boat was right where it had been the night before. Weird. Why would he anchor on the *bajo*? And why had he towed Mac's boat out there? Maybe they wanted to do a night dive, in spite of rumors of squid attacks? And even so, why wouldn't either of them answer the radio?

And then there was that conversation we recorded the night before between Javier and his boss.

When the phone rang and on the other end we heard a gruff, "*¿Bueno? ¿Quién habla?*"

"*¿Capitán? Teniente Morales aqui.*"

I hit the pause button and tried to shut my mouth, as did Jan. We aren't easily shocked, but I'd say this certainly did the job. We said, at the same time, "*Lieutenant* Morales?"

Jan circled her finger impatiently, urging me to hit PLAY again.

I did, but paused every few words for her to translate, as I was only catching about every third word of the rapid fire Spanish. Basically it went like this:

Javier: "Lieutenant Morales here."

Captain (after a long pause): "Where are you?"

Javier: "Caleta Partida, aboard *Raymond Johnson*. The women are here, but not Mr. Ignacio. His boat is gone. What are my orders?"

"Is he expected back tonight?"

"He was not expected to leave. The women seem surprised he left and even more worried that he has not returned. Do you wish me to go out and look for him?"

"No, I think not. We will stay with the original plan."

"Okay, then. I have been invited to stay on Raymond Johnson for the night, but I declined."

"Good you did. I understand those *gringas* can be devious."

"I believe this to be true. They really want to get the pouch, I can tell. They have suggested we go look for Mr. Ignacio tomorrow morning."

"Play along. But be careful and—How are you calling me? There is no cell service out there."

"The satellite phone on the *Raymond Johnson*."

"*¡Mierda!*"

The line went dead.

"Devious, huh? Well, I guess he's got *your* number, Hetta."

"My number? Pot calling the kettle black, if you ask me. So, obviously looks can be deceiving. Javier, whom we thought to be a sweet, gullible little fishing panga dude, is a freakin' lieutenant in something or other. What? Navy? Police?"

Jan threw up her hands. "Got me."

"Which branch of the service might matter. I hear the Navy is more trustworthy than, say, the Federal Police."

"Which means they probably wouldn't be working with Nacho."

True, Nacho is not the guy you want dating your daughter, but after I got over the fact that he might not be a real drug dealer—when he saved my life by offing one—I also know he's no choir boy. He has, however, hidden virtues. Well hidden.

For now, I just wanted to find out where he was, and what he was up to. Javier, whether some kind of fed or not, and his blue panga, were our best bet for locating Nacho. Even though we now knew Javier was a lying sack of ca-ca.

Chomping at the bit to get underway, we bolted down breakfast at the speed of Po Thang, tossed some sodas, cheese, and bread into a cooler in case we didn't get back for lunch, and took off.

"Where do we go?" Javier asked as we exited the anchorage.

"The *bajo*. And don't even try to ask me where it is, you little twerp."

"*¿Mande?*"

"*Mande*, my ass. You heard me."

"*¿Mande?*"

I wanted to strangle the dude, but Jan elbowed me out of the way and smiled at him. "To the *bajo* northeast of here," she said sweetly. "I will show you the way."

"I'd like to show him the way straight to hell," I mumbled, but neither Jan nor Javier heard me over the roar of the engines when Javier pushed them to full speed.

I turned my back to him and took a peek at my GPS tracker. Jan mouthed, "No change?"

I shook my head; Nacho's boat remained right where it had been since last night.

Jan stood next to Javier, he pretending to let her show the way, she pretending to show him where to go, and me pretending I didn't long to pull Nacho's 9mm from my backpack, stick it in his ear, and force him to tell us everything he knew. I hummed a few bars of, "The Great Pretender" by the Platters. Jan gave me a thumbs up.

"There!" Jan yelled, pointing to Nacho's boat.

Po Thang scrambled out of a deep sleep to bark in that direction. The boat looked ominously deserted, no movement on board I could discern. There was, I knew, a very small cuddy cabin under the steering console one could, in case of extremely violent weather, cram into, but you wouldn't want to stay there for long. And there certainly was no room to lie down.

Javier skillfully brought us alongside. The deck was deserted and the little cabin door had swung open. There was obviously no one aboard.

I caught my breath when we saw the mess. "Oh, hell, Jan. Please tell me that blood is left from when you guys caught the fish on the way in yesterday."

"You know it's not. Nacho scrubbed the boat down."

I started to board Nacho's boat, but Javier grabbed my arm, holding me back. "No!"

"What's wrong?" I said, a pretty stupid question in light of blood all over Nacho's decks. And just as I said it, something moved, and what looked like a huge worm writhed its way in our direction. All three of us jumped back in alarm, knocking Po Thang, who'd seen the thing and lunged toward it, for a loop.

It stopped coming at us, but still squirmed, contorting as though in pain. Not a worm, I realized, but an eight-foot tentacle, leaking blood and what looked like ink from where it had been crudely hacked off.

Jan scooted as far away as she could, dragging Po Thang by the collar. He, too, squirmed, but only half-heartedly tried to get away after he got a good look at that horror on Nacho's deck.

Javier unclipped his boat hook and prodded the tentacle, which wrapped itself around the handle and jerked. Throwing hook and all at the monstrous thing, he joined us on the other side of his boat. With three adults and a dog huddled on one side of his panga, we listed dangerously close to the water. Water I had no intention of getting dumped into.

If I was as pale as Jan, I figured we were both in shock. Javier was a couple of shades of brown lighter himself. Po Thang knew something was drastically wrong, and whined in sympathy.

I said it first. "You don't think Nacho...." I couldn't finish.

"Oh, god, I hope not. What are we going to do?"

We both looked at Javier, who picked up his radio. Now that we were out of the anchorage, he could reach La Paz. "*Capitanía del Puerto la Paz, Capitanía del Puerto la Paz, este es Treinta.*"

When they answered almost immediately, he told them, in lightening fast Spanish, of a deserted boat found anchored on the *bajo*.

He did not mention the still squirming *tentáculo*. And I tucked away, in my still fear-numbed brain, the number identifying his boat, *Treinta*. His boat was *La Paz Thirty*. Sounded official, but what branch of official?

The rest of our morning was rife with officialdom, several members of which looked at me with suspicion, as this was the second time in just a few days I'd been associated with a boat abandoned under mysterious circumstances.

Heck, I was feeling guilty myself.

They bagged the tentacle, which had finally quit moving, swore each of us to secrecy about its existence, and finally, around one, we were allowed to return to *Raymond Johnson*. We diverted straight for the nearest beach for a way overdue potty stop for dogs and humans alike. We could have jumped in the water for a pee, I guess, while we were out there by Nacho's boat, but what with that tentacle as evidence of very large Red Devils about, no way.

We didn't talk much on the way to *Raymond Johnson* even though Javier wasn't running full speed, and we could hear each other. What could we say? Nacho had most likely met a grisly death out there, and there was no explaining it. What was he doing at the *bajo* last night, and why did he go without telling us? Or at all. And even more confounding, why did he tow *Full Kilt Boogie* from the anchorage, and just where were Mac and his boat anyway? All questions we had no answers to.

We had not informed the authorities, or Javier, about Mac. Why complicate the whole thing and involve a guy who probably had nothing to do with Nacho's disappearance? Or did he?

Javier came aboard for a sandwich when we got back, but said he had to leave almost right afterward for La Paz. His cell phone had pinged a signal just as we were about to turn into the anchorage entrance, so he slowed the boat and made a quick call. He repeated to someone (the Captain?) exactly what he'd told the police and navy dudes, but this time he mentioned the tentacle. He quickly held the phone away from his ear as we all heard a blast of cursing from the other end. He listened until the guy calmed down, and told him he'd be back in a couple of hours.

As I made him another sandwich to go, Jan gave him a Coca-Cola Light and tried to convince him to show us what was in the packet still tucked into his shorts pocket, the reason he came out in the first place. We'd concluded that Nacho was our friend and perhaps whatever was in there might help find his...him.

Javier steadfastly refused to give it up.

Okay, it's not like we didn't try.

# Chapter Twenty-three

Pantsing, or debagging, had it's origins at Oxford University when students wore loose fitting slacks called Oxford Bags. They became the target of pranksters.

It was still practically Dorm Pranks 101 when Jan and I went to college, despite being labeled a form of sexual harassment back in the seventies. The seventies? That decade was reputed to be a cesspool of free sex, drugs, and debauchery, which Jan and I lamented not being old enough to participate in. Seems like a little pantsing was fairly mild by comparison.

So, along with Jan's goat roping and hog tying skills left over from a misspent youth in 4H, she'd refined the art of the pants. However, now that we knew we were dealing with a trained soldier of some sort, we had to be fast. And devious.

Jan opened her arms wide to hug Javier goodbye, much to his surprise. He stood with both arms hanging down, looking at a total loss for what to do when she captured him in a bear hug not unlike some chick in a World Wrestling Entertainment's Diva Division match. As soon as she had him fast in an iron clutch, I stepped around them and yanked his cargo shorts down around his ankles.

Po Thang, liking the looks of this new game, lunged, clamped his teeth onto the shorts and proved to be a pretty slick yanker, as well; he threw both Jan and Javier off balance. Both went down cussing to beat the band while Po Thang held fast and continued to play tug of war. I, on the other hand, filched the pouch from Javier's pocket, ran into the cabin and locked the door behind me.

We'd already placed my computer right inside the door, so within seconds I downloaded the thumb drive from the pouch into my computer, and was back on deck, winded but chuffed with success. The man/woman/dog pile was still untangling themselves—mostly due to Jan, who was watching for my return—so I grabbed a joyously cavorting Po Thang by the collar while stuffing the pouch back into the shorts my dog had pulled completely off Javier.

I handed Javier his cargo shorts, which he snatched and shimmied into while grumbling and hopping on one foot, then the other.

"*Gringas*! Gah!" he spat, and jumped into the boat and escaped.

FYI, Javier is a tighty whitey guy.

"So what next?" Jan asked as Javier left the anchorage, shooting us a one-fingered salute on the way out.

"I dunno. I guess becoming best buds with Javier is out."

"We'll be lucky if he doesn't come back and slit our throats in the dead of night."

"The man has no sense of humor."

"Let's take a look at that thumb drive. Maybe it will give us a clue as to our next move."

The thumb drive was identical to the last one we stole, with much of the same content. After comparing the screens side-by-side on our computers we were no more enlightened than before. We even slowed it down, synchronized the shots on both our computer screens, but saw little change. Maybe a few white caps that were not present in the sister screen, but nothing else jumped out at us and yelled, "Aha!"

Jan went to the galley and returned with two iced teas just as I finished going over those videos for the fourth time. "Anything?"

"Nope."

"Not even a panga?"

"Not even." I took a sip of tea and stood to stretch my neck. I'd been hunched over the screen for over an hour, playing with the images any way I could.

"So, what should we do? Stay put and hope Nacho surfaces?"

"Oh, Jan, that was such an inappropriate choice of words," I scolded, then in spite of trying to maintain some modicum of decorum, burst into laughter, which devolved into deep sobs. Tears brought on by unfitting laughter, sadness, or just plain old hysteria, I wasn't sure. "God, I'd kill for a Valium or three."

Jan patted my shoulder. "Hetta, Nacho isn't the kind of guy who ends up dead at the tentacles of a giant squid."

I wiped my eyes, and took a ragged breath. "You're right. He's almost surely destined for a firing squad."

"See? Always look on the bright side."

"What time is it?"

She glanced at her bare wrist. "Five o'clock somewhere."

With our master mixologist missing, we reverted to plain old wine before dinner. The way I was feeling it might be *instead* of dinner.

We watched pelicans diving for their own evening meal, gliding in circles, their bellies glowing green from a reflection off the turquoise water, and marveled at a National Geographic moment when an osprey dive-bombed the surface and scooped up a large pipe fish. It was touch and go for awhile, with the fish thrashing wildly while the bird fought to gain altitude. The bird won.

The anchorage had cleared out some, and I counted only six boats besides us. We listened to the Happy Hour on ham radio to find out what the weather guessers had to say, and learned we might get a pretty good blow in a couple of days.

"I guess we'd better make a decision before the blow if we're going to move."

Jan, who was trying to capture action shots of the Pelicans downing fish nodded. "Yep. Once the wind starts we're stuck. If you can call anchored out in paradise, stuck."

"Right now I'm a little skeptical about the paradise thing. Shall I recap?"

She put down her camera and grabbed her wine. "If you must."

"This is such a hot mess I hardly know where to begin."

"Never stopped you before. How about starting on that day you had the harebrained idea to buy a boat? Or then take the boat to Mexico? Or—"

"Wontrobski!"

"Bless you."

"Smarty pants. We need to call Wontrobski. He's the one who started this whole thing."

"Actually your parents did, much to their dismay, I'm sure. But right now I think you're right. After all, he's the one who set up this charter."

We went to the Satfone and called the Trob. He and his wifey poo, our friend, Allison—along with a wee one I secretly called a Trobite—were preparing to debark for their new home in Dubai, where Jenks was doing the ground work for relocating Baxter Brothers Corporation, my former employer, from San Francisco to the Middle East.

"Yo, Trob," I said when he answered from his office high atop the Baxter Brothers building in downtown San Fran.

"Hetta, Jan, what can I do for you?"

The Trob is a man of few words, and even fewer social skills, so no small talk necessary. "You can tell us about this freakin' charter you arranged."

"What's wrong? You run out of wine?"

Jan and I exchanged a look of amazement. Was that a joke? Good grief, fatherhood must be working miracles. But then again, I'm sure the little tyke was uninterested in discussing algorithms with her dad, the genius.

"Wow, a touch of humor. I'm dumbfounded."

"Hetta, why did you call?"

So much for chitchat. "Nacho is missing, his boat has been towed into La Paz by the Mexican Marines and several federal agencies, it looks like he might have been attacked and killed by a giant squid, and we don't know what to do next. We're anchored north of La Paz where he wanted us to be before he went missing. Do you think we should stay here and wait, or return to La Paz?"

"Who is Nacho?"

"Houston, we have a problem," Jan drawled after we moved back outside to watch the sunset and discuss this surprising, and possibly really ugly, turn of events.

"No kidding. At least the Trob is on the job trying to follow the money, but without a client telling what he wants, what are we to do?"

"I vote we sit tight until after the blow. If we haven't heard from Nacho or who ever the hell set this charter up, we go back to La Paz, run him to ground like a feral hawg, and beat the truth out of him."

"I like your style, Miz Jan. Okay, doing nothing is up for a vote. All in favor say Aye. All opposed, find another boat."

We clinked glasses.

"However, there is one thing we have to do that cannot wait much longer. We gotta dump our holding tanks, and we'd better get 'er done early tomorrow in case the wind gets here before the weather guessers think it will."

We decided to pass by the *bajo* on our way to dump our black water tanks, a necessity of boating in Mexico that would give the United States Coast Guard a heart attack, but there is no choice.

Unlike many boaters in Mexico who don't even have holding tanks or have the annoying habit of dumping into an anchorage or even marinas, I have steadfastly done my best to go out at least three miles, on a strong outgoing tide, to dump mine.

*Raymond Johnson* has two heads, and two holding tanks. Normally I use one for pee, which is highly diluted with water and I have no problem dumping overboard, and the other for #2. No toilet paper goes into either system.

What with Nacho staying in the guest cabin, both heads were used for both functions, so it was time to go out to sea and purge the tanks. My waste management system uses only fresh water, and I treat the tanks with an additive that kills bacteria, so what it left is a brownish liquid that doesn't smell wonderful, but is designed to do no harm except to the sensibilities.

I know, *way* Too Much Information!

# Chapter Twenty-Four

We headed out for our black water dump just after first light, hoping to avoid those first swells from the north that show up before the real wind actually arrives in the southern area of the Sea of Cortez. We had already listened to an early ham net that had boaters reporting winds picking up overnight in San Felipe, in the far northern section, so we knew we only had a few hours at best before things started getting lumpy.

Even though we steered for the *bajo* as soon as we rounded the north end of the island, as expected, there was nothing to see. Evidently the powers investigating the strange disappearance of Nacho had done everything they intended to and left. Had this kind of thing happened in the States, there would still be divers down and boats stationed on site for days, but this is Mexico. 'Nuf said.

After the dump, we returned to the *bajo* and lingered long enough to drop a couple of treble hooks to see if we could snag any of the brown stuff we tried to get the last time we were here in my pangita. On her third try, Jan yelled, "Hetta! I've got something!"

I'd been holding the boat in position as best I could in a growing swell and running tide, so I couldn't leave the bridge. "Whacha got?" I asked, leaning over the rail to see.

"A piece of something we've seen before. I'll bring it—Oh, hell!"

While I wasn't paying attention a williwaw out of nowhere caught my boat, and a large swell hit us right on the beam. The boat took a big enough roll that I worried we hadn't secured for sea like we're supposed to, and the entirety of my fridge's contents were splattered all over my galley floor. Po Thang would be delighted.

I quickly steered into the swell, stabilizing the boat, and looked back to see that Jan had grabbed a railing. Po Thang, however, who had been leaning over the gunwale watching Jan try to bring up what he hoped was a fish, was gone. Jan's cursing and calling his name raised my worst fear; he was overboard, and visions of that tentacle flashed into my mind.

"Where is he?" I yelled.

"I'm on it. I'll get him. I've got a visual!"

"Dammit I should have tied him up here. I'm going to neutral so we don't hit him with a prop. Hold on tight, cuz we're gonna roll for a few minutes!"

I took the engines out of gear, deployed the anchor from the bridge, and let it run out faster than usual in my haste to get us stopped, but I knew the wind was pushing us back fast enough for the chain not to foul the anchor. We were only in twenty-five feet of water on the sea mount that rises from hundreds of feet under the sea, so I stayed put at the steering station, playing out a hundred feet of chain before stopping the windlass. The anchor bit firmly and we swung bow-in to the swell with a satisfying tug. As least something was going our way for the moment. Grabbing two life jackets, I went down to help Jan.

She'd already pulled the pangita to the swim platform in case she had to go after Po Thang. Since we were securely anchored, I lifted the dawg overboard life sling from its stanchion mount while Jan kept an eye on Po Thang, just like they taught us in Coast Guard classes.

Holding the 150' of looped line in one hand, and the horseshoe shaped floatation collar in the other I asked, "Where is he?"

"There!" Jan yelled, pointing about three boat lengths behind us. I'd trained him to swim to the float, making a game of it. So Po Thang, looking totally unconcerned at his sudden dunking, paddled happily towards the yellow collar against a strong current and wind. He's a powerful swimmer and had on his life jacket, so I wasn't worried he'd drown; my worry was a monstrous slimy Red Devil that may have already devoured Nacho was looking for dessert.

While I pulled the collar with the line, keeping it just out of reach in front of him, much like the fabled carrot-and-stick trick, Jan stood on the swim step, egging him on with sweet talk.

In a burst of speed, he outfoxed me, gained on the float, and threw his front paws over it. I pulled in the line, hand over hand, as fast as I could, and breathed a sigh of relief while Jan clapped and cheered.

Twenty feet behind the boat, he yipped and suddenly dipped under the surface.

Jan was in the water before I could even register what happened. She made a clean dive and popped up eight feet out, yelling, "Hetta, stay put! You may have to haul both of us back!"

Feeling helpless, I quickly retrieved the sling, then, when Po Thang popped up I threw it at him so Jan could see it. He ignored it and swam in circles, as though searching for something beneath him. I tied off the ring and ran for the gun.

By the time I got back on deck, Jan had Po Thang by his harness and her arm looped through the ring. "Pull, damn it! There's something in here with us!"

Terrified, but certainly no more so than my best friend had to be, I hauled as fast as I could, fighting the drag of the water and the combined weight of Jan and a sopping wet dog. Terror, however, has a way of making one super strong and I had them to the platform in two minutes.

Cleating off the ring, I clambered down the steps to the swim platform, where Jan was attempting to boost Po Thang's furry rump to safety. He wasn't cooperating, and kept trying to go back into the water. I grabbed his life jacket harness and clipped him to a leash I leave permanently affixed to the back rail just in case of some kind of fiasco like this one.

"Come on Jan, you get out of the water. We'll haul the bugger up whether he wants to come or not. Then, when he's safe, I'm going to murder him!"

It took both of us to drag his contrary butt onto the main deck, where I shortened the leash so he couldn't go anywhere. He struggled against his restraints, barked and yelped, looking back into the water.

"Hetta, there is definitely something down there! Shoot it! I've got the dog."

She didn't have to tell me twice.

My hands were slick and shaky as I assumed a two-handed stance and searched for a target while trying to maintain my balance on the now pitching deck.

"Jan, we don't have time for this, we gotta go before someone gets hurt."

"Okay, wait, there!"

By some miracle, considering the river of adrenaline coursing through my system, I didn't commit dolphin-cide when Bubbles broke the surface, vaulted skyward, and gave us a pirouette.


"Dolphin repellant. We need dolphin repellant," Jan groused as we got underway.

Po Thang whined and strained against his leash. Both he and Jan were still dripping salt water all over the bridge, so I had a major clean up on my hands when we got back to the anchorage.

I was already running the watermaker at full capacity to ensure we had enough fresh water for the job, with enough left for a few days. According to the weather gurus, it would be at least five days before we could go back out again, and I don't like to make water in the anchorage, especially when there's a blow stirring all kinds of stuff up in the water.

"When we get back in, let's call your Doctor Chino and ask him if there is such a thing. I have heard of shark repellant. Bubbles is becoming a real pain in the back fin."

"Or, you know what? She might have saved Po Thang and me? We still don't know for sure she wasn't protecting us. Maybe there was a squid down there with a mind on Dawg Burger."

"Or Jan Burger. What were you thinking, jumping into the water like that?"

185

"Obviously, I wasn't. I just reacted. Won't happen again." She patted Po Thang's soggy head. "You hear that? Next time you're on your own."

"For sure. The ever-unanswered question is, did he jump or did he fall?"

"Uh, I think that's, 'did he jump or was he pushed'?"

"Is Nacho dead or just missing?"

"Or, is he et up? Or just a floater?"

"Nice imagery, Miz Jan."

The wind was increasing little by little, as were the swells, both giving us a great sleigh ride back to the anchorage. My two wet friends were shivering in their towel wraps, but I found the breeze refreshing, as it cooled my raging blood pressure. This cruising stuff ain't all Margaritas and mariachis.

I put on a few turns, anxious to put the hook down and let my dog and best friend get a warm shower.

Our favorite spot was still open, mainly because no one else likes the shallow water. I did move us a little to the east, into twenty five feet of water, to soften the yank on our ground tackle during the big gusts. I also let out extra scope as extra insurance we'd stay put. The bottom in this part of the anchorage was pretty good, but I'd dredged up a rock or two on previous outings, so I backed down with more gusto than usual. Only when I almost jerked us off our feet was I satisfied that we were firmly entrenched for the duration.

I shampooed Po Thang while Jan went inside for a hot shower, then began the boat clean up to remove all the salt water. I knew that with the gusts throwing salt spray during the upcoming norther we'd be coated again, but at least, for now, we wouldn't be tracking salt into the interior.

Keeping salt off a boat in salt water is like trying to keep Po Thang away from food. A lost cause, but I do my best.

"I'm starving," Jan declared when she showed up to help me scrub the decks and wipe down the brightwork I'd de-salted.

"How's about you make us something wonderful while I finish up here. I'm Jonesing for...well, good grief, look what the storm dragged in."

Jan turned as *Full Kilt Boogie* sidled up alongside, gave us a wave, turned into the wind, and anchored nearby. "He's got some nerve! Hetta, just shoot him."

"Whoa there. He doesn't know we saw Nacho's boat towing him out of the anchorage. Let's play stupid."

"Right now I'd call that typecasting."

# Chapter Twenty-five

Mac secured his boat, dinghied over and was greeted with a one wagging tail and two large doses of skepticism. Our plan was to let him do all the talking, maybe incriminating himself.

"Ahoy, *Raymond Johnson,* permission to come aboard?"

"Permission granted." Somehow that Scottish brogue had lost much of its charm, but I was determined not to give that away. Just yet, anyhow.

Jan had just placed a large platter of ham sandwiches, pickles, and chips on the table. The Scot, like many single-handling dudes, has a knack for arriving when food is afoot.

"Take a seat, Mac. Want a beer or three?" Jan said, for all the world like his new best friend, but I knew better. She'd been below sharpening a large carving knife.

"Sure would," he sat down and Fickle Dug put his head in his lap. So much for dogs picking up on bad vibes; Jan and I were barely able to keep from jumping him and beating the crap out of his handsome face.

He lifted his ice cold Tecate into the air. "A toast to lying, cheating, stealing and drinking! If you are going to lie, lie for a friend. If you're going to steal, steal a heart. If you're going to cheat, cheat death. And if you're going to drink, drink with me."

We automatically lifted our glasses, then he looked around, "Say, what have you done with Nacho?"

I'm sure my jaw dropped as far as Jan's. To cover my surprise, I took a glug of beer.

Jan blurted, "What have *we* done with Nacho?"

I kicked her under the table. "We thought maybe you knew."

"Me? I haven't seen the lad since day before yesterday."

"Here?"

"Well, yes, and when he cut me loose. After we had lunch when you returned from La Paz, you Lassies left in your new dinghy, and I invited him over to my boat for a wee dram. I told him I wanted to go up to San Francisco Island for a few days, but there was no enough wind and I'm running low on petrol. He told me he was going out to fish for an hour or so, and would tow me a good part of the way, which he did. At the north end of this island, the wind freshened and I sailed up to San Francisco."

I tried to think back to what we knew for sure. We'd tracked Nacho's boat as it headed north, passed by Los Islotes and then turned out to sea, almost due east. Then, later on, the boat stopped at the *bajo*, and stayed there. The next morning we found the boat, abandoned, with that nasty piece of bloody tentacle on board.

And now Mac was telling us Nacho towed him north, then cut him loose to sail to San Francisco Island? Was he lying through those gorgeous teeth? And why was he back so soon?

"Why are you back so soon?" I demanded. No one had used the word, subtle, when writing me a character reference. Now that I thought about it, no one ever wrote me a character reference.

He swept his arm toward the anchorage where, behind the boats, tiny white-topped wind waves were being whipped up by ever-strengthening gusts. "Was a wee crude in the nor'maist anchorage."

"Huh?" Jan asked.

"I've got this one," I said. "You said it's crowded in the north anchorage, right, Mac?"

"Aye. D'ye speak Scots then, Hetta?" He said this with a crooked grin, as though we hadn't spent enough time together for him to know.

"Just good at understanding accents. But do us a wee favor and lighten up on the brogue, bro?"

"Aye." He eyed the bottle of wine on the sideboard, and Jan asked if he'd like some instead of beer. "Juist a wee...small bit would be appreciated. Am I sensing a problem here with Nacho?"

"Aye," I said before I could catch myself. I am a natural born mimic and it was kicking in fast. "He's disappeared."

"Where to?"

"If we knew that he wouldn't be missing, would he then?" I swear, I said that with a slight brogue.

"Sairy. Tell me what happened."

Jan and I related the whole story, leaving out a few details involving a large handgun and a pantsing. Mac sat quietly sipping his wine and frowning. When we finished he said, "He said he was going to fish, maybe dive. I dinna kin where. This is very disturbing."

"Yes, Mac, it is. As they say in the movies, you might have been the last to see him alive."

"Help ma Boab! I hope not."

I didn't know who or what Boab was, but Mac sounded and looked sincere enough.


After Mac left, Jan and I went over everything he said, which, by the way, we had recorded. On playback, we agreed his story was believable.

"If we were somewhere in the States, CSI would be all over that *bajo*. They'd have had divers down, and Mac would be a person of interest, for sure."

"Well, yes, *if* we'd told either them, or Javier, about seeing Nacho tow *Full Tilt Boogie* out of the anchorage the day Nacho went missing. But you said not to."

I threw up my palms. "This is Mexico. Witnesses, and that is what we'd be if we spilled the beans on Mac, are considered somehow guilty most of the time. And what if, like he says, Mac is entirely innocent. And me? I've already been seen at the scene where two dudes disappeared off their boats. I don't want them getting ideas and throwing me in the local lockup."

"So, what now?"

"I have an idea, but don't know what to do with it."

"Oh, hell, Hetta. This never bodes well. What is it?"

"Well, when I was on that first sailboat, I stepped in what looked like a mix of squid slime and blood. For some reason, I bagged those shoes, mainly because I was too lazy to wash them. And today I purposely stepped into the goop on Nacho's boat again. I now have DNA evidence from two crime scenes on two separate pairs. If this keeps up, I'm gonna be barefoot, but I have evidence. Of what, I'm not sure."

"Fat lot of good that's gonna do us here. I'm not sure they even have labs for such things. Maybe in Mexico City, but with only one in ten crimes being reported and only one in a hundred solved, that means only one in one thousand crimes are punished, which means their DNA data banks are probably a mite on the slim side."

"I was thinking about the squid."

"Probably don't prosecute them either."

We had a giggle, made some really silly jokes about squid crime rates, crimes against squid—fried calamari being at the top of the list—and the like. It felt good to laugh after the past two days.

"Okay, really. What can we do?"

"Call a doctor."

Jan hung up after a lengthy chat with her amour, Doctor Brigido Comacho Yee, a.k.a. Chino.

"He's still not real pleased about us being out here in a blow, but I think I smoothed it over some."

"Not mentioning Nacho probably helped."

"It's not that Chino doesn't like Nacho, he just doesn't know what Nacho does, and doesn't trust that."

"Ha, he can join the club."

"Anyhow, Chino says he keeps in close touch with some marine biologists he met at a conference he attended a few years back about the endangered hammerhead shark."

"Endangered? Hammerheads? I thought I just saw a National Geographic thing about thousands of them in the Sea of Cortez."

"They're being caught by the hundreds, their fins cut off, and then they get thrown back in to sink and die. All for a bowl of shark fin soup in China."

"That's awful. You know I'm no shark fan, but someone needs to stop this."

"Chino's working on it. Anyhow, back to what we were talking about. Evidently they can now take a small piece of fin in China and trace it back, using DNA, to where it was killed. It's a big step towards protecting the hammerheads."

"Good for them. But, what about squid? If we have some of their DNA, can't Chino at least figure out if it comes from the same family? Like a couple of sisters gone berserk?"

"What the hell would that matter?"

"I don't know exactly. I guess it would at least tell us if this is a sociopathic family of angry squid on a rampage. Kinda like Ma Barker and the gang."

"Where do you get this stuff, Hetta?"

"From Chino. He's the one who speculated the squid might be hunting in packs, killing everything in sight, didn't he?"

"No, that was some of his colleagues, but he admitted it was a possibility. Ever the scientist, he won't commit without facts. Why does the pack thing even matter?"

"I'd just feel better knowing whether it's only a few renegades, or if every giant squid in the Sea of Cortez is hell bent on killing me."

"You are so weird. You know who Werner Herzog is?"

"No, is he weird, too?"

"Some might think so. He's a German film maker I studied in a class I took that gave me credits for watching movies."

"I took contract bridge once. So, what is it that brings old Werner to mind?"

"He said, "What would an ocean be without a monster lurking in the dark? It would be like sleep without dreams.' "

"Dreams? This is turning into a freakin' nightmare!"

A gust rocked the boat and Jan looked out at the whitecaps behind us. "Nightmare or not, we can't do squat for a few days, cuz we are plumb stuck. Let's batten down the hatches and get out the DVDs and popcorn."

# Chapter Twenty-six

The first norther of the year turned out to be what I call a *righteous* norther; one that blows a steady twenty-five to forty knots—gusting sometimes to fifty—day and night for three days straight. There are no clouds, just bright blue skies during the day, with dazzling star-studded nights.

During blows I take the nighttime anchor watch because I can't sleep anyway. I sit in the main cabin, where I can repeatedly peer out the large windows to check our position in relation to other boat's anchor lights. *Raymond Johnson* is equipped with all sorts of alarms should we drag anchor, but I've never been able to put my complete faith in them, even though Jenks, the pilot, says to trust your instruments. Some might say I have trust issues?

And those dazzling stars I talked about? They slide wildly by as the boat swings like a yo-yo on a string, until we reach the end of a fast sixty-degree arc, the double anchor chain snubber line groans, and the boat, stopped suddenly, shakes like Po Thang worrying a bone. Then, after a few seconds of lull, with small waves lapping innocently against the hull, we do the same thing all over again in the other direction.

When Jenks is on board during one of these wind events, as the weather people like to call them, he sleeps like a log. Po Thang sleeps like a dog. Jan just sleeps. I surf the web when I have it, or read, as a distraction, but my concentration lags as vertigo grows. After the first long night of this norther, I finally fell asleep at dawn, only to have Po Thang wake me an hour later for his morning pee, which, for some reason I'm required to witness.

No amount of cajoling, threatening, or bribing gets Po Thang out on the front deck to use his pad during a storm. He has, however, devised his own method using the swim platform and some extraordinary balancing tricks, even though he gets pretty wet in the process as the boat slides sideways through the small fetch.

Once Jan got up to take the watch, I was able to tuck myself in for some good restful ZZZs. As you can imagine, after a day or two, I get a lit-tle cranky.

Everyone else in the anchorage was hunkered down in their boats, their boredom only occasionally broken by listening in on radio conversations between other boats, and bulletins announcing wind velocity, like, "Holy crap! That gust pegged my anemometer at thirty-eight knots!"

The ham nets were lively, with cruisers all over the Sea trying to one-up each other with wind speeds, wave heights, and the like. Being in the southern part of the Sea, we were not getting the worst of it. One boat up north, whose owner sounded like he might have broken into the emergency rum stores, claimed a sixty-mile-an-hour gust almost laid him over. Hey, I've been there.

And then there were the smugger-than-thou cruisers on the Mexican Rivera reporting eighty degrees, clear skies and warm water. After that report I checked our water temp and saw it had dropped overnight from seventy-seven to sixty-nine. Puerto Vallarta was starting to sound better and better until the same boater said a crocodile just swam by with an unfortunate dog clamped in its jaws.

It's always something.

As these storms often do, it died suddenly, but it takes a couple of days for the seas to abate. We'd had no news of Nacho, even though we'd asked Javier to let us know what he heard. In fact, he never even answered our e-mails. Mayhaps he was still a touch annoyed with us dainty damsels?

While trapped in the anchorage, we were not, however, idle.

A call to Rosario, our expert hacker dude, giving him the number Javier called from my Satfone, garnered a clue who he worked for. The phone number was traced to PGR_BC. When I heard this, my blood ran cold.

PGR_BC turns out to be Procuraduria General de la Republica de Mexico, the equivalent to the Attorney General's office in the United States! The question is, was Nacho working with them, or maybe against them? And either way, what in holy hell had I gotten involved in?

"I guess this kinda puts the kibosh on counting on Javier as my best friend, huh?" I said, trying to make light of my deep fear. "He's a freakin' fed, for crying out loud. He's royally pissed off, and I'm firmly on his radar."

"I doubt he'll tell anyone about that little incident, what with the Mexican male ego and all, but he could be holding a serious grudge. He doesn't write, doesn't call."

I smiled, in spite of my inner turmoil. Jan and I had a long history with men who did neither. "This is very worrisome. I do not in any way trust the Mexican judicial system, or their agents. Matter of fact, what I should do, while I still can, is take this boat back to the States. Do not pass GO, do not collect two hundred pesos."

"Can we do that? I mean, just leave? Run for the border?"

"Yep. No one will miss me or my boat for at least a week, and by then I could be in San Diego."

We spent the next hour calculating distances, fuel usage, and the like.

"Here it is, in black and white. Running at slow speed, one engine at a time, I can get to Magdalena Bay with the fuel I have in the tanks. I don't dare pull into Cabo for more. But Chino can arrange diesel for me in Mag Bay, and then I'll make it to Turtle Bay for one last refueling before making a beeline for San Diego. I'd rather not stop in Turtle, but I won't have a choice. If everything, and I do mean *everything*, including weather goes well, I could be in the good old US of A in under a week. It would be a grueling trip, but it could happen."

"Okay, so it's doable. What about cars?"

"My guess? Mine is a write off. No way do I dare retrieve my truck. But you'll be okay. I'll drop you off near La Paz and you can beat feet back to Lopez Mateos. No one will even know you were here. Well, except Javier, and he doesn't have any idea you are working at a whale camp. As far as he knows, you're just visiting me from the States."

"And just who is gonna help you take this tub up the coast? Po Thang?"

"Maybe I could find crew." I glanced out the window and nodded toward *Full Kilt Boogie.*

She followed my gaze. "Mac? Are you nuts? He might have offed Nacho. Or fed him to the squid."

"Oh, come on. We don't know what happened to Nacho, but he's gone, and it won't take the federales long to trace him right to us. Me."

"I don't like the whole thing, but I agree you might want to get the hell out of Mexico until this mess blows over."

"And speaking of blows being over, let's take Po Thang to the beach. He's way overdue for a run, and there is no way any of those Parque Nacional dudes are gonna slog into the slop to get out here this morning. I'll talk to Mac on the way back."


Mac was more than willing to help me get to Mag Bay, but not all the way to San Diego.

We discussed my run for the border all afternoon, hashing out details and what everyone's role would be. Going over charts, time frames, and the like, we came up with a plan, but there were still a few holes, the main one being crew from Mag Bay north after Mac returned to La Paz.

Mac left us to work on that while he went back to his boat and prepared to leave for La Paz as soon as possible. He would meet us the next morning at either Tecolote Beach or Balandra, depending on how much the seas calmed. He'd drive down in Jan's Jeep, she'd go to Lopez Mateos to meet Chino, and then I'd meet both of them, and refuel, at Mag Bay. And make my run for the border. It was going to be a verrry long week.

As for crew north from Mag Bay, Jan suggested she and Chino join me there and the three of us continue to San Diego, but I nixed that idea. "No way. If I get boarded by the Mexican Navy for leaving the country without checking out, they'll arrest us all, and you two have way too much to lose."

"I've gotta talk to Chino and come clean. He'll have ideas. And Hetta, you have to call Jenks and do the same. He won't like it, but we don't have time to do anything else. Unless you agree to get on a plane and leave the boat here."

"Not a chance."

"That's what I thought. Okay, here goes what could be the end of a lovely romance."


As predicted, Chino was majorly pissed, but when he calmed down he agreed my escape plan might work. Being a Mexican, he knows the saying, round up the usual suspects, is the way any government entity, and especially law enforcement, works down here.

"And, he had a grand idea. He'll get at least two of his cousins to crew. You'll have to drop them off somewhere before you cross into American waters, though. They don't have any papers and we don't have time to get them. If by some chance you are stopped, they'll just say you hired them in Mag Bay and they had no idea you were a criminal."

"I prefer international fugitive, thank you."

"Whatever. What about P....the d-o-g?"

"What about him?"

"You taking him with you?"

"Why wouldn't I?"

"Have you considered what the authorities would do with him if they snag your butt and throw you under the jail?"

That thought made my stomach sink. Mexico is not the kind of country where the kindly Animal Control dude shows up at a crime scene and takes the pets to safety. "You're right. I can't take that chance with him. He goes with his Aunt Jan."

We went back over the whole trip, using a large printed calendar to schedule day by day. If all went as planned, I'd pull into Mag Bay in under three days, offload Mac, load up on fuel and cousins, then head for Turtle Bay for the final refuel. Weather would dictate where I put Chino's cousins on the beach, but there were all kinds of places where fish camps abound, and these guys would know how to get home.

It was a daring caper, and the enormity of what I was about to do came crashing down on me in a sudden wave of dread. There were just so many ways this escape plan of mine could go horribly wrong.

Perhaps I should say *more* horribly wrong than most of what Jan calls my harebrained schemes.

However, caught between the Devil and the deep blue sea, I choose the sea.

# Chapter Twenty-seven

My escape from Mexico plan was fraught with all kinds of danger, some of which I really didn't want to think about. Like going down with my ship when I hit a rock in the dead of night. Or....

"Hetta, you okay? You've gone all white and wonky looking."

Po Thang, sensing something was not right, put his head in my lap and whined. Tears stung my eyes at his empathy. Swiping my face with my sleeve, I admitted, "I guess I'm a little skeered."

"Just a little? Hell, I'm terrified, and I'm not even going with you. Let's try to look at the bright side, okay? Your crew from Mag Bay north will be Chino's cousins, who were born to the sea, and one, at least, will be a master mechanic. You couldn't ask for a better bunch."

"This is true. They proved their merit working with us on the dive boat last summer."

She ticked off a finger. "Po Thang will be safe and sound with me, which will make the trip so much more worry free. I'll bring him up to the States as soon as you get safely there and settle in. And, when I take Mac back to La Paz, I'll have someone with me to get your pickup. Win-win."

"Now that you put it that way, I guess everything is as good as it can be, under the circumstances. Damn that Nacho! He got us into this and I can't even hunt him down and emasculate him with his own gun."

"That's my Hetta. Uh, speaking of guns, if you get stopped by the Mexican Navy on the way up to the States, and they find the 9mm, which they will, they'll nail you for it."

"In for a peso, in for a pound. That gun and I are going into battle together."

"Remember the Alamo and all that, huh? Your call, Chica."

"Ahoy, *Raymond Johnson*!"

We went outside to wave at Mac as he left for La Paz. "See you tomorrow, Mac!"

"Are you absolutely sure you're comfortable taking Mac with you to Mag Bay?" Jan asked after he motored away.

"He's the only game in town."

"I could come along."

"No, you have to take you-know-who," I tilted my head at Po Thang, "to Lopez Mateos and help Chino get ready to refuel and crew me."

"Somehow the way you put that sounds slightly naughty."

"Ha. Okay, let's get this tub ready for a major ocean voyage. Mac is going to bring more oil, and the like, but although I'm sure we could feed a small third world country from our larder, let's inventory the pantry, just in case I need you to bring us stuff at Mag Bay. After all, we're only looking at a week here."

"Yabbut for sure you'll need tortillas and beans. I don't imagine Chino's cousins are gonna be much for hummus and pita."

"Maybe you can get Chino's Granny Yee to stir up a pot of her famous beans for the freezer. Boy, can that woman cook."

Jan nodded. "Good idea. The cousins won't have to eat your cooking. Danger of mutiny there."

"Hey, I'm not that bad. You're just better, and so is Grans Yee."

"We all have our talents. I just had another idea. Remember all those fifty-five gallon fuel drums in Granny Yee's shed. We used them last summer to refuel the dive boat before you went and sank it."

"For the millionth time, I didn't sink that boat. Intentionally."

"Yeah, yeah, yeah. Anyhow, couldn't we strap them down on *Raymond Johnson* so you don't have to make a stop at Turtle Bay?"

I went to my desk, and the growing pile of spread sheets, lists, schedules and charts for planning my trip back to what I now thought of as the promised land. "Okay, San Diego is a little over a thousand miles from Mag Bay, so if I top off there, I'll need at least four extra drums to get me to California, and not be running on fumes when I get there. Of course, two-hundred and twenty gallons of diesel adds around fifteen-hundred extra pounds of drag to the boat, and I'll have to run the generator some, but I figure four drums will get 'er done.

"If, and this is a big *if*, everything goes well with the boat mechanically, and the seas and weather cooperate."

"Gee, thanks, I need all the encouragement I can get."

"Sorry, I'm just worried. I swear, if Nacho isn't dead and he shows up, *I'm* for sure gonna kill him for getting us in this mess. How *dare* he exploit our inherent greed."

I grinned. "The bastard!"


We arrived without incident—something increasingly rare lately—at the Puerto Balandra anchorage, just outside La Paz.

As soon as we picked up some signal bars, we called Mac with our ETA. He reported he was on his way from Marina Palmyra, where he was leaving his boat at my expense, to get Jan's Jeep out of hock from a parking lot near Marina de la Paz. He'd meet us at the anchorage, even though the road was a little rough. We knew Jan's Jeep could easily handle the unpaved dirt track to the anchorage.

While we waited for Mac, Jan packed up her things, and I gathered Po Thang's stuff. It was amazing how much paraphernalia a dog can collect. Once again, tears stung my eyes as I stuffed dog food, leashes, toys and the like into duffle bags. Po Thang hovered, paced, hovered and paced. Something was up, he didn't know what, but he did not like it. His humans were projecting doom and gloom, and there was packing going on. At one point he raided his own bag and unpacked his toys, which gave us a little moment of levity.

"It's okay, baby," I told him as I gave him a big hug. "In just a few days we'll get back to normal."

Actually that was a little white lie. Once I arrived in San Diego, *if* I made it to San Diego, what then?

Jan must have read my mind. "Hetta, you can get a job anywhere. Your boat safe is jammed with valuables and your bank account runneth over thanks to Nacho. You'll be better off in the States until this whole thing blows over. You can always come back to Mexico, ya know."

"*If* I don't get arrested at the police dock in San Diego for smuggling contraband."

"Hey, better a California jail than a Mexican jail."

"You're a real barrel of sunshine today."

"Just looking for a silver lining. Hetta, you have to call Jenks, right now, and tell him everything. You owe it to him. If something were to happen to you, he will be devastated that you took off on this debacle, uh, offshore cruise, in the Pacific damned ocean without letting him know what you have planned."

"You mean I should call to say goodbye, don't you?"

"No, that's not what I mean at all. I have every confidence everything will go smoothly. But let's face it, stuff happens at sea. Call. Him. Now. Or I will, the minute I leave this boat."

Jenks was far from happy at first, and demanded I wait until he could get here to go with me to San Diego, but I convinced him there wasn't enough time; I had to get gone before the feds came looking for me. I laid out for him what I hoped sounded like a well-planned trip, adding that from La Paz to Mag Bay I'd be accompanied by an experienced blue water cruiser who'd sailed all the way from Scotland single-handedly.

"And when I pick up fuel in Mag Bay, Chino's cousins will come aboard for the rest of the trip so I'll have at least two great mechanics with me. If the weather holds, and according to the ten-day forecast, it will, I'll be in San Diego in a little over a week. On top of that, Jan says she's going to dog us by road all the way, so we'll have backup on land. She's even going to carry extra diesel, and can meet us at any anchorage if necessary."

The more I worked at persuading Jenks what a piece of cake this whole thing was going to be, the more I almost convinced myself it was true.

What was Joseph Goebbel's propaganda strategy during WWII? Oh, yeah. *"If you tell a lie big enough and keep repeating it, people will eventually come to believe it."*

# Chapter Twenty-eight

It was with a heavy heart that I ferried Jan and Po Thang to the beach while Mac stashed his belongings in the guest cabin, and then, after tearful goodbyes, I went back to prepare to leave.

By the time I returned to the boat, Mac was out on deck and had the heavy duty motorized davit system ready to lift *DawgHouse* out of the water, and into the chocks on the sundeck overhead behind the flying bridge.

I'd planned to have new chocks made to fit my new pangita, but we'd have to make do with what was already there. The existing cradle was well-built, but designed to hold a rigid-bottomed inflatable, not a fiberglass boat with a deeper chine. However, Mac turned out to be a master rigger, and lashed *DawgHouse* down snuggly.

While we worked on securing the dinghy, we discussed our watch schedule. We agreed I'd take the first shift, since it was already two in the afternoon and I really, really, hate night watch, especially on the first night out. He'd get some sleep and relieve me around nine, man the helm until just before first light, then I'd take over again. Once we rounded Cabo Falso and headed north, we'd be far enough offshore that I'd feel more secure with taking a night watch.

As I sat on the flying bridge, we entered the San Lorenzo Channel, cleared the land mass, and I entered a proper waypoint on the boat's GPS navigation system, setting a course directly for Punta Arena. Jenks had, bless his heart, marked all the way points from La Paz to Mag Bay when we made this trip from the other direction the year before. Yes, there are all kinds of charts and cruising guides out there with the latitude and longitude of anchorages, hazards, and that sort of thing, but I prefer the ones marked either by Jenks or me on site. With my own GPS coordinates, I can confidently return to any place we've been in heavy fog or dark of night.

These waypoints, entered only a year ago, brought on a wave of despondency. Was it only a year? Seemed both like yesterday, and eons ago.

I don't normally get depressed, hold onto feelings of sadness very long, or feel sorry for myself more than a few hours, with the exception of when my dog, Raymond Johnson—RJ to his friends—died. That set me on my rear for several weeks. I finally got over it by buying a forty-five foot yacht, a therapy I highly recommend. Watching the Baja peninsula—a place I'd learned to love—slide by, I had a presentiment that things were not going to go well for me in the near future.

Making matters worse, I'd so looked forward to making this return trip with Jenks when he finished up in Dubai, and here I was, on the run, alone. Well, not totally alone, for Artherrrr MacKenzie Gra-ham, Mac to *his* friends, was with me, but after talking with Jenks earlier I realized any attraction I had for the handsome Scot had evaporated.

Yes, he was attractive, and yes, I was grateful he was willing to help me, but he wasn't Jenks.

I wanted Jenks.

I wanted my mommy.

I wanted my dog.

I wanted to be anywhere but running for the border!

Much to my relief, Mac joined me on the bridge early, just as the last light faded and I was already getting a little anxious. We'd just passed Ensenada de los Muertos—Cove of the Dead—which the new developers didn't think sounded good for business and had renamed Bahia de los Suenos or Bay of Dreams. It will, however, remain Muertos to boaters for years to come. Jenks and I had anchored there for a few days and gone ashore to a boater potluck which is something cruisers throw together at the drop of a sombrero. As I looked longingly at the boats in the anchorage, I recalled how clever cruisers can be at putting together casseroles from just about anything on board.

Unfortunately, the Bay of the Dead wasn't on the itinerary for my voyage of the damned.

We were making ten knots at Jenks's insistence. He said my bright idea of running one engine at a time wasn't all that good for the transmissions, especially on such a long voyage like I was undertaking. He was right. The last thing I needed right now was a transmission failure. We'd slip into Cabo for fuel around three in the afternoon, a busy time when fishing boats are returning and the harbor bustles with activity. If anyone bothered to ask, we'd tell them we were fishing our way to La Paz, then hopefully get underway again by five and do an overnighter to Mag Bay. Putting on a few turns, doing twelve to fourteen knots, would put us into Mag Bay by the next afternoon.

Jan and Chino were going to have to hustle to have fuel, extra fuel barrels, crew, and hopefully some of Granny Yee's victuals ready by the time we arrived.

I nuked frozen beef stew and toasted left over pieces of garlic bread for our dinner, and unearthed a box of Oreos for dessert. Mac made us both a cup of tea before I went to my cabin, which I politely drank even though he put milk and sugar in it. Yuck.

Finally back in my cabin, the long day of emotional turmoil caught up with me. Exhaustion, mainly due to the stress involved in my latest fiasco, sent me into a deep sleep. I woke once, barely able to fight myself out of a comatose-like slumber, made it to the bathroom and then back into my bed before going out again.

Brilliant sunlight woke me.

I looked at the clock and saw it was after nine. I'd slept twelve hours straight! So much for my eight-hour watch. *Some sea captain I am. Poor Mac has had the helm all this time and must be beat to hell.*

My head hurt from so much sleep, and I felt woozy. The boat was bucking some, so I surmised we were running into a Pacific swell. Throwing water in my face, I glanced out the window, into that bright morning sun.

Whoa. The sun should be behind us, not to our starboard side. Oh, hell, had my crew fallen asleep on the job? Cursing a blue streak I rushed my cabin door, only to find it locked. From the outside.

As Dorothy Parker wrote, "What fresh Hell is this?"

I almost overrode the lock and opened my door from the inside, but changed my mind. The year before, after a bad guy locked Jan, our friend Topaz Sawyer, and Chino's then medical assistant, the Devine Doctor Di, in my cabin, I fixed it so that it could not happen again at the insistence of Topaz, who is a cop back in Arizona. I'm pretty sure that she and Nacho had a little fling at one time, but he won't admit it, and neither will she. I guess the cop/criminal thing didn't work out.

Anyhow, I rigged a system kind of like those escape pulls in case you get locked into a car trunk.

The reason I changed my mind about opening the door this time was that I needed to reach deep into my foggy brain and think things through. Through that same fog, it finally dawned on me that Mac had drugged my tea, and then locked me in my cabin. Okay, got that much.

Peering out the portholes on both sides of my cabin, I couldn't see anything but water on the starboard side, and just the tops of mountains to port. With the excellent visibility in the Sea, I figured we were at least fifteen miles out, cruising due north, and therefore back up into the Sea. If there's one thing I hate, it's waking up on the wrong side of my boat.

I sat down with a large glass of water, hoping to dilute whatever Mac fed me.

So, Mac is indeed dirty and probably had something to do with Nacho's disappearance. But why? What I didn't know would fill an encyclopedia.

But then again—and this made me smile—Mac was not really aware of who he was dealing with. Nor was he cognizant that:

1. I can open that door.

2. I have security cameras throughout the boat, and can activate them from my cabin.

3. *Raymond Johnson's* physical location can be tracked via that same security system, and both Jan and Jenks know how to do so.

What else? I jumped up, suffered a head spin, and leaned on the bed to steady myself. When the boat stopped doing loops, I lifted my mattress and opened the hidey hole containing my safe, Nacho's 9mm handgun, and sixty rounds of ammo.

My smile broadened and my head cleared.

Oh, and Mac was also ignorant of the fact that:

4. Drugs don't last on me. Ask any poor dentist who has had the unfortunate experience of trying to deaden a tooth.

5. My big butt can actually shimmy through my aft cabin portholes.

6. I am armed and dangerous.

7. I have been known to serve up some serious badassery when provoked.

8. I was provoked.

# Chapter Twenty-nine

I waited another hour locked in my cabin, listening carefully for anything other than engine noise, but aside from moving water, heard nothing. I tested whether the generator was running by turning on an AC lamp in my cabin that was not connected to my inverter system. Yep.

With AC, or 110V current in the boat, my security and satellite communication systems had good power, and was waiting for someone, namely *moi*, to hit the ON button. It was time to take a peek at what that bottom feeder was doing with my boat.

Switching on the flying bridge camera, I saw he was not up there. Watching the wheel closely, I saw no movement, which indicated we were on autopilot. I wished I could read the GPS coordinates, but couldn't quite make them out.

Okay, so where was the *pendejo*? What with it being broad daylight, and cruising in an area where there are few boats, he was most likely in the main cabin.

Turning on the living room—in boat-speak, the saloon, but pronounced salon for some reason only known to ancient mariners—camera was a little trickier. Unlike the one on the bridge, it swivels, and when first activated, usually does a scan. There is only a slight movement, but no light comes on to give it away. He would probably never notice, but there was always the off chance he'd catch the motion.

Holding my breath, I hit the switch.

And there he was in all his glory, sound asleep on the settee.

There goes *his* bonus.

Okay, so maybe there were no boats about, and the radar alarm, if he set it, would sound when anything got within two miles, but sleeping while on watch on *my* boat? This is a keelhauling offense. Drawing and quartering would be way too good for him, and feeding those quarters to the sharks, justified. Or squid. Whichever got them first.

I was so angry I considered breaking out of my room and shooting him in his sleep—or somewhere much more personal and painful—but calmed myself down. Dead, he couldn't tell me what he was up to, or what he'd done with Nacho. On the other hand, if I didn't kill him outright, there was always a chance he'd overpower me and throw me overboard.

What I really needed to do was get a message to Jan, but I'd already searched the cabin for my laptop and it was gone. He'd obviously taken it after I passed out. My cell phone was also missing.

I stared at the panic button on my security system, but it probably wouldn't do me any good unless the master satellite system was turned on. I'd used that button once back in the States, and it saved my life, but I wasn't sure it would even get anyone's attention way down in Mexico. I pushed the button anyway. About ten times.

I always keep extra lifejackets in my cabin, just in case I ever had to leave via those undersized—in my opinion—portholes. After Po Thang moved in, I'd stashed one for him, as well. Three of them are equipped with Personal Locator Beacons, great devices if you are just off the beach and your boat sinks. In that case the boat's EPIRB will also go off, and the Emergency Position Indicating Radio Beacon can be picked up by the United States Coast Guard, even from down here.

Every once in awhile the ham net and cruiser chat included reports of an EPIRB going off somewhere in the Sea of Cortez, leading to a search by boaters, the Mexican Navy and even the US Coast Guard, for the vessel it belongs to. I'd seen a low-flying American search plane in one case that ended tragically despite an intensive hunt. Normally, however, the whole incident is due to a malfunctioning unit, or someone turning one on by accident. It is just nice to know that should yours go off, someone might be searching for you.

The PRBs like the ones I had attached to those life jackets, on the other hand, are really meant to send a signal back to your own boat so overboard crew can be located. However, figuring I needed all the help I could possibly use, I quietly opened the porthole, activated one PRB, and threw it into the water. I saved the others, because they only have a twenty-four hour battery life and who knew what was going to happen. I had no idea if any of them would have anyone looking for me, but figured doing something is better than doing nothing.

As I shut the porthole as quietly as possible, I heard a sound at my cabin door. I flipped off the security system, dove under my duvet, cradled the handgun, and let go with the best snores I could muster. I sensed Mac entering the room and standing near the bed, watching. Evidently satisfied I was still out cold, he left.

The second I heard the lock click behind him, I reactivated the system and watched as he went to the galley and rummaged in the fridge. Which reminded me I was hungry. I eyed a bag of Po Thang's treats I kept in my cabin, but I wasn't quite that desperate yet. Besides, they were chicken flavored; he'd eaten all the Beggin' Strips.

It occurred to me I couldn't play possum forever, so maybe I could play stupid? Yes, I know what Jan would say about that.

After a shower, brushing my teeth, and even putting on a little blush and tinted lip gloss, I was ready for my close up.

It was ten thirty in the morning, and we were scheduled to arrive in Cabo at three.

Maybe I'd had a sixth sense about Mac, or perhaps it's just my nature not to trust my fellow man, or—and this is more likely the case—my control freak habits kicked in. Whatever the case, I'd made a call even Jan didn't know about.

After I'd waved goodbye to Jan and Po Thang, I used my cell phone to beg a favor from the boat, *Me Too*. They'd helped me with the abandoned boat, *Carpe Diem*, and then we reconnected back on the dock at Marina de la Paz. I knew, just from our short acquaintance, that I could rely on her and her hubby, Clay. Telling Jill where to find the hidden magnetic box containing an extra key to my truck that any car thief could locate in moments, I asked her to meet me at the fuel dock in Cabo. If I didn't show up, she was to call Chino. And if Chino said Jan and Po Thang hadn't arrived at Lopez Mateos, he was to alert the port captain, the police, and maybe the United States Marines.

Yes, I might face some angry officials if Chino had to make that call, but at least both Jan and I wouldn't just disappear into thin air. I also told Jill who was going to be my crew, just in case I was right about Mac being shady. Which I now knew he was, for sure.

Dang, I hate it when I'm so right.

# Chapter Thirty

Screwing up my courage, I pounded on my locked cabin door and yelled until Mac finally opened it.

"Oh, thanks," I gushed. Jan majored in Southern Gush at the University of Texas and passed the skill to me. "I sa-wear, I cannot for the life of me figure out how I managed to lock myself in. And please, Mac Honey," I lightly touched his arm with my hand because I was fresh out of silk embroidered hand fans, "can you possibly forgive me for oversleeping?"

Clearly taken aback, he stammered, "Uh, not to worry." Then, because he probably couldn't think of what to say next, he added, "I just had a nosh, but you must be starving."

"Oh, yes, I surely am. Where are we, by the way?"

"Still on schedule. Making good time."

"That's wonderful. I am sooo lucky to have you helping me." I made a point not to look outside as I sashayed down to the galley. I had one goal in mind before I had to give up the game, and that was to turn on the master security system, and push that panic button again, hopefully activating the reverse GPS locator back at Jenks's security company's office in San Francisco, where one of his staff would maybe pick it up. Maybe.

I made iced tea for both of us, adding fresh mint, while daintily nibbling on a piece of cheese that I wanted to bolt down a la Po Thang. Mac watched me, somewhat warily, but I stayed in character, making us both a cheese and cucumber sandwich—of course trimming away the crust—then added exactly three chips to my plate and carried everything to my desk. Brushing papers to the side, I sat to eat.

Jenks had designed this system for just this kind of situation. Both a hidden switch and the panic button were under the desk, and I hit both of them with my knee. I had no idea whether it did any good, but it was all I could do for now.

Mac ate his sandwich while standing behind the lower steering station. I still studiously refrained from looking out any of the windows as I took my empty plate and glass to the galley, then joined Mac, standing just out of his reach. It was time to call in his cards. "Say, are you sure we're on track? Shouldn't land be to starboard, not port?"

"Yes, Lass, it should. However, there is a change in plans, and here is what they will be. For the next twenty-four hours, you do as I say. I dinna wish to harm you or anyone else, but if I must, I will."

I tried to look helpless, and whined, "I don't understand."

"You will. Now, sit down," he pointed to a folding metal chair I use for my Chair Yoga practice. I noticed a piece of line conveniently placed next to it on the settee and pictured myself, tied hand and foot into that chair, sinking into the depths of the sea, holding my last breath until my lungs exploded.

Nope, not for me. It was time to make a move.

No more Miss Nice Girl.

"Oh...oh...why? What are you doing, Mac?" I wailed.

He gave me a little push toward the chair and as I pretended to stumble, I grabbed the chair's back and swung it, catching him right in the gut with one of the legs. I'd aimed lower, but, oh well.

Doubling over and groaning, he rushed me like an angry bull, but I wasn't where he thought. I'd stepped to one side and behind him, put my considerable weight into a roundhouse swing, and whacked him again, this time connecting with his neck and the back of his head with the chair back. He went down hard, but he was tough and was trying to get back on his feet when he looked up and found himself staring down the barrel of a 9mm. He sank back to his knees. "Crikey, they warned me about you American women."

"Whoever *they* are, they've obviously never been to Texas. Anyway, you should have listened. Get up, vurrry slowly, Laddie, if you prefer to put a tilt in your kilt ever again."

He did as he was told, never taking his eyes off the gun. I didn't like that. He reminded me of a cobra, tracking my hands, waiting for a chance to strike.

"Shut your eyes."

"What? Why?"

"Because I said so, and I'm the one holding the large semi-automatic."

He shut his eyes.

"Turn slightly to your right. Yes, that's fine. Now, take five baby steps."

He took four steps and banged face-first into the port door frame.

"Oooow."

"I said *baby* steps. Okay, put your hands on your head, keep your back to me, open your eyes, step out on deck and walk aft."

He did, stopping at the back rail.

"Now, GET OFF MY BOAT!" Harrison Ford would be so proud.

"What? Are ye daft?"

"Yes, I am. Jump!"

"We're miles from land!"

I fired a round over his head.

He jumped.

"I'll be back," I growled.

Was I having a Hollywood kind of day, or what?

I let the boat continue forward at ten knots until I'd put a quarter mile between the boat and the Scot treading water, and probably trying to figure out how many hours he'd have to swim before reaching shore.

Cutting back to engine speed, I went to neutral and waited. He swam my way. I went out on deck and let him get within hearing distance.

"Where is Nacho?" I demanded.

"I dinna know."

I climbed to the bridge, put the boat in gear and pushed the throttles forward, leaving him in my wake. Then I stopped again, and waited as he swam my way.

"Where is Nacho?" I asked again.

"I—"

I didn't give him a chance to lie. I took off, got some distance between us and stopped. But this time when I did, I opened the deck chest freezer and rummaged inside for the good stuff.

When Mac almost reached *Raymond Johnson* again, I didn't even bother asking the question; I dumped three pounds of chum into the water, went back to the bridge and moved out, leaving him surrounded with quickly thawing fish guts.

Even over the engine noise I heard him howl. "Okay. You win."

I circled back, and waited at a safe distance.

"He's fine. Nacho's safe. God's truth. We dinna want to harm anyone. I was taking you to him."

"That so?"

"Aye."

"And where would he be, exactly?"

"Let me on board, and I'll tell you."

"Uh, last I checked, you were in no position to make demands. Tell you what, you swim a little longer and think about telling me what you've been up to, and why, and with who. Whom. Whatever. When you're ready we'll have another chat." I pulled away, slowly. He cursed and fell in behind. I figured another five or six miles might do the job.

Checking the GPS, I located the last waypoint entered, and it wasn't one of mine. Something, or someone, was ten miles to the north. Nacho?

I adjusted the radar, expanded it to cover twenty miles out, and lo and behold, right where Mac was headed, there was a boat. On the *bajo*. I felt like I was living the movie, "Ground Hog Day," returning over and over to the same spot. All boats lead to the *bajo*, but why?

During the next couple of hours we played our cat and mouse game, Mac the Mouse protesting he was badly tired and not that good a swimmer, but I still didn't trust him on board. He was big and strong, and unless I had the gun trained on him every second, he had the advantage.

I slowed again. "Think you can make it to the *bajo*, Mac? It's only another nine or so miles and, what a surprise, it looks like we've got company up there. Who? And why?"

"A gang of rubbish, that's who!"

"There's the pot calling the kettle black. I guess you didn't hear the word, *why*."

As I motored away, he yelled, "Wait! Pearls!"

# Chapter Thirty-one

Pearls?

Someone went to all this trouble to steal my stupid pearls? Good grief.

I turned back and sidled up next to Mac as he treaded water. "How did you know I found pearls?"

The minute I said it, I had a flashback to San Francisco Island, where I discovered Bubbles being dragged down by what I thought at the time was a fishing net. It turned out to be netting woven into box-like oyster cages.

"You wanted the net, and helped me cut the dolphin loose to get it?"

"I saw you diving and figured you'd spotted the net and were going to take it. But then I realized it was an animal you were trying to save."

"And then I kept the net you wanted on my boat, right? Are you trying to tell me you entered into some kind of stupid plot that has gotten us to this stage in order to recover a handful of pearls? That makes no sense." I turned toward the bridge and that set him to hollering.

"No! Hetta, don't drive away again. It is pearls, but not yours. There are many, many, more. I can make you rich."

Now he was speaking my language. I leaned over the rail. "Okay, you can climb onto the swim platform, but one false move and you'll be singing soprano." I'm not sure where I got that line, but I always wanted to use it.

I released the swim ladder and kicked it down so Mac could pull himself out of the water. He was shivering and seemed winded, but I didn't drop my guard. "Turn around and sit down."

He leaned up against the transom and pulled his feet out of the water, hugged his knees to his chest and closed his eyes. That Mac is a fast learner.

"Good boy. Stay right there. If I see a hand, or even a finger, on this rail," I patted it, "I will use my machete. Do you understand?"

"No worries, there. I canna barely move."

Backing away so as to keep an eye on Mac, I reached into a locker and pulled out the bikini design fleece snuggle blankie Jan gave me. Throwing it down on his head, I told him, "Put this on. Slip your arms into the sleeves and wrap yourself up."

It wasn't easy, considering his size and the narrow area he had to work with, but he eventually got himself tucked in. His shivers subsided, and he was quickly regaining color in his face, not a good thing in my book. I looked around for a piece of line, but could I trust him to tie himself up? Nah.

I pulled the nine pound Danforth dinghy anchor with twenty feet of line and six feet of chain I'd used on

*Se Vende* from another locker. "Tie this around your ankles."

"Are ye mad, woman? If I fall off this platform I'll sink like a rock."

"Aye, that you will, so I suggest you do not do that. Now, wrap 'em up tight like a good boy."

Cursing under his breath, he wound the anchor chain around both ankles, tied the line around his waist, then pulled the anchor into his lap, as instructed.

"Well done. Now, very carefully, hand me the end of that line." I lashed it to the rail, and pulled over a deck chair. "Now that we're comfy, let's have that little chat. How is it you're gonna make me rich?" I know, I should have been asking more about the fate of poor Nacho, but I do have my priorities.

He tilted his head back so he was gazing up at me with those intensely green eyes, which would have been incredibly sexy had he not been wrapped in that bikini blankie. "I'll tell you, but first can I ask a question?"

"Okay. One."

"If we both live through the next few days, will ye marry me?"

"I thought ye'd never ask." I love a man with a sense of humor.


His story sounded somewhat believable, but then again, I'd fallen for his kind of crap before. And, I am admittedly a really lousy judge of character when the man is tall, dark, green-eyed and looks good in a kilt.

My dilemma for the moment, however, was not whether to believe him, but what to *do* with him. I couldn't keep my eye, and gun, on him all the time, and didn't want to get close enough to tie him up properly, especially since my knot-tying skills run to the crappy side. Jenks teases me all the time about using granny knots on a boat.

So, short of shooting him in a foot or something, I needed a way to keep him at bay without tossing him back in the water. I didn't trust him one iota, so letting him back on deck was out of the question. Where the hell was Jan and her handy handcuffs when I needed her?

And speaking of Jan, I had to contact her as soon as possible and let her know where I was, and how things had gone all to hell. But in order to call her I had to go inside, and until I secured the Scot, that made me uneasy. He might look like a half-drowned rat right now, but he was still a rat.

I glanced at the ship's clock mounted near the bar. It was nearing one o'clock, and my accomplice from Marina de la Paz should be arriving in Cabo to see if we showed there. If we didn't, Jill would most likely call Chino by five, who would then call the authorities. What had I been thinking? *Mexican* authorities?

Looking to Heaven for some kind of divine revelation, I got one. Sort of. Actually, I spotted my dingy riding in its chocks on the sundeck's hard-topped cover.

"You sit and stay," I told Mac, and then I walked a few steps over to the davit controls.

Normally, all I'd have to do is release some tie down straps and let the motorized davit swing the dinghy over the side and lower it into the water. Then, I'd release the painter, or the towing line, and walk the dinghy to the aft for boarding. However, *DawgHouse* was sitting on chocks not designed for that particular boat, and my captive had lashed it all ways from

Sunday. I'd have to spend way too much time up on that sundeck, untying the skiff while trying to keep an eye on Mac. Luckily, the seas were quite calm, but even so, I'd be up there trying to work while the boat lolled in the sight swell. A little too much multitasking.

"Okay, Mac, you better hang on!" Putting the boat in gear, I headed into what little swell there was and turned on the autopilot, ignoring Mac's bellows of protest.

As soon as we had a better ride, I went back to check on Mac, who had gone silent. Everyone who owns a dog knows this can bode badly. Or, maybe the CO2 fumes got to him. After all there is that warning sign on the transom.

But, sure enough, he was working on the lines tying him to the anchor.

"Bad! Stop that!"

He looked up, startled. I guess he figured I was busy doing something on the bridge and this was his chance. I'd seen that same look from Po Thang.

"I was just trying to get comfortable," he whined. "Besides, we're underway and my butt is getting soaked again."

"Better than getting plugged, Podner. Now hear this. Do not move, you hear me? I am a devout coward, I am afraid of you, and if I have to shoot you to protect myself, I damned well will. You got that?"

He glowered but nodded.

I took a dive knife from my locker, rushed back to the bridge, climbed carefully out on the sundeck roof, and slashed all the lines but the painter. This bit would cost me when I got back to port. Checking on Mac, I saw some wiggling going on, so I fired one right behind the boat, raising a spout about three feet from that wiggling leg. Two spent, plenty left.

Mac let loose with a string of foul language and protested his innocence, but he stopped moving.

Putting the boat into neutral, I rushed back to the davit control panel and swung *DawgHouse* over the starboard side, but now we were swaying again and the dinghy started banging into *Raymond Johnson's* hull. Fearing something would let go and I'd lose the dinghy, I quickly secured and lowered two large round buoys I keep on board to mark my anchor's location, as fenders.

After a few more minutes of fiddling with all the lines, I tied off the dingy to a rail, and unhooked it from the davit. The large hook swung back, threatening to conk me in the head, but I grabbed it in time and winched it back into place.

The dinghy's painter was too short for my purposes, so I added a long piece of line and played it out until *DawgHouse* rode about thirty feet behind *Raymond Johnson.*

"Okay, Mac, show time. I'm going to let you pull the dinghy up to you and you are going to place your anchor in it, gently, of course, and then roll yourself in. No funny stuff."

I didn't like the way he looked somewhat pleased with this idea. What had I overlooked?

"Let's see, have I overlooked something that would allow you to make a move I wouldn't like? No? Okay, into *DawgHouse* with you. And by the way," I reached in my pocket and waggled a squiggly red plastic cord holding the outboard's "key." It is designed to loop over a driver's wrist, so if they are thrown out the "dead man's switch" is pulled out, stopping the motor. It is also used as a safety to prevent the motor from starting unless it is inserted.

"Yes, Mac, you will have a dinghy and outboard, but no gas, and the motor won't start without this little doohickey, anyhow. Oh, and I removed the paddles." That wiped any smugness from his face.

"Now, pull the dingy to the swim platform and get in." After he was settled onto the floorboards, the dingy began drifting back. I sissy-pitched a couple of bottles of water in with him. "Drink up, you'll figure out how to manage those bottles. And fasten your seatbelt, Darlin', it's gonna be a bumpy ride."

Back on the bridge, I tooled up to fifteen knots, which is pretty much redlined in my book. Once we settled on course, I engaged the autopilot and went below to make a bunch of important calls.

I had to use the Satfone, because I had no signal on my cell, which I'd found in the main cabin. As I made the calls, I watched my dingy bouncing erratically along behind us. I'd misjudged the distance and Mac was jouncing off the floorboards as *DawgHouse* slammed into *Raymond Johnson's* wake instead of riding the swell. My bad.

Neither Jan nor Jill answered, so I left messages. I really wanted to call Jenks, but knew better until I had this particular situation under control .

As soon as I hung up, I decided to give Mac a break and pull the dinghy closer to the boat. Poor guy was hunkered down under the blanket, getting beat all to hell while being soaked with salt spray. I doubted he was able to even think about working on those lines, but he boded watching.

At fifteen knots, it is extremely hard and dangerous to pull in a dinghy, and requires the upper body strength I simply do not have. I spotted Nacho's electric reel he'd mounted on a rail, and decided to give it a go. It was designed to haul in a few hundred pounds of fighting fish, so why not a bounding dingy. And then, if Mac acted up, I could just release the brake and out he would go. The catch and release system just took on a whole new meaning.

With Mac and dinghy riding smoothly behind, I moved to the bridge to check our position, and that boat on the *bajo*. I figured if I could see him on my radar, he most likely saw me, as well. But then, he was expecting Mac, wasn't he?

When we were two miles out, I stopped again and reeled the dink in. I had no choice but to put Mac on the bridge where his cohorts in crime—even though I still wasn't sure *what* crime—could see him as we neared the meet.

What came next, I had no freakin' idea, but at least I'd know who else was involved.

And maybe find Nacho?

# Chapter Thirty-two

A mile from the *bajo*, I halted the boat once again, pulled the dinghy against the swim platform and cleated it off. "Come out, come out, wherever you are," I trilled.

Mac extricated himself from under the soggy, salt-encrusted blanket and snarled, "Very bloody clever, Hetta. What now?"

"I'm glad you asked. Take off the blankie so I can see what you've been up to."

"Shrew!"

"Now, now, compliments will get you no where. Disrobe for Hetta."

He peeled off the blanket and, as an act of defiance, threw it overboard. Dang, I loved that snuggly fleece. As I suspected, he'd managed to unwind the anchor chain from his ankles.

"Okay, you know the drill. Retie that line, but only to one ankle this time. Tight."

He grumbled, but secured it around his left ankle. "Good boy. Tie the other end around your waist."

"You *are* a daftie. Absolutely baurmie." He pronounced it barmy.

"Not crazy enough to let you get back on this boat without some major impediments, Mate. Run the line around your neck and waist and tie them together. Cinch the anchor up against your belly button."

I let him stand and grab a cleat on the transom, but when he took a step up onto the platform, an anchor tine gouged his knee. "Ooowww."

"That's gonna leave a mark. You'll get the hang of it. Nice and easy does it. Up the ladder, maybe backwards. You'll figure it out. Hetta and her best friend, Mr. Springfield XDM, will be watching very carefully."

"Hure."

"I heard that. And for your information, I am not a hoor. I've never been paid for my favors."

It took some time, and a little pain on his part, but I finally got him all the way to the bridge, and into a dry shirt and hat I'd found in his cabin. From a distance, he'd look downright jaunty.

Letting him take the helm, which was an honorary position since we were on autopilot, I warned him of dire consequences should he try any tricky maneuvers as we neared the rendezvous site. Hunkering down with my back against the gunwale, I was out of sight from other boats, but somewhat vulnerable should Mac manage to jump me, anchor or no. In fact, the more I thought about it, the more paranoid I became.

The truth of the matter was I was very tired, and feared that eventually I'd drop my guard long enough for him to strike.

I threw him an extra long bungee cord I use in all kinds of handy ways when battening down the hatches for a blow. "Sit down in the captain's chair, wrap this around your wrist and the arm rest, and then throw both ends over your shoulder."

He slumped into the seat and didn't protest this latest order. I was pretty sure he was much more fatigued than I. Or at least I hoped so. The difference between us is I'd had twelve hours of sleep, thanks to whatever he put in my tea, and he'd been swimming, cold, and wet for over three hours. Still, a little insurance never hurts.

Pulling both ends of the bungee cord by the end hooks, I ran them over a rail and fastened them together. "Hey, yer cutting off my blood flow."

"You're lucky that's all I'm cutting off. Turn up the radio with your other hand."

I listened as boaters hailed each other and I knew some of them. I considered asking them for help, and they would come as fast as they could, because that is what cruisers do, but if I did, whoever waited for us at the *bajo* might hear me, as well.

Suddenly realizing my attentiveness had strayed, I snapped to attention and saw that Mac had shifted his weight, turned his head, and was intently eyeballing me. It reminded me of the book, *Life of Pi*, where an Indian boy was trapped in the Pacific Ocean in a life raft.

For two-hundred and twenty-seven days.

With a Bengal Tiger.

"Don't even think about it."

"I dinna do anything."

"You looked at me."

"My sincere apologies."

"Sarcasm will get you shot."

He grinned. "Well, then, I wouldn't have to look at you again, would I?"

*Touche!*

Why, oh, why are all the bad ones so damned charming?

Half a mile out, the radar revealed there was not one, but two boats ahead. And I picked up a third, larger, making a beeline for the *bajo*. Crap! Sure, I had a gun, but I wasn't Wonder Woman. Of course, Wonder Woman and I have never been seen in the same room, so there could be some doubt there, huh?

Anyhow, so much for arriving in stealth mode. Scanning with my binoculars, I saw the boats already at the bajo were pangas. One was white and just a regular old everyday panga, but the other was a super panga I knew well. Nacho's boat. What the hell? It had been hauled away by a contingent of Marines, and now it was back?

Oh, and the other boat coming our way? A shrimper, just like the one we'd seen hunkered in Partida during the blow. In fact, *exactly* like the shrimper in Partida during the norther. I zeroed in with my binoculars and confirmed that it was the same one Jan had scored shrimp and some *lenguado*—California Halibut—from: *Pelicano.* Were they part of this passel of punks? Or could I count on them as allies?

I told Mac to throttle back and let us drift until I could see whether *Pelicano* was actually in route for the *bajo* or was merely crossing the Sea. Many of these boats come from Mazatlan and San Carlos, on the mainland, so it was possible that's where he was headed.

I checked aft to make sure the dinghy's polypropylene tow line was floating on the surface. The last thing I needed right now was for it to sink and get wrapped in the prop. I'd customarily snug the dinghy to the swim platform to avoid this, but I was loath to leave Mac alone on the bridge.

We lingered, observing both the radar screen and the pangas. The two small boats at the *bajo* were stationary, moored, in fact, as I could see anchor lines descending from the bows. The shrimper was steaming at a pretty good clip towards them, and I'd know his intentions within a few minutes. If he passed by, it was one less thing to worry about, and I could surely use a break about now.

So, of course, the big boat slowed and headed straight for the *bajo*.

Oddly, Mac cursed under his breath. I interpreted this as a good thing. Was I gonna get that break, after all? Was the *Pelicano's* crew *not* in cahoots with the others and was just checking out the two boats? In which case, I needed to get there, pronto, in the event I had to ask them for a helping hand. Or a hand grenade.

"Let's go, Laddie. Put us in gear and bring her up to fifteen knots. If I'm going to engage some bad guys then at least I'll have witnesses."

Mac gave me a look I could only read as entirely sincere, and said quietly, "Ye do na know what you're about, Lass. Better you let me go. I'll swim in, and you can leave."

"Oh, sure. And with two go-fast boats in pursuit I wouldn't even make it to the anchorage."

"I can ensure you do. Let me go, and I promise no one will come after you. You have my word on it. Only one thing though, I will need *your* word you will remain at the anchorage for three more days, and you canna tell anyone *anything* about your situation. And, if you promise to do as I say, Nacho will be returned to you."

"Your *word*? Which we both know isn't worth a bowl of spit? Do I look that stupid?"

He refrained from answering that last question lest I force him back into the drink with that anchor still attached.

As we approached the growing flotilla at the *bajo*, someone waved at us from Nacho's boat. "Wave back, Mac. Make them think all is well, and whatever crappy plot you jerks have hatched is working. And why three days? What's happening during that time?"

He clammed up.

"Okay, then, tell me this much, at least. Is that Nacho's boat?"

"Yes."

Okay, he was telling the truth there. "How did your partners in crime get it? The last I heard it was being towed into La Paz by the Mexican Navy."

"Trust me, Hetta, the less you know, the better."

"I never like knowing less. In fact, I want to know it *all*."

"Aye, you are that."

I let his dig slide. If this mysterious "they" only needed three more days to accomplish something that involved kidnapping, and perhaps murder, it must be coming to a head fast. Maybe that is why he couldn't take the time to go all the way to Mag Bay with me? Or, did I have something on board they wanted? Or, was it my boat he wanted?

Too many unanswered questions, along with a narcotic hangover, made my head throb. I was far too fatigued and under-gunned to engage in a dust up at sea with an unknown number of bad guys.

"Okay, Mac. I'm going to gamble and trust you, which is probably the stupidest thing I've done since day before yesterday when I trusted you."

He looked like he couldn't believe his good luck, so I let him know I meant bidness. "Here is what is going to happen. I'm going to let you swim to your nefarious friends, but if I see anything at all that alarms me, and I mean anything, I'm going to run you down with this boat. Those Red Devils can't hold a candle to what mayhem a couple of bronze props at high rpm can do. Got that?"

"Aye."

"You will tread water for thirty minutes before swimming for the *bajo*. I don't think we have to synchronize our watches because if you leave that spot before your time is up, I will be on the radio calling in the gendarmes and everyone else in this area, so whatever you guys are up to will go to Hell in a handbasket."

"Ten minutes."

"You're *bargaining* with me?"

"I just know what will work. Fifteen."

"Deal."

"You will no regret this. There is much more at stake than you know."

"You could tell me, but obviously you won't. So, for now, I'll let the bungee cord go, and you work your way to the back of the boat, nice and slowly." Like he had a choice, what with an anchor around his waist.

The bungee cord was stretched to its very limit, and I had trouble unhooking it from the rail. When I finally worked one end loose it went flying and the plastic-coated hook hit Mac in the back of his head quite smartly. "Watch it!"

"Oops. Stand up and move on down."

"I canna swim with this albatross of an anchor around me."

"I know that. But you can walk with it, so get to it."

He executed a Quasimodo lurch down to the back deck, each step punctuated with a curse as the anchor hit him in some personal places. Then, under the watchful barrel of my new best friend, he unwound himself from his trusses, dropped the anchor onto the deck, and before he dove overboard, turned and said, "Hetta, thank you for your trust. I haven't earned it, I know, but if something happens to me, I want you to know it wasn't your fault." Before putting the boat in gear I yelled back, "It might be if you doublecross me!"

He shook his head and hollered. "Haggendass!" as he swam away.

Wondering what manner of Scottish slur he'd besmirched me with as a parting shot, I waved him my own single-digit gesture, redlined the tachs, and hauled ass for Partida.

*Pelicano* had turned north and put on some speed as well, but as I pulled away, it turned back. Hells, bells

Turning on the autopilot, I kept an eye on both Mac and the shrimp boat with my binoculars. Mac, the rat, didn't tread water for more than a couple of minutes before striking out for the pangas. So much for *his* word! *Never mind, Hetta, you'll be out of sight around the end of the island before he can even reach the* bajo, *and the shrimper couldn't catch me now if he wanted to.*

For insurance, however, I picked up the mic on my VHF and turned the radio power on HIGH. "Any vessel vicinity of Isla Partida, this is *Raymond Johnson.* I am inbound to the north end of Partida with an onboard emergency. Request medical assistance."

The radio sprang to life with a jumble of responses.

Now I had a posse on the way, and the last thing Mac and company wanted was a bunch of witnesses if, or more likely when, they came after me in those fast moving pangas. But, I wouldn't sic the gendarmes on them. Yet. After all, I didn't exactly want the authorities on *my* tail, either.

However, I was going to have to come up with a convincing medical emergency, because crying wolf to other cruisers is a sure-fire way to end up on the receiving end of a verbal flogging as well as getting a bad reputation. Okay, so maybe it was way too late for that bad rep thing.

Or, perhaps I could explain to them that I didn't think yelling, "Pearls!" was a very effective distress call?

# Chapter Thirty-three

Tucked safely back at the Partida anchorage, surrounded by other vessels and concerned boaters, I was shaky, but relieved. And exhausted.

And although I assured her that my chest pains had abated, a nurse in the fleet insisted I endure a cautionary medical exam. My blood pressure was a little high, but whose wouldn't be if they'd lived in my flip flops for the past twenty-four hours? Make that forty years.

I provided cold beer and other drinks for those who gathered on *Raymond Johnson*, eager to show support. When my own three beers caught up with me, I began yawning and they politely left, but assured me they were only a radio call away.

My need for sleep was superceded by an urgency to talk to Jan, as I was unsure she had even reached Lopez Mateos. Much to my relief, she answered.

"Hetta! Thank goodness. Where the hell *are* you? Jill called and said you wouldn't be in Cabo, but she's worried even though you told her not to call the feds. What's going on? We're expecting you to arrive here tomorrow afternoon."

"I'm back at Partida."

"What? Why?"

I told her of my horrible day, thanked her profusely for stealing Nacho's gun, which probably saved my life, but was too tired to share all the mean stuff I'd done to Mac, even though I knew she'd be delighted. I did let her know I'd cut Mac loose at the *bajo* on his promise to return Nacho if I didn't squeal for the feds for at least three more days.

"And you say they had Nacho's boat back out there?"

"Yep. And Mac told me Nacho was fine, and if I just wait it out, it'll be over in a few days. Whatever *it* is."

"And, of course, we should believe the lying sack of *caca*."

"Which I don't, but I checked that GPS tracker on Nacho's boat as soon as Mac swam away, and for sure it was his."

"Interesting. The Navy towed it off, and now it's back? I smell a large rat."

"Yeah, that's what I thought."

I heard someone in the background and Jan added, "By the way, Chino says you owe him a bunch of money for diesel fuel. It's all stored in fifty-five gallon drums at Granny Yee's."

"Who knows? I might need it yet. How's Po Thang?"

"Pouting. Ever since we left you at Balandra."

"Put him on."

She held the phone for Po Thang, I sweet-talked him for a couple of minutes, and then Jan got back on. "Yuck, there's dog slobber all over my phone. Have you called Jenks yet to let him know you aren't headed for the border?"

"I left a message."

"Did this message you left contain anything resembling the truth?"

"Not exactly. I said I had boat trouble and had returned to Marina de la Paz."

"You better grab an extinguisher, Chica, your knickers are ablaze."

"Hey, I feel bad, but I figure if he thinks I'm safely at a marina it'll settle him down. It's not like he can do anything to help me from over there, you know."

"Hetta, you already told him the feds were after you, and you had to leave the country! What part about you *not* leaving the country is going to make him happy? He'll be worried. You just gotta learn to keep your stories straight."

"Okay, I'll tell him the feds are no longer interested in me. It might even be true. Hell, maybe they never really *were*, and I panicked without reason."

"Oh, I think you had plenty of reason, and still do, but we're back to square one."

"I know. Look, why don't you have Chino phone that number Javier called when he was on the boat and see who answers? Maybe he can talk to someone, you know, feel them out about me."

"Who does he ask for? Lieutenant Javier of the blue panga? That doesn't sound very official."

"It's Lieutenant Morales. I peeked at his drivers license when we pantsed him. We should' a kept the *pendejo's* chorts for making us believe he was just a courier."

"Yeah," she drawled, "I know how much you abhor artifice. Anyhow, I'll ask Chino to make the call."

"Good. Uh, and I need a really, really big favor."

"Your favor karma has reached critical mass, and not in a good way. What now?"

"Can *you* call Jenks and tell him it was all a misunderstanding, and the feds don't want me for anything? *You*, he'll believe."

"Maybe that's because I've never lied to him?"

"But you've ratted me out to him from time to time, so he trusts you. You'll be doing him a favor. He's a good guy, half-way around the world, and there's no sense in keeping him worried, right? I mean, he can't do anything anyhow, because the one guy he calls when we're in a jam is Nacho, and that ain't gonna happen, may he rest in peace."

"I thought you said Nacho isn't dead?"

"Okay, so maybe he isn't, but Jenks still can't call him for help."

"Standby, gotta talk to Chino."

While I waited I checked the GPS tracker on Nacho's boat. It was still at the *bajo*. What if he was on it, hurt, and needing help? It was high tide, I *could* go out through the cut in *DawgHouse,* and if the other boats were gone, check it out. But night was fast approaching, and I was dog tired. Maybe in the morning?

Jan came back to the phone, "I'll call Jenks. I'll lose any credibility I've ever had with him if this thing goes badly, but I'll fib to him for his own good, just this once. But only if you stay put. Chino and I will be there by tomorrow afternoon. We'll hire a panga in La Paz to bring us out. Agreed?"

245

"Yes, yes, and yes! Cross my heart and hope to die I will not leave this boat. You'll bring Po Thang?"

"Of course."

"And some of Granny Yee's *carnitas*?"

"Don't push your luck. Will you be okay there by yourself for tonight?"

"Yep. I didn't go back to our usual anchoring spot, so I'm smack dab in the middle of the fleet. And, they are keeping an eye on me because of that TIA."

"What the hell is a TIA?

"Transient Ischemic Attack. I'm all better now."

Silence. Then a big sigh. "I don't *even* want to know."

# Chapter Thirty-four

As weary as I was after being drugged, then waxing devious, and being a downright bully-dame, I was restless. Actually, I'd kind of enjoyed the bully part because Mac deserved it, but I guess I was feeling a tweak of conscience for the fake TIA I'd conjured up to justify declaring a medical emergency to my fellow boaters.

Or maybe my inability to sleep was the aftereffect of whatever Mac slipped in my tea, which I could have used a tiny hit of again. I had a bad case of the heebie-jeebies. Every little noise sent me leaping out of bed and peering outside. I'd checked all the locks on the doors several times, and couldn't stop watching my security cameras. I missed my guard dog something awful.

Sometime after midnight, I took a slug of Nyquil and moved from my comfy queen up to the main cabin settee. Less comfortable, yes, but at least I could easily see outside while I awaited Nyquil's surefire wave of nirvana. To quote one of my favorite lines by Blanche Deveraux in the *The Golden Girls*, I was as jumpy as a virgin at a prison rodeo.

Before turning in for what proved a restless night, I'd poked around in the guest cabin, snooping through Nacho's and Mac's belongings they'd left behind. Mac's gallon-sized plastic zip bag held toiletries, and a wallet containing a drivers license confirming the story of his home town in Scotland, and five thousand pesos, which I stuck in my pocket. Call it dues.

Nacho's aftershave was Canoe. I'd wondered why every time he showed up showered and shaved for cocktail hour I got a case of nostalgia; there was this baseball pitcher from the Dominican Republic...but I digress.

I dabbed a little Canoe behind my ears.

Mac had stuffed his shorts and tees into a raggedy duffle bag, Nacho's clothes were neatly folded on shelves. Nacho wears tighty whities, Mac evidently wears nothing at all, which brought to mind that kilt thing. Looked like Nacho was reading a Lee Child novel (of course) and Mac? One of the Outlander series (of course).

Why is it the men in my life are so unpredictable and not more nerdish? Even Jenks's touch of nerd-dom is overridden by his adventures around the world, which are why he is seldom around. Nacho lives a shadowy existence straddling both sides of the law, and Mac? Suffice it to say, I have permanently erased him from my dance card.

Nacho must have been keeping his important things—the ones he didn't want me getting into—on his boat because I found no wallet, computer, or paperwork of any sort in the cabin. Another good reason to go get that boat.

I checked the GPS tracker again. Yep, still out there but a low battery warning let me know I wouldn't be able to track Nacho's panga for much longer.

Chino and Jan were due out the next day, so when they arrived, I figured we could take the boat they'd hired to run out and retrieve Nacho's panga. Along the *malecon* in La Paz, pangas are lined up every day, their drivers waiting hopefully for some one to hire them for a run to the islands, so I knew the driver would appreciate some extra cash. Lucky for him I'd just happened upon five thousand extra pesos. Coincidence? You be the judge!

After dawn, I finally got a few hours sleep, but later in the morning concerned boaters began stopping in to check if I was okay. They were all so nice, bringing me muffins, cookies and herbal tea, I almost came down with a case of the guilties, but evidently we mini-stroke victims recover quickly from the burden of telling the truth.

Jan called about halfway out from La Paz, while she still had a cell signal, to let me know they were inbound with even more treats in hand. And, she added, she had a surprise for me.

I hate surprises and Jan knows it. I figured this little tease was the first of many ways she planned to torment me for...well, everything.

Yep, surprises suck.

Jan, Po Thang, Chino and, uh-oh, Javier arrived just before lunch. That's *Lieutenant* Javier, of the blue panga, Nacho connection and pantsing. I couldn't help noticing he wore a belt now, perhaps as less of a fashion statement than a security measure.

As they neared I saw Po Thang leaning against Javier's leg, gazing up in adoration. Perfidious cur. Then I noticed Javier was both driving the boat and eating a candy bar, a multitask which my dog hoped would result in dropped chocolate. Javier, however, stuffed the last of the candy into his mouth and a disappointed Po Thang immediately turned toward me, as though my presence was a complete surprise.

His exuberant, "OMG, it's you!" act was less than convincing, but I was so happy to see him I went along. He bounded up the stairs and almost flattened me, whining and bashing me with that tail of terror. I bent down on one knee and buried my face in his fur. His breath was chocolaty.

I sniffed and gave Jan, who was second to board, a frown. She shrugged and whispered, "Javier gave him a tiny piece before I could stop him. He'll live. You? Maybe not. What the hell have you gone and got us into this time?"

"Me?" I hissed, "You're the one who brought the fed."

"Chino did it. We traced the number from Javier's telephone conversation with some captain, and Chino called in a few favors. He is, after all, a highly respected Mexican with lots of contacts, which we sometimes forget because he doesn't throw his weight around. Something *one* of us could take a lesson from. Anyhow, the good news? What I told Jenks wasn't a lie. According to Javier, the feds have no ax to grind with you."

Chino joined us, his arms full of grocery bags. "¡*Hola!* Hetta. What are you two whispering about? And where do you want the carnitas?"

"In a tortilla, stat!"

Javier arrived with overstuffed arms, as well. I eyed his shorts and he grinned. "Do not think of it!"

I gave both guys a hug around the bags, and Po Thang didn't like that much. He grabbed the bottom of a plastic bag and tugged. It broke open, but to his dismay, only oranges rolled out.

We all scrambled to catch rolling *naranjas* before they went overboard, and Po Thang, eager to get in the game, dashed about barking and nipping at other bags. Jan grabbed him by the collar, snapped on a leash, and clipped him to a rail.

The entire crew collapsed into deck chairs, howling with laughter. Po Thang howled as well, but in frustration at being tethered. I popped up and got four beers from the deck fridge, so we put off taking the groceries down to the galley.

As we relaxed, a panga roared into the anchorage way too fast, throwing a rooster tail and a very dangerous wake. And it was headed directly for us.

"Isn't that Nacho's boat?" Jan yelled.

Javier, Chino and I all spoke at the same time.

"*Si.*"

"Yes."

"*Mierda!*"

Only Chino flew into action. Faster than I thought possible, he jumped down into Javier's panga, untying it on the way, started the engines and hit the throttles just after Javier made his own graceful leap to join him. Their lives spent in pangas made this action look easy, but I would have broken my neck.

"Get ready to jump if he hits the boat!" Chino yelled over his shoulder at Jan and me. "We'll try to head him off."

Like stunt men out of a Western or action movie, they caught up with the speedster, pulled alongside, and gave it a bump, diverting it from *Raymond Johnson*, but toward the fleet. It was bearing down quickly on all those anchored boats when Javier leaped into Nacho's boat and instantly pulled back the throttles. The boat settled into it's own wake so fast that water almost swamped the outboards.

Chino veered off, very nearly clipping Nacho's boat, and then throttled back himself.

The two boats had created a mini-tsunami, which hit *Raymond Johnson* first, then continued into the main anchorage. Masts began a slow metronome-like sway, becoming more pronounced until the boats were both rolling gunwale to gunwale and wildly yawing at the same time as they rotated on their vertical axes. Some of the smaller ones shipped water, but our wind-assisted buddies are somewhat used to that. I just hoped no one was seriously injured. Screams and curses echoed throughout the anchorage, and from the fish camp behind us as the beached fishermen's pangas were washed up onto the rocks.

Po Thang, when the wake hit us, was still tied to the rail and almost skidded overboard, but I threw myself flat out on the deck and grabbed him by the tail. We were both in danger of taking a plunge when Jan, both feet wrapped around the base of a deck mounted table, latched onto my feet.

A refracting wave from shore hit us again on the other side of the hull and I skidded in Jan's direction, dragging Po Thang with me and almost strangling him with his collar in the process.

Crashing sounds from below told of a nasty cleanup in our immediate future. However, if the reefer's contents were all over the galley floor, Po Thang was the man for the job.

When the surge finally calmed down enough to stand, I worked my way forward, holding on to handrails all the way and checked out my ground tackle to make sure all that turbulence hadn't chafed the snubber lines, or dislodged the anchor. Po Thang, still coughing and gagging from his near hanging, dogged me and whined until I dragged his pee pad out of its hold. After the past few minutes I totally sympathized.

Both pangas worked their way slowly back to *Raymond Johnson* and we tied Nacho's alongside the transom. Javier cut the engines, and Po Thang bounded into the boat and began giving it a goodly sniff. After a couple of minutes he zeroed in on the locker where Nacho kept his gun before Jan liberated it, barked, and then went on point.

Jan and I looked at each other with dread, knowing whatever was in there couldn't be good. I stepped into the cockpit, and while Javier pulled Po Thang away, I opened the door. Inside was a large black plastic bag, closed with duct tape.

Just as I reached in to drag it out of the hatch it squirmed and I jumped back so fast I banged into Javier, almost knocking him down. His superior balance kept both of us on our feet, but my scream brought Chino on the run.

Whipping a knife from his cargo shorts pocket, he said, "Everyone, stay back. Hetta, please take Po Thang away. Secure him on the deck, then come back down here. You, too, Jan. Then, while Hetta and Jan pull out the bag, Javier and I will be ready to fend off whatever is in there."

"Like a giant squid?" I asked. Everyone nodded, all of us evidently sharing a common fear.

Po Thang didn't go easily. It actually took both Jan and me to wrestle him up the ladder and clip him to the rail. Even then he was struggling so hard he was choking himself again.

*Someone* was gonna have a really sore neck later today.

I ran inside, took the gun from its hidey hole and stuffed it into my shorts pocket. The heavy weapon threatened to pants me, ironic given that Javier was back. I also brought back Po Thang's life jacket and harness to make sure he didn't slip out of that collar and add to whatever chaos was coming.

Back in Nacho's panga, I asked, "Chino, can you let Jan and Javier pull the bag out and open it." I brandished a nasty looking gaff I use to land large fish. "If whatever is in there attacks, you and I can nail him." I wasn't about to reveal that gun unless necessary in front of a Mexican federal officer. Just one bullet can get you five years in the clink.

Jan looked like she was about to protest, but then noticed the sag in my shorts and smiled. "Good idea. Let's do this."

While Chino and I stood to either side of the console, me behind the opened door, Jan and Javier grabbed the bag by the duct tape-wrapped opening and tugged.

"Heavy," Jan proclaimed. Javier nodded.

"On three?" I suggested.

Everyone agreed.

"One. Two. Three!"

The bag slid out faster than anticipated on the wet deck, and wedged behind the removable driver's seat and the console. Why hadn't we removed the damned chair? Oh, well.

Jan and Javier moved back while Chino grabbed the bag and cut the top off with one quick slash of his dive knife. Another wiggle inside the bag scattered us, but Javier recovered fast and moved in, lifting the bottom of the sack. He gave it a hard yank and it slipped down far enough to reveal a set of bare, bloody feet held tightly together with plastic tie wraps.

I helped Chino cut away the tough tie wraps while Jan and Javier shredded the plastic bag. Concentrating on holding down the legs lest they move and Chino sliced into the victim, I heard Jan say, "He's breathing. Forget the feet, let's turn him on his back and sit him up."

"On three!"

"One. Two. Thr—Oh, hell!"

Nacho struggled to sit himself up and gave me a grin that, even though in a blood-splotched face, was charming.

" Café," he croaked, "I want a refund. This is the worst cruise I've ever been on."

# Chapter Thirty-five

We dragged Nacho up onto the main deck and Jan gave him water while Chino and I finally released his feet. The plastic had cut into his skin, but that was not the source of all that blood.

I was so glad to see him again that I wanted to give him a hug, but he'd obviously been in that bag way too long. Even Po Thang strained against his leash far enough to give him a sniff, but quickly backed off.

"What hurts?" Chino asked while wiping the stinker's face off with fresh water.

"Nothing too serious. Mostly my pride," he croaked and signaled for more water. "Uh, do you think I could have a beer?"

"*Absolutamente*, Señor Ingacio," Javier said, reaching into the fridge.

Jan drew a large pot of warm water in the galley and brought it up so Chino could wash away blood and gore while looking for wounds.

Nacho chugged the beer. "Please, help me up and take me to the shower, Chino. I am not hurt. It is not my blood. And *por favor*, another beer."

"Yes, please, someone get him into that shower," I cracked, but fetched two bottles out of the deck fridge for him.

He chugged both beers, then grabbed his head. "Brain freeze!"

For some reason this wimpy gripe struck us all, including Nacho, as funny. Here he was, dehydrated, filthy, and most likely starving, and he was complaining about a brain freeze?

The men helped him to the outdoor shower—no way was he going inside my boat smelling like last month's fish—and Jan and I left him to his dignity while they helped him strip and wash down. Jan made him soup and toast, I found him clean clothes.

By the time we got him fed, it was time for our own dinner, during which I'd hoped to learn where Nacho had been all this time. Unfortunately, he was so exhausted from his ordeal he went straight to bed.

While we ate, several boaters stopped by to ask what the hell the boat chase was all about, looking for someone to blame for being whacked about so rudely. Chino explained to them that we'd witnessed the runaway panga and gone after it, only to find that the driver had passed out and the boat was on autopilot. And no, he wasn't drunk, but had suffered a dizzy spell.

There seemed to be a lot of that going around.

So, instead of being targets for derision, we were now heroes, and we left it like that; we powerboaters get enough guff without adding fuel to the fire.

After dinner, I volunteered to wash the dishes, Javier went to crash on the upper bunk in Nacho's cabin—and keep an eye on Nacho—Jan and Chino took my cabin, and I ended up, once again, on the settee. After they all went to their respective cabins, Po Thang and I did the dishes.

It was nice to have my pre-rinse and garbage disposal device back on board.

Somewhere around four in the morning according to the clock by the settee, Po Thang's thumping tail woke me. Nacho was in the galley, rummaging in the fridge, so we joined him.

"Lot's of good stuff in there. What's your pleasure?" I asked.

"I cannot have what I really want," he said, giving me a meaningful look that set my tummy jumping. Then he grinned and added, "However, I have dreamed of mac and cheese for days, as well."

Whoa, can this dude make a girl all gushy, or what? "Well, lucky for you I froze an entire casserole and hid it in the back to preclude marauders."

I found the dish and popped it into the microwave. While it cooked, I poured a glass of wine for each of us and we settled at the dining table. Nacho downed his and held out his glass for more. He was still pale and a little shaky, but he sure smelled a lot better.

"How are your ankles?" I asked. We'd applied an antibacterial ointment and bandaged them.

"They will heal."

"How about the rest of you. How do you feel?"

"Like I spent more than one day in a black plastic bag."

"You kinda look like that, too. Where'd the blood come from?"

"I think they'd had fish in there. Old fish."

The microwave dinged and I went to give the macaroni a stir. When I returned he was pouring more wine.

"You might want to pace yourself there, Buddy. Dinner will be ready in five minutes."

"Maybe some water, as I am still very thirsty." He started to get up, but I pushed him back into his chair.

"I'll get it. You take it easy."

He smiled that smile that always gives me a little flutter here and there. Mostly there. "I should get kidnapped and stuffed in a bag more often. You are being nice to me."

"There's been many a time I longed to tell you to get stuffed. Don't get used to me being nice. It will pass."

"Of that I am certain."

We clinked glasses and laughed.

He inhaled half the mac and cheese straight out of the casserole dish, washing it down with alternate gulps of water and wine. Po Thang stood by, attentively watching the fork's movement, his head and eyes following. I gave him a treat. "Nope, you ain't getting any, Matey. Pasta gives you gas and much as I missed you, I did not miss your hellacious farts."

Nacho stopped eating and gazed into my eyes. Okay, reading the occasional romance novel may have influenced that description, but anyhow he looked at me, and his eyes glistened. Tears? On Nacho? He wiped his eyes with his napkin and said, "I cannot tell you how much I have missed both of you. I thought...well, I was almost certain I would never see you again."

I patted his wrist. Po Thang put his chin on my arm, pinning my hand to Nacho's arm. I quickly pulled back from a little too much contact. Nacho stroked Po Thang's snout and cocked his head at me. I guess it was my turn to get schmaltzy. "Okay, I gotta admit, I missed you, as well. Seems we've both had quite an adventure. You tell me yours and I'll tell you mine.

"Isn't that supposed to be, *show* me yours and I'll show you mine?" he asked with that unhinging grin of his.

"I didn't miss you *that* much."

# Chapter Thirty-six

We talked until first light reminded us we required more sleep.

And even after all that time, I wasn't so sure I got the whole story. But, of course, neither did he.

Nacho claimed Mac had slipped him a Mickey—I sure didn't doubt that!—right after Jan and I took my new pangita out to the *bajo* that fateful day nine days before.

"And I woke aboard a large vessel I knew to be a shrimp boat by the smell. I worked on one during summers when I was in college, and it is something you never forget."

"You went to college? Where?"

"Café, I have been held hostage all this time, my life in danger, and you want my scholastic credentials?"

"Sorry. You just don't seem the type."

"Because," he asked softly, "I am Hispanic?"

"No, because you're a criminal."

"You obviously have not spent much time with graduates of the Harvard School of Business."

His quip gave us both a chuckle.

"So, where the heck have you been for the past nine days?"

"Until yesterday, on that shrimp boat. They actually treated me quite well, considering I was a prisoner, and locked into a tiny dark compartment in the engine room. I may never eat shrimp again."

"It was the *Pelicano*. That boat was here, in the anchorage, during the norther. Jan even went over and traded Spam for shrimp and halibut. Who could have known you were on it? And I saw the shrimper at the bajo when I was out there yesterday. They looked like they were leaving, but then they turned around."

"I felt them make a sharp u-turn, and hoped it was for the good. Up until then, I figured they were headed out to sea to dump me overboard. When they stopped, stuffed me into that bag, and carried me out on deck, I feared the worst. And I was right. They shoved me over a rail and I thought it was the end. But, I landed on a hard surface. My own boat's deck, as it turns out."

"So, how did you get in that little locker?"

"Someone rolled me in there, then started the boat. I realize now that when they stopped again, we were outside the anchorage here. They must have set the autopilot and jumped overboard for another boat to pick them up. If Chino and Javier hadn't come to the rescue, I would have had a really nasty landing on the beach."

"But, in your estimation, not a fatal one."

"Probably not. The boat is sturdy, and I was inside that cubby hole."

"So they evidently didn't intend to kill you. If so, they could have done that any old time in the past few days. They just wanted you out of the way."

He nodded. "I think so."

"Why?" I demanded, perhaps a little more sharply than I intended. After all, I had been promised Nacho in return for staying put and shutting up. But was he part of the plan to keep me from yelling for the authorities that something afoul was afoot on the *bajo*?

"I really have no idea."

"Why don't I believe you? You've been up to something, searching, and don't deny it, because Jan and I *know* you were. You ran a grid at the *bajo*, and Javier gave you an assist."

"How do you know this?"

Oops. "Uh, well, Javier came looking for you after you disappeared, so we figured you were in cahoots." I thought that sounded much better than, *we bugged your boat, put secret agent double-OH-dawg on the job, stole your thumb drive, and pantsed your accomplice.*

His eyes narrowed. "And just what have *you* been doing the past nine days? Besides, of course, worrying about me."

"Yeah, like that happened. I dunno, we did all kinds of stuff. Mostly drank up your expensive booze."

He shook his head and gave me a two-handed, come on, give it up, sign. "Day by day, Café."

"Nacho waxing poetic? Lemme think. Okay, after we saw your boat towing *Full Tilt Boogie* out of the anchorage—"

He cut me off. "You did not think this strange? Why did you not intercept us and ask where we were going?"

"We were stuck. When the wind came up we returned via the cut, and ran aground. Had to push and pull the boat through, and by the time we were finally free, you were long gone." I didn't think it prudent to mention we were tracking him with a GPS locater Jan had planted on his boat.

"And then what?"

I told him we waited, hoping he would return, but then Javier showed up looking for him and we decided to go out the next morning in his panga. "Javier took us to the *bajo* and we found your boat anchored there, with this...*thing* on it."

"What thing?"

"A bloody, slimy, twitching, tentacle. Big. And throwing blood and gore all over the place. You were nowhere to be seen, so Javier called for help from La Paz, and all kinds of people showed up. They sent a couple of divers down to search for you, then took your boat to La Paz, and that was that. Well, until Mac showed up."

"*¡Pinche pendejo!* Where is he now?"

"I dunno, but if I ever see that SOB again, I plan to hand him his *cojones*."

Nacho squirmed in his chair and covered his lap with his hands.

"Whose pockets you gonna pick, Hetta?" Jan asked, stretching and yawning as she entered the main cabin and made a beeline for the coffee pot.

"Mac's."

She shuffled up to us with her coffee cup and plopped down on the other side of Nacho. "I'll help you, Hetta. That guy sure had *you* fooled."

"Hey, how was I to know he was a...whatever he is. We need to find out, you know. He's obviously up to no good, but he isn't here to ask what."

"More's the pity, as he would put it."

"On the other hand, Miz Jan, look who *is* sitting here, on my boat, and *is* without a doubt up to his neck in this pile of crap we've had to live through for the past...what? Two weeks?"

We both scooted closer to Nacho, sandwiching him tightly between us. He tried to stand, but Jan grabbed him by the belt with her free hand, and jerked him back, none too gently. "Whoa there, Podner, you got some 'splainin' to do."

Nacho was saved by Javier sticking his head out of their cabin.

"*¡Javier! ¡Ayúdame!* These women are molesting me."

"You are lucky." Javier went straight for the coffee, poured a cup, added three tablespoons of sugar, and cream, took a sip, then smiled at Nacho. "*Pero*, you still 'ave your *pantalones*."

"Of course he has his pants. What do you take us for?" Jan huffed.

"What's going on up here?" Chino asked as he came up the stairs from my cabin. "Who needs help?"

"Me," Nacho answered. "I am under attack."

"Not yet, you rat," I said. "You are at the root of this entire screwed up mess, and I want to know why, or we will hurt you. Badly. *¿Entiendes?*"

"Yes, I understand. But, there is not much to tell. Ask Javier. We were just investigating the diver attacks, trying to find out if the Red Devils were becoming a serious danger."

"Why you? Why not hire a full-fledged, world renowned, Doctor of Marine Biology." I put my finger to the side of my face and tilted my head. "But, where oh where could you possibly find one of those? Oh, that's right, you actually know one." I pointed at Chino, "Doctor Brigido Comacho Yee, in the flesh."

Chino took a bow. "At your *servicio*."

Javier frowned at Nacho. "Why did you not suggest him?"

Nacho sighed. "Because it was too dangerous. Look at what's happened."

"Yeah," I said, "Just look at what...hey, exactly what *has* happened?"

"I was drugged and kidnapped. People are missing."

"And so you quite naturally decided to drag me into it, but not Chino?"

He shrugged. "You had a boat, and were in La Paz. There was no plan for you to even leave the anchorage. A marine biologist, on the other hand, would have to go out in search of the Red Devils."

I threw up my hands. "Squid, squid, squid. I'm sick of them. Anyhow, that slimeball, Artherrrr MacKenzie Gra-ham, said it was more to do with pearls."

Chino coughed, almost spitting coffee. "Art Graham? What on earth has he to do with anything?"

# Chapter Thirty-seven

"Art? Art?" I blurted when Chino called Mac, a.k.a Arther MacKenzie Graham, Art.

"Someone throw Hetta a fish," Jan quipped, then added, "Art?"

We were all staring at Chino, waiting to hear what he had to say about this turn of events. "I know *an* Art Graham. Actually *Doctor* Art Graham, a fellow marine biologist. Is that who you are talking about? He is here?"

"Oh, boy, is he! But we had no idea he's a marine biologist. You *know* him?"

"Yes, we met years ago, when I was studying in the UK. I attended one of his seminars in Glasgow, and then he visited me in Lopez Mateos to help with the whale count one year. And now you say he is here?"

"Hell's bells," I said, "no wonder he couldn't show up in Mag Bay on my boat. He knew you would be there, Chino. This is getting weirder by the minute."

I narrowed my eyes and zeroed in on Nacho. "I smell a common denominator here, and for once it isn't just me."

Nacho stood, swayed a little on his feet and plopped back down. "Could I please have some water?"

"How about a nice comfy water*board*?" I snarled.

"I'll pass."

Jan patted his hand and scowled at me. "Hetta, have a heart. The poor man has been through a horrible ordeal. I'll get him a nice glass of ice water, and *then* we'll waterboard him."

Chino and Javier smirked, but Nacho knew we were fairly serious.

"I can explain," Nacho said after he had a sip of water.

"Oh, yes, you surely can," I told him. "From the beginning?"

"We, well, *I*, hired Mac."

"That doesn't sound like the beginning to me, how about you, Jan?"

"Nope."

Nacho rolled his eyes and looked to Chino and Javier for backup, but they gave him blank stares.

"Okay, okay. As you have heard, giant squid have been killing divers."

Chino shook his head. "The *diablos rojas* have been *accused* of attacking people. I have my doubts."

"So does Mac, but something is going on. Anyway, about a year ago, two Mexican navy divers disappeared, then washed up on the beach, torn to shreds, bruised all over with dark round spots. All the signs of a squid attack."

"Yes," Chino said, "and when I was sent the coroner's report and photos of these poor men, I expressed doubt. The cause of death was drowning, which I certainly was not qualified to contest. My misgiving, and I expressed so in my response, was that a hungry squid would not leave so much...uh, well...."

"Meat on the bone?" I asked.

Chino grinned. "Ah, Hetta, what a way you have with words. That is it. If you ever witness what is left of prey after a true attack, you will know what I mean."

My stomach did a flip. "Uh, I think I'll pass on that experience."

Nacho agreed. "I have no wish to witness such a sight. Anyway, we needed an expert in our investigation, and for obvious reasons, I did not wish to engage you in the investigation, Chino."

"What obvious reasons?" I demanded.

"Chino is local. If it turned out there was no squid to blame, whoever staged such a gruesome murder is very dangerous, and Doctor Yee would be a sitting target out there in that fish camp. Unless of course," he raised his hands and shivered in a campy *I'm so scared move,* "Hetta was visiting."

"Jan, fetch the waterboard. It's right next to our jar of leeches."

"So," Chino said, "you brought Art Graham and his wife all the way from Scotland?"

"Wife?" Jan and I screeched, banshee-like, in unison.

Chino, used to our outbursts, ignored us, but Nacho shrank away and Javier grabbed his belt buckle. "Yes, Johnnie is his partner. They work as a team."

I caught Nacho giving Chino a shut up sign, but it was too late.

"Mac is *gay*?" All of this information overload had me blurting before thinking, not at all a rare circumstance.

"No, Hetta, not Johnny. J-o-h-n-n-i-e, as in female."

"Oh." Eloquent.

"They came from Scotland to help you?" Chino asked again.

"No, luckily they were already here, working with some biologists in La Paz at the university. That is how we were introduced. They are sailing and working their way around the world on a two-year sabbatical."

"So, just where is this wife?" I wanted to know. I'd never seen hide nor hair of her, either at the dock or out in the islands.

"We do not know. They were helping us investigate the Red Devil attacks, and then Mac reported she was called back to the UK on a family emergency, but something did not seem right. Chino, do you know anything about their, uh, relationship?"

"No, I have not seen her, or him, in years. Why do you ask?"

"Rumor has it there was a ruckus on their boat the night before she left. Loud yelling, that kind of thing. And," he said, somewhat ominously, "there is no record of her flying out of La Paz or Cabo."

Now Javier bobbed his head in agreement, then regretted it when I zeroed in on him. "Just what is your part in this, anyhow?"

He pressed his lips together and gave his shoulders a twitch.

Nacho and he exchanged a look. Javier sighed and tilted his head in a reluctant, "Oh, what the hell," gesture.

"I guess we must share what we know. Javier is with the PGR, which is somewhat like the United States Department of Justice. What with squid attack reports, and the possible disappearance of a renowned Scottish scientist working on the investigation, it was only a matter of time before someone put the two together, and SECTUR, the Mexican Secretaria de Turismo, wanted to have answers before the story hit the headlines."

"What you mean is they want it covered up?" I said, remembering that veiled threat towards me by the port captain's office. "And they want it bad enough to hire someone like you, who walks a fine line on the tightrope of legal? Right, Nacho?"

"Yes. But of course, Café, that is why I then hired you."

Jan laughed and slapped Nacho's knee. "Nacho and Hetta, *como dos gotas de agua, verdad?*"

"Did you just call us goats?" I demanded.

"No, I said you and Nacho are like two drops of water, two peas in a pod."

I guess I can't really argue with that.

# Chapter Thirty-eight

"And to think, that rat Mac asked me to marry him!"

Jan scoffed. "I think he was being facetious, what with him having a wife and all."

"A missing wife," I reminded her.

We were on a tiny patch of beach around the corner from the anchorage, where the Parque Nacional guys wouldn't likely spot us. I'd tucked the dinghy in behind a mangrove and let my dog run wild.

Beside himself at being off the boat, and free, he raced round and round the playa, then into the water and back out again. Only after a good half hour of this exercise in pure joy did he begin anointing whatever vegetation was available. We watched him carefully, garbage bag at the ready for the big event.

"That's circle number three, so a squat and number two is eminent," Jan noted. "Don't make eye contact or he'll never settle on a spot."

In my peripheral vision I saw him hunch and grin. "Bingo. When he comes back I'll go bag the goods."

"So, while we await his nibs to unload, what do you make of Mac now after all we learned this morning?"

"Danged if I know. Nacho and Javier seem to suspect he may have done in the wifey poo."

"I certainly wouldn't be surprised. There but for the grace of a 9mm, go I. I'm convinced he planned to dump me and take my boat. But where? And why?"

"I disagree, Miz Hetta. If he was gonna dispense with you, why didn't he do so while you were drugged? After all, when you didn't show up in Mag Bay, it would have taken days to search for you, and he could be long gone."

"Good point. So, we're back to ground zero. When we get back to *Raymond Johnson*, I'm going to Google Dr. Johnnie Graham, and Mac. And, don't forget, he told me all this skullduggery is connected to pearls, and all he needed was a few more days grace. I got the idea all would be revealed after that. Also, he did send Nacho back, as promised."

"Wonder where Mac is now?"

"*Pelicano*, according to what Nacho said, doubled back and dumped him onto his own boat. My guess is Mac is on *Pelicano*. Let's go up to the top and see if we can spot that danged shrimper." I pointed up at a sheer rock cliff.

"Go ahead. I'll wait here."

"Chicken. There's a path and Po Thang has gone up it before. We can follow him."

"Hetta, we're in sandals."

I grabbed my backpack and pulled out two pair of thick socks. "My motto: be prepared."

"Socks and sandals? How very Berkeley. Someone call the fashion police!"

The climb up the steep path wasn't for sissies.

The unstable volcanic rock rained down in a mini-avalanche of pebbles as Po Thang raced ahead, then back, and danced in place as if to say, "You got a problem there? Get a move on, Maggots, I haven't got all day, you know. Chop, chop!"

Panting, dusty, bruised, and thirsty, we finally reached the summit where we collapsed onto a flat rock and reluctantly shared our water with our doggie drill sergeant. After catching our breath for a few minutes, we plodded on a blessedly level trail along the top of the cliff to the other side of the island. From there we could see forever—all the way to San Francisco Island, the *bajo*, and parts of the anchorage.

*Pelicano* was nowhere in sight, nor were there any other boats on or near the *bajo*. which we easily identified by the yellowish color of the shallow water.

"Wow! What a view." Jan walked to the edge and pointed back to where we could see my boat. "And there she be."

Sure enough *Raymond Johnson* looked like she was floating in light blue glass. "Let's backtrack as close as we can for photos, because I am never, ever, climbing up here again. I'll post 'em on Facebook."

"Better than those bazillion pictures of Po Thang you've got on there already."

"Oh, good idea! Why don't you take one of Po Thang and me with the boat in the background?"

Po Thang and I grinned and struck poses for our millions of fans as Jan captured the moment in time. Just as she took the last one, her phone dinged, startling her. "Whoa, we got cell service up here! I'll post those photos on Facebook right now."

While she busied herself with her phone, I checked mine. Three bars. Biting the bullet, I made a very expensive call to the Trob, because I wanted to talk to him far away from the three men on our boat. He answered on the second ring and I quickly outlined what had happened, who was involved, what we suspected, and the entire situation at present, assuring him I was safe, even though he didn't ask. Matter of fact, he didn't pose any questions at all, saying, "Okay," after each detail.

When I hung up, Jan patted me on the shoulder. "That was very concise, straight to the point, and not one single lie or obfuscation. Either you're losing your touch, or you are really skeered."

"I'm skeered. We are not out of the woods yet, until Mac is behind bars. He's got partners in crime, and we don't know who they are. Let's Google Johnnie Graham while we have a signal. I wanna get a look at Mac's wife."

"Jealous?"

"Very funny. I'm worried about her. Her husband is a freako psychopath and she's missing. Maybe we can find an e-mail address or something? Who knows, she might actually be back in Scotland, but what with Mac doing his Jekyll and Hyde act, she also might be fish food. Which would be pretty danged ironic for a marine biologist."

"Okay, but first, let's call Doctor Di. The international marine biologist club is fairly chummy, so maybe she knows Johnnie, or has heard something about her. Chino is hopeless when it comes to dishing the dirt. He takes everyone at face value."

I was batting a hundred today. Not only did Chino's former assistant know of Doctor Johnnie Graham, she knew the couple personally. Evidently these Jacques Cousteau types swim in a rarified pool. She told me about Johnnie's brilliant career, her work with Mac—a fabulous man as well as scientist—and ended with, "Why do you ask?"

I knew that was coming. "I sort of hoped you had a telephone number, or some kind of contact address. Jan and I are doing a little work for Chino." So much for that obfuscation thing.

"Hang on, I'll get what I have in my computer."

I counted the pesos rolling by as I waited. Oh, well, Carlos Slim was probably running a little low on yachts. That thought reminded me of something I'd read recently, that one of the reasons he was one of the richest men in the world wasn't only his monopoly of the communications industry in Mexico. Or that his rates are exorbitant. What really fuels his coffers is the twenty billion bucks a year that head south over the US border, sent to families of migrants, both legal and illegal, so they can have a cell phone and keep in touch.

Doctor Di broke into my deep thoughts on a world of finance that totally escapes me. "Okay, Hetta, here goes. You have a pen?"

"Uh, no. I'm on a bluff at Partida. Can you send me a text message with all the info? "

"Sure thing. You and Jan having fun out there?"

"How did you know Jan is with me?"

"She just posted a picture on Facebook, and it showed the location."

Now *there's* something I need to remember, should I continue my wont for steadfast equivocation.

# Chapter Thirty-nine

Since we were already at the top of that dastardly cliff, we took more selfies, and pictures of *Raymond Johnson* resting below. Po Thang, always ready for his close up, grinned and drooled for us and we clicked off even more great shots of boats in the background.

I was making a video surely destined for National Geographic when a sudden movement under the clear water caught my eye. I zeroed in just as Bubbles pirouetted behind *Raymond Johnson*, making a loud splash probably intended to call her BFF out for a romp.

Unfortunately, it worked.

Po Thang barked and dove right off the top of a very steep slope created eons ago when the volcano blew and created the crater that was now an anchorage.

Jan and I screamed, "Noooo!" but he was gone.

With my heart in my throat, I rushed to the edge, prepared to see a broken lump of fur on the rocks two hundred feet below. Which is where I would have ended up if Jan hadn't grabbed the back of my shirt and shorts and yanked me back.

"Hetta, for cryin' out loud. Get a grip."

"But, Po Thang!"

"It sure as hell won't help him to have your big butt land on top of him. Now, very slowly, we'll crawl to the edge and take a peek."

"I'm too scared to look. You do it."

"Okay, stay behind me and hold my feet. What's that noise?"

Hoping she hadn't heard yelps of pain, I cocked my head. "Sounds like...rocks falling?"

Jan shimmied to the edge. "It is. I think he's found a path!"

I scooted over to join her, losing skin in the process. Sure enough, just as I dared look down, Po Thang, preceded by a mini-avalanche of stones and dust, rolled ass over teakettle onto a stretch of rocky beach, gave a mighty shake, and bounded into the water to meet his BFF.

"I swear, I'm going to shoot that damned dolphin," I said, as Jan and I rolled onto our backs and caught our breath Then we began to giggle, which is what we always do when in this kind of situation.

Finally composing ourselves, we stood, yelled, and waved our arms when we saw Chino, camera in hand, come up on the flying bridge to see what the brouhaha was all about. He waved and then focused in on us as we posed and vamped, camping it up for his camera.

And that's when we saw the Parque Nacional patrol boat headed for Raymond Johnson.

"Oh, crap. They won't arrest Po Thang will they? Let's go!"

"Take it easy, Chica. First off, because Po Thang is the designated search and rescue dog at our fish camp, he's registered with the parks department."

"Po Thang is registered with the Mexican government?"

"Had to. Dogs are not allowed at the lagoon, so Chino pulled some strings. He's kind of a park ranger himself. And even if he wasn't, can you imagine those dudes down there trying to take your dog from Chino, Nacho, and Javier? No way are they any kind of match for those three."

Even with those assurances, we made our way back to *DawgHouse* as fast as we could navigate that torturous trail, and while we didn't have to put up with Po Thang showering us with rocks and dust, we slid a good part of the way on butts and stomachs. We arrived back at *Raymond Johnson* looking as though we'd just competed in a mud wresting match.

The park rangers were a little taken aback with our appearance when Jan and I arrived, but from the questions they asked us—Was Po Thang our dog? And was he swimming only, and not going to the beach?—it was obvious they had little interest in busting anyone for allowing a dog on the island. Matter of fact, they seemed much more interested in a dolphin and dog playing with each other than whether said hound had broken their rules. Both men took photos and made videos. One of them also snapped off a couple of Jan and me.

When they motored on toward the main anchorage, waving as they left, I breathed a sigh of relief. "Whew! I was sure we were collared."

Chino, looking us over said, "Maybe they thought you two had been beat up enough for one day." He snapped another photo of his own.

"Hey!" Jan made a grab for his iPhone, but he deftly stepped aside.

"Oh, no. I must share this on my Facebook page for others to enjoy."

"Glad to be of service," I grumbled. "I need a beer."

Javier, looking way too pleased with our dishevelment, at least handed me a cold Tecate. I sank into a deck chair and examined my scraped knees. Lord only knows what my butt looked like.

Nacho, who hadn't said a word since our return and didn't seem to share Chino's glee at our muddy selves, moved into the chair next to me. "Hetta, we have had news." From his facial expression, I surmised it wasn't *good* news.

"What now?"

"Another body has been discovered east of here. Very torn up. And, he was wearing a kilt."


After Bubbles left and Po Thang, Jan, and I were cleaned up, we threw together lunch while the guys made calls and checked the Internet for any more details on this latest victim.

"Ya know, Hetta, it might not even be Mac."

"Yeah, right. I hear kilts are all the rage in the Sea of Cortez."

"I guess the bright side is, whatever was up is over. We can go back to La Paz, and Chino and I'll head back to camp and get ready for the whale season. And you?"

"I don't really know. I'll call Jenks and—" I lowered my voice to a whisper. "Oh, hell, you think Nacho will want a refund?"

"Hadn't thought about that. Lemme think. We've been working on this cruise of his for...thirteen days. I'd say the most he could ask for is less than half. Which is still a pretty penny."

"Ain't happening. Just for starters, he got me kidnapped, and forced me to try to flee the country, incurring extra costs in fuel and...upset."

"Upset? Think that'll hold up in court?"

"Matter of fact, now that I think about it, he owes me *more* money."

"I love the way you can turn any crappy event to suit your bank account."

"It's what I do."

We high-fived. "Anyhow," she said, "if Nacho's still working with Javier and Mac—make that *was* working with Mac—to investigate the Red Devil thing, I guess he'll stay on the case, and he'll want to do so on your boat. I can hang on for a little longer if you like, but I want to get paid up front, just in case you go and get yourself kilt."

# Chapter Forty

We were hooting over Jan's extremely irreverent, inappropriate, tasteless, and just plain bad, kilt line when I caught a movement in my peripheral vision and Javier materialized behind us. "Can I be of help?"

Startled, Jan, who was multitasking as a standup comic and master chef, whirled on him, paring knife raised in threat. In one deft move, the knife was in Javier's hand.

"Don't do that!" Jan screamed.

Po Thang, who had been hanging around hoping for a dropped quart of ice cream or something, tucked tail and took a powder just as Chino rushed to the galley and put his arms around Jan. "Sweetheart, what's wrong?"

Jan, her cheeks flushed, shook off a combination of chagrin and embarrassment. "Nothin'. Javier startled me, that's all."

Chino turned on Javier and saw the knife in his hand. "What did you do to my darling Jan?"

Javier was speechless, so I jumped to his defense. "Your *darling* Jan pulled a knife on a federal officer, and he disarmed her. Pretty danged slick move there, Javier. Can you teach me how to do that sometime?"

Nacho joined us. "What's going on? Po Thang jumped into my lap and almost knocked me from my chair."

Po Thang who had slinked back behind Nacho, leaned up against my leg. I scratched his ears. "Jan yelled at Javier, and this poor dog thought she was scolding *him*. Everyone just calm down and grab a dish. Lunch is ready."

Jan, carrying a bag of potato chips in one hand and a bottle of wine in the other, growled, "Gee, thanks for your unflagging support."

"Well, you did look like you were about to filet him."

"He shouldn't sneak up on people holding knives."

"Did anyone bring the Valium?"

Jan pouted throughout most of our lunch, only un-pooching that bottom lip when the conversation turned to Mac.

"I am very confused," Chino said. "Mac told me he and Johnnie might visit the whale camp again soon, but I did not know they were already in La Paz. And Hetta, how did you meet him?"

Nacho spoke up, sidestepping Chino's question. "I think we need a timeline here. I will start it; divers began to be killed by what appeared to be *diablos rojas* attacks. So, let us start with those Red Devils, and the deaths attributed to them."

We all nodded, but no one spoke up, so Nacho continued. "Javier, your group contacted me to hang out with the cruising fleet and keep my ears open for clues, since some of the men who died were on foreign boats. I also came up with the Grahams to help with investigating what was going on with the squid from a scientific viewpoint."

"Yes, that is so," Javier agreed.

"Who did Mac report to?" I asked.

"To me," Nacho admitted.

"Did you know Mac had helped me free a dolphin from a fishing net?" I wanted to know. "And if so, was he already on your payroll at the time?"

"Ah," Chino said, "it was Art who helped you. Good for him."

"Yes, it was," Nacho continued. "He was actually looking for the dolphin. It had already been reported that an animal in distress was spotted near San Francisco Island, and he went out to find it. But the dolphin came to Hetta for help." Nacho said this with a crooked grin, as if to question the dolphin's judgment. "However, at the time Mac did not know you and I were acquainted."

"But, when he told you we'd met, and how, you then decided to hire my boat to infiltrate the cruising community?"

"It seemed reasonable. At the time."

"Was his wife with him then?"

"No, she was already gone, but we did not know why, or where to. However, when he returned to La Paz right after the dolphin rescue and, instead of returning to his slip at Marina Palmyra, he ended up next to your boat at Marina de la Paz, we became curious as to what he wanted from you."

Jan perked up. "Oh, you know how men flock after Hetta, what with her fatal charm. But then when he kidn—yahhh! Hetta, what the hell?"

I dabbed iced tea from her face, muffling her mouth in the process. "So sorry, Jan, I tripped." I hauled her out of her chair and herded her down into the main cabin. "Let's get you into some dry clothes."

Over my shoulder, I said, "We'll be right back."

At the bottom of the steps Jan balled her fists and attempted to swing on me, but the heavy towel over her head threw off her aim.

"Jan," I hissed, "ix-nay on the earls-pay. There are two men out there we cannot entirely trust."

"Oh, orry-say. Okay, I got it." She dried her hair on the towel. "At least you don't use sugar."

"Let's go back up. No pearls, no guns. No nothing, let *them* talk."

Jan wrapped the towel into a turban, which on her looked great, and pasted a big smile on her face. "We're back. No harm, no foul. Hetta's clumsy."

Po Thang, always leery of shouts and unscheduled liquids, was hunkered down between Nacho and Chino, who both had that look of discomfort men get when women act up. Javier, on the other hand, was the picture of suspicion.

"Now, where were we?" I asked cheerfully.

"Jan was saying something about Mac?"

"It's not important. Let's stay with the timeline. Nacho, who contacted the Trob in order to charter *Raymond Johnson*?"

"It was arranged through the Mexican justice department. At my suggestion."

"So now that you and Javier were in cahoots, investigating the diver deaths, you were also still working with Mac, whom you suspected may have offed his wife?"

They both nodded.

"Why were you at the *bajo*? What is out there?"

"Actually, he didn't know he did it, but Mac led us there. We had him under surveillance, because we were suspicious that he was covering something up. Maybe the death of his wife, but we were also beginning to wonder if he was trying to protect the squid."

"Protect the squid? How nuts is that?" I blurted.

Chino shook his head. "Not so nuts. I, too, was reluctant to blame the squid in an attack reported near Loreto, and that story has since been proved a hoax. Unfortunately, I was one of the scientists who caught a poor innocent squid for testing. It has to be the low point of my career."

Jan patted his shoulder. "You didn't know. By the way, did you ever discuss this incident with Mac?"

"Not personally, but I addressed the situation in an article in the MarineBio Newsletter, and he probably read it."

"So," I looked at Javier, "you hired the Graham team to get the truth about the squid attacks, and something went awry?"

He was clearly not understanding the word, awry, so Chino quickly translated.

"Yes." He scowled, as though unhappy with Mac's findings. "He seemed certain the squid were not to blame, but we disagree. Since the *Tourista* Bureau," his emphasis on *tourista*, almost spitting it, made clear his feelings for one of the most powerful offices in Mexico, "never wants bad, uh, *publicidad* they prefer to bury the truth. We have made no progress and divers still die."

Jan and I exchanged a grin at his use of *tourista*, a euphemism in Mexico for Montezuma's Revenge.

I looked to Nacho for the story to continue, but he tilted his head, cut his eyes skyward and lifted his palms in a *¿quien sabe?* gesture. Who knows?

"Okay, then, Nacho. Answer this. What next?"

Javier spoke up. "I suggest we all return to La Paz."

I shook my head. "Not for a few days. I have, uh, things to do out here." There was no way I was telling this fed I'd made Mac a promise I'd stay put. "Anyone who wants to leave better go with Javier."

My loyal crew and friends all said they were staying with the ship, so Javier gathered his things and left.

As soon as he was out of the anchorage, Jan asked, "Okay, tell me again why we aren't heading for port."

"I told Mac, as part of the deal I made with him, I would stay here a few days. He kept his end and returned Nacho to us, or at least I think he did, so I'm staying put."

"Hetta, he's probably dead."

"Doesn't matter. I said I would, and I will. If you don't want to stay, Nacho can take you in when you're ready. Right Nacho?"

"No."

"No?"

"I think we must all stay to protect you from yourself. It is surely more than I can do on my own."

# Chapter Forty-One

I was still stuck sleeping on the settee, but I had to admit I was soothed some by Jan, Chino, and Nacho remaining on board. There were still too many unanswered questions, and possibilities for trouble, for me to feel totally at ease hanging out for no apparent reason, waiting for heaven only knew what.

But, a deal is a deal.

And, Mac did mention making me rich. 'Course, him being dead might put a kink in that scenario, but hope springs eternal.

Going over the timeline, cast of characters, and possible reasons for the whole mess, didn't do much for my sleep patterns, and I found myself at all hours on the Internet, researching people, boats, agencies, and even giant squid rumors—anything at all connected to me for the past month.

When I did finally drift off, Po Thang invariably snored, twitched, and dream-yipped. At one time I let him have the settee and caught an hour or so on the floor. I awoke feeling like I'd slept on a floor. Go figure.

Back at the computer, I started to Google, for at least the fourth time, Doctor Artherrrr MacKenzie Graham. This time, however, I left off the *Doctor* title and, on page four, hit pay dirt. Art Graham had competed in the 1996 Olympics in, of all things, long distance swimming. Hello? The guy who wanted me to think he was going to drown when I threw him off my boat? That Art Graham? I read more. Yep, that be he.

I added this interesting, but useless, information to my growing file, made a note that Dr. Graham is a sneaky devil, and went on to look into Javier's group, the PGR, and what the Justice Department in Mexico actually does. What a surprise: they investigate stuff.

"What are you looking for?" Nacho said over my shoulder, danged near scaring the pee out of me.

"For crying out loud, don't do that!" I screeched. Po Thang looked guilty, and Nacho backed away, hands up defensively. "I am sorry."

"You sure are. Make coffee, at least."

He hurried to the galley and, while loading the coffee pot, asked, "Did you know, Café, that the PGR is headed by a woman?"

"You were reading over my shoulder. Not nice. Isn't having a woman as the head cop a bit progressive for Mexico? And anyhow, what's that got to do with anything?"

"Many did not like it when she took over."

"Dissention in the ranks?"

"Yes. They think she is soft on crime."

"I'd say that wouldn't be one of the best qualifications for the head of the Justice Department. So, is she soft on all crime, or just the cartels?"

"Ha. Without the cartels, Mexico would just be a nation of petty criminals. I long for the days when all you had to worry about was your hub caps."

"Those guys all moved to East LA."

"Hey, I resemble that remark, Café."

"Speaking of that, just where are you from? Your fake drivers license says Los Angeles. But then again, that one has a fake name, as well."

"If I tell you, I will have to kill you."

Jan wandered in. "Thank goodness. Someone needs to."

"What did I do now?" I demanded.

"You ate all the ice cream."

"I did not!"

"Then where is it?"

I went to the galley and rummaged in the freezer. No ice cream.

Po Thang followed on my heels and I almost stepped on him when I turned back to Jan. "That rat, Mac. He ate it all! If he wasn't already dead, we'd have a case for justifiable homicide on our hands!"

"We could dig out the ice cream maker, but I need cream to make French custard," Jan said, "and milk. I need fresh milk, not canned."

"Or," Nacho suggested, "we could do without ice cream for the next two or three days?"

"Blasphemy!" we shouted.

"Ooor," Jan pointed at Nacho, "*one* of us could make a run into La Paz. It's not like you have anything else to do. You can fish on the way and, quite frankly, we're tired of you hanging around here all day. Take Po Thang and Chino with you so Hetta and I can have some girl time. Maybe we'll take a nice beach walk."

He sighed in resignation. "Do you want fresh cream, canned *crema*, or milk?"

"All. One cannot be too penurious in such matters."


After our trio of guys left, one of them wagging his tail in glee at the prospect of a boat ride, Jan and I gathered up all the gear required for a day at the beach. It was easier without a dog to pack for, so I decided to do some fishing, maybe even catch something. Hey, it could happen.

"Okay, Hetta, we'll drag a line around for awhile, but, in the off-chance you catch something besides bottom, you clean it."

"Deal." I stuck my handy filet knife in my pocket. "I'll get us the bait. We have some squid in the fish freezer," I volunteered, even though the idea of squid was not all that appealing after all the horror stories of late. On the other hand, maybe there was a soupçon of justice there?

I dug down into the chest freezer, holding my breath because of the lingering scent of old seafood that no amount of cleaning gets rid of, searching for a bag of squid pieces. At the very bottom I found cartons of designer ice cream. What kind of idiot puts ice cream in the fish freezer? Especially when a pint of the stuff costs twelve dollars in Mexico?

"Hey, Jan, I found the ice cream. It's in the bait freezer."

"Well, yuck. Why on earth did you put it there?"

"I didn't." I took out the cartons, but they didn't feel right. "I'm almost afraid to open this. God knows what fishy ice cream smells like."

Jan grabbed one. "I'll do it, you chicken. Crimeny, Hetta. You eat kimchi, how much worse can this smell?"

She ripped off the top and almost choked.

"Ha! Told you."

She gagged again and held out the carton. "Look!"

I held my nose and moved closer. Nestled in the carton were bits of previously rotted oyster that, even frozen, stank worse than, well, Po Thang's farts.

And there were pearls.

Lots and lots of pearls.

We completely forgot about going to the beach.

# Chapter Forty-two

We soaked all those lovely pearls in a bucket of salt water, then cleaned them carefully, one by one, rubbing them with table salt and a towel to remove oyster yuck. Once they were dried, we put them into a good-sized plastic mixing bowl. It took a couple of hours to complete the job.

"Holy moly, Hetta, we gotta have several hundred pearls here. Maybe a thousand. Wanna count 'em?"

"I *told* you Mac said he'd make me rich. And the last time I saw him—" I had a flashback of Mac swimming away from the boat, and calling me a name. "Oh, my, God! He yelled at me and I thought he had come up with something more colorful than hoor. He shouted, 'Haggendass.' Haagen-Daz! As in, ice cream! Where are those cartons?"

"In zip-bags. I wrapped them in garbage bags, then in zip-bags, and they still stink, so I threw them into *DawgHouse*. I'm gonna take them to shore and burn them."

"We need to see if we missed anything. He knew if I found them, he was probably a goner. In that case, don't you think he'd leave a note of some kind?"

"Get out the rebreathers if we are to survive."

Even breathing oxygen, the rotten oyster smell sneaked through, but at least it wasn't as bad as first hand. On the bottom of the first carton we found written, with a black marker pen, the name, Johnnie, and a boat name, *Pelicano*. That shrimper again.

"You think he meant to tell us they have Johnnie?"

"That's my guess. It's all about pearls, Miz Jan. Pure and simple. Gathering pearls is illegal and, obviously, they are doing it on a grand scale. If this is only a smattering of the take, there's enough moola involved to make any lying, murdering, kidnapping, schmuck salivate."

"You're drooling, schmuck."

I wiped my mouth. "Oh, hush. Let's check the other cartons and then get to countin'."

The second carton was marked, HETTA FOR EXPENSES, the third, CHINO: NOT THE SQUID, PROVE IT.

"Uh, Hetta, we mixed the cartons up and dumped them together. How do we know which is whose?"

"Elementary, my dear Watson. We sell them all and divide by three."

"What if we can't find Johnnie?"

"We will because now we know where to look."

"The shrimp boat, *Pelicano*. As soon as Nacho gets back, he'll know who to contact to find that boat. I'll betcha, since he was held prisoner on it, he already

294

has someone tracking them down. He's not one to take being kidnapped lightly. What time is it?"

Jan gave me a crooked lip twitch. "You got a train to catch, Chica?"

"No, smarty pants. I was just wondering how long the guys have been gone."

"Lemme think. About three hours. They should be back any time now."

"The sooner the better. I have the distinct feeling that if Johnnie is still alive, her time might be running out."

"I agree. What can we do right now?"

"Drink wine and count our good fortune?"

"No, silly. I'll try to call Chino on his cell phone and tell him what we found, meanwhile…hey, isn't that Javier's blue panga?"

I followed her gaze. "Yes, it sure is. Jan, hide the pearls somewhere good. He'll be here in a couple of minutes."

Jan was back just as Javier rushed up the ladder.

"Hetta, Jan, you must come with me! There has been a terrible accident!"

"What? Where? Who?"

"Calm down, Jan. Let the man talk. What? Where? Who?"

"Chino and Nacho have been gravely injured."

"Oh, no! What about Po Thang?"

He shook his head and my heart stopped. "I do not know."

"What do you mean, you don't know?"

"He has not been found."


We quickly closed up the boat, grabbed extra jackets, a first aid kit, and backpacks before jumping into the panga with Javier.

As we sped away from *Raymond Johnson*, Jan sobbed loudly, but I was too numb to do anything except pat her shoulder and say everything would be all right.

When Javier turned right, and north, out of the anchorage, I worked my way next to him. "Where are you going?"

"The *bajo*. That is where they are."

"What the hell are they doing there? They went to La Paz."

"I do not know. We received a call. Perhaps they decided to go there on the way back from La Paz."

"Oh, okay." I sat back down next to Jan, but something was off.

I leaned in close and said into Jan's ear, "Go smell Javier."

Her reddened eyes widened and she honked into a piece of paper towel. "What? Are you nuts?"

"Just do it."

Even though the water was fairly smooth, our speed made for a bumpy ride. Holding onto a rail for support, she reached Javier's side and leaned into him, asking a question.

He answered, she nodded, and then worked her way back to me and sat down.

Holding her nose, she said, "Shrimp."

"That's what I thought. Nacho said even *being* on a shrimper for any time made you smell like the little critters. Coincidence? You be the judge."

"Wanna take him down now, or wait?"

"Let's see where we're going first. Maybe Chino and Nacho are actually out here and in trouble. You got the gun?"

"Is there a .30-30 in Texas?"

"Uh-oh. Speaking of shrimp." She jerked her head toward the front of the boat.

I stood and looked forward. About two miles away was a shrimp boat that looked like the *Pelicano*, right on top of the *bajo*.

"How we gonna play this? There are only two of us and heaven knows how many of them."

"You take his right, I'll take the left. You distract, I'll grab the wheel. We have to take him down fast. He's a trained cop, but we have the element of surprise."

"We do?"

"Yep, Miz Jan, we do. He doesn't know we suspect a thing. Or that you were a goat ropin' champ and have blue ribbons in hawg tyin'. Military training's got nuthin' on 4H."

Per our quickly hatched plot, I untied a line from an aft cleat and handed it to Jan, who looped one end and tied a lasso. Or a hanging noose. Whatever floats your goat.

As it turned out, Javier never knew what hit him. When he woke up, he'd easily figure out it was a 9mm semi-automatic barrel, since I probably wouldn't have time to clean off the blood.

He fell toward Jan, so she obligingly stepped back to let him hit hard on the deck. I took the wheel, she dragged him out of my way, and trussed him up tighter than a gobbler on Thanksgiving morning.

"What now, Hetta?"

I slowed the boat. "Uh, I have no idea. Maybe we should—"

Jan cut me off. "Listen!"

Throttling back even more, I shut down the motors. A breeze blew our way, and sound carries well over the water. "What did you hear?"

"Shush."

We drifted, waiting. Then I heard it. "That's Po Thang! I'd know his bark anywhere. He's on that shrimp boat!"

# Chapter Forty-three

I rummaged around and found binoculars in a watertight hatch.

"It's Po Thang, all right. He's out on deck with a couple of what look like Mexican fishermen. Unfortunately, he's alerting them we're out here."

Jan who was still looking through the locker let out a whoop. "Pay dirt! Looky what we got here."

I put down the binocs and craned my neck to see what she found. "Yeah baby! I think that's an Uzi. I actually shot one once. Someone should tell Javier not to leave automatic weaponry lying around when we children are present. Here, Jan, you take the helm and move us slowly toward *Pelicano* while I check this lovely gun out."

Picking up the submachine gun I reached into my memory banks for that day in Texas when my cousin let me fire his Uzi. He'd used 9mm ammo, which I happened to have with me on Javier's boat, but was it the same for both my gun and this one? I unfolded the stock and it clicked in place. The bolt was closed. Rats, empty.

On my own 9mm, when the bolt is open, it is empty, but an Uzi is just the opposite.

Checking the locker, I found a metal box with six fully loaded magazines.

Moving next to Jan, I told her, "I'd say we're ready to rumble."

"Yeah, how's that? You just gonna open fire on a boat that has your dog, and maybe my boyfriend, Nacho and even Mac's wife on board? And, doncha just think they might, like, shoot back?"

Picking up the binoculars once again, I scanned the deck. Po Thang was running back and forth, barking and staring our way. So much for a stealth landing. However, I didn't see he was being threatened, nor did I spot any guns. The men looked more curious than anything.

"Let's sit Javier up in the captain's chair and tie him in."

While she did the deed, I found a yellow foul weather jacket, put it over his shoulders and jammed a hat on his head, which was lolling to one side. Not very convincing.

"We need to prop his head up. He looks like the dead guy in that movie, *Weekend at Bernies.*"

Looking around, I grabbed a paddle and we shoved it down the back of the jacket's collar and Jan used a bungee cord to fasten Javier's head to it, but he started falling forward. Another short piece of line fixed that problem.

I stood at Javier's side, steering the boat with one hand. We were getting close enough to the

*Pelicano* for them to make us out, so I gave them a friendly wave with my free hand.

"Jan, sit in Javier's lap and steer the boat."

"What? He's a criminal."

"*Now* you get choosey? Have you forgotten about Jean Claude?"

"Hey, he's out on good behavior."

"Just do it. We need these guys to think we're one big happy family until we can get the drop on them. I still only see two crew on deck. Do you remember how many you saw when you bought the shrimp?"

"Six, and I think that was all of them, cuz they all wanted to get a gander at the blonde *gringa*."

"So, four of them are...somewhere. Veer off and let's circle at a safe distance until we can figure something out."

"Gimme a cushion. I do not want to make contact with this guy's lap." She stared down and pointed. "Uh, I think he's waking up."

Jan circled toward the aft of the big shrimper and we made a discovery: Nacho's boat was side-tied to the starboard side. Through the binoculars I saw several large plastic bags on deck, and they looked ominously full.

"What do you see, Hetta?" Jan asked.

"Uh, not much. Don't get any closer."

"Javier's wiggling. Can't you whack him again?"

"I'm afraid I'll kill him. Lemme think."

"Hey, look, a dive flag. Maybe the rest of the crew are all underwater."

"Oh, man, what I'd give for some dynamite or a depth charger."

The diver waved, swam to Nacho's boat, threw a dive bag on deck, gave us a two-thumb's up, and went back down.

"What's in the bag?"

I fiddled with the binocular lenses. "Oysters. They're harvesting pearls."

"If we had any doubts about Javier here being behind everything, I suppose this puts it to rest. Let's take out those two on deck, find our people and get the hell out of here. Let the authorities deal with this scumbag." She poked him on the nose and he groaned.

"Think if we whistled Po Thang would hear us?"

"Maybe, but that's a mighty long drop from the shrimper's deck to the water. He might get hurt."

"If we don't get him off there, it could be worse. It's a chance we have to take."

We both began whistling, Jan better than me. She'd mastered that two finger thing I never got. Po Thang stopped in mid-pace, tilted his head, and without hesitation, jumped off the boat. It was a long fall.

Holding my breath, I waited for what seemed forever until he popped up and began swimming toward us. "Yes! Come on boy, you can make it."

As Po Thang swam toward us, I looked up at *Pelicano* and saw the two crewmembers had disappeared, but not for long. When they rushed back to the rail, they were brandishing weapons and took aim at Po Thang.

We were about fifty yards away and I had no idea whether it would do any good, but I put the Uzi in fun mode—fully automatic—executed a spray-and-play, and the men hit the deck as splinters flew.

I reloaded, put it on semi-auto, and told Jan to move us closer to Po Thang and put the boat between him and those rats on the ship. However, the gunfire had confused my dog and he was swimming away, back toward the enemy.

Jan whistled, and Po Thang changed direction toward us again, but suddenly went under.

"Hit it, Jan. We gotta get him. Maybe he's hurt."

"Hold on, Chica."

I tried to keep aim at *Pelicano* while maintaining my balance as we went in hot to where Po Thang went overboard, and twenty feet out he bobbed up, but he had company. A diver held him with one hand and brandished a dive knife in the other.

Jan veered off, the sudden boat's movement to the side throwing me to the deck. I lost my grip on the gun and it skittered away. Javier fell sideways, knocking Jan hard into the stainless steel steering wheel. She grunted, doubled over, grabbed her ribs, and gasped for air before she lost her balance as well when she was forced to let go of the wheel.

I crawled over and brought back the throttles, almost swamping us in the process, and by the time I could make my way back to retrieve the Uzi and stand up, Jan was nowhere to be seen. On *Pelicano,* the armed crewmen were upright again and waving their guns from side to side, trying to decide who to shoot at first. A short burst from my gun sent them sprawling on the deck again.

The panga tipped and I whirled, hoping to help Jan back on board, but a diver in a black wet suit had propelled himself over the gunwale. I swung the Uzi, but not fast enough. He tackled me and I went down hard on the right side of my head. We struggled for a few moments, but I was no match for him. He was strong, and the slick, wet, Lycra of the suit made it hard to hold on to him.

He was reaching for the Uzi when Jan materialized behind him, launched herself over the gunwale, and landed on both of us. I rolled away and he tried to stand, but our two-on-one pileup took him down.

Jan whopped him unconscious with a boat paddle and tied him hand and foot. Now we had two restrained perps on board and were running a tad low on lines.

"You look for Po Thang and that damned diver with the knife. I've got to keep those guys on *Pelicano* pinned to the deck, and I've only got four magazines left for this gun."

A yell and a yip caught our attention. The diver with my dog was trying to tell us something, which I surmised was, "Drop the gun or the dog gets it," or something to that effect. Po Thang struggled against his hold, and I was afraid the diver would stab him to stop the fight.

I held the Uzi high overhead in a gesture of surrender and whispered for Jan to stay low, where he couldn't see her while she slipped the 9mm from of my jacket pocket.

I pleaded with the man holding Po Thang. "Let the dog go and I'll throw the gun in the water."

The diver shook his head.

Po Thang shook *his* head, whopping the man across his mask with a wet ear.

The man cursed and raised his arm as if to knife Po Thang when Bubbles took to the air and whacked him with her powerful tail. The diver was laid out, face down, and only his suit kept him afloat.

We motored over and dragged both Po Thang and the unconscious diver on board, but it wasn't easy, what with me having to pin down the men on *Pelicano* every few minutes, Po Thang wanting to go back into the water with Bubbles, and the diver having indulged in a few too many tacos and beers in his life.

By the time Jan tied Po Thang to a rail, and bound the second diver, we *were* out of rope. So many bad guys, so little line.

# Chapter Forty-four

I was checking Po Thang over for wounds when a gunshot caught my attention, but we'd backed away and the crewmen's small handguns were totally useless at this distance. I gave them a short burst to calm them down. "These guys are slow learners."

But just as I said this, they made a liar out of me, which doesn't take much doing. One of them leaned over the side and aimed at the black plastic bags in Nacho's boat, confirming my unwanted fears. I had half-hoped the bags contained nothing but oysters.

Jan, who hadn't seen the black bags yet, was confused. "What is he doing?"

"You don't want to know." I put the Uzi on semi-automatic and took aim, afraid if I sprayed on fun mode I'd hit Nacho's boat.

I nailed him with my second shot and he fell overboard, landing in Nacho's boat. The other guy took a bead on us and we instinctively ducked even though we knew he couldn't hit us from that distance, but when he pulled the trigger there was no report. He looked stupidly at the gun and stupidly threw it at us.

"Just like in the movies. Out of ammo? Throw the gun. Janster, I think we might just be winning this here war. Four down, two to go."

Jan tried to laugh, but grabbed her side and blanched.

"Are you all right?"

"I," she gasped, "don't think so. It hurts to breathe."

"Okay, we gotta get out of here, but first we have to get Nacho's boat."

She didn't have the breath to ask why.

Nearby there was a geyser of water and Bubbles, a mask and mouthpiece in her beak, took to the air nearby. A few seconds later, a diver surfaced, gasping for air.

"Make that five down, one for the Bubblenator."

"Ooh, that has a nice ring to it," she said, but with difficulty. "Or, how about, Hettanator."

"Jan, do not talk. Go sit down and let me handle things."

We both turned at the sound of the shrimp boat's engine firing up as the anchor chain clanked over the chocks.

"Oh, hell, I sure hope he doesn't come this way. We gotta go get Nacho's boat untied from him before he takes off with it!"

"Wh...why?" she finally managed

"I think maybe our people are in it."

She just nodded, not having enough breath to do more.

"I don't know for sure, but I saw several plastic bags like the one Nacho was in when we found him. I'm going to take us over there next to Nacho's boat, but you will have to steer this one while I jump in and cut it loose. Do you think you can manage?"

She tried to say yes, but grimaced in pain and gave me a thumbs up sign instead.

"Okay, here we go." I pulled the filet knife kit from my pocket. "Always be prepared."

While I maneuvered the boat with one hand, I kept aim with the other, but it was obvious the crew member only wanted to get away.

*Pelicano*, with only a small amount of anchor chain deployed, took off before its anchor even cleared the water. The water depths just off of the *bajo* plummeted, so he was immediately at full speed, with Nacho's boat banging against the hull and in danger of being swamped by the shrimper's bow wave.

We caught up, but realized I had overestimated my ability to leap from one moving boat to another. It looks so easy in the movies.

Each time we got close enough, I chickened out, and Jan, it was soon obvious, had been seriously injured. She was white as a fish belly and gasping for air while trying to control the boat.

I looked at my dog. Where was Lassie when I needed her?

Nacho's boat was tipping to the point of almost dumping the black plastic bags overboard. If my hunch was right and our friends were in them they'd sink like rocks.

I took a deep breath, said a little prayer, and jumped, landing hard on one knee, which made a loud noise, sent a shock up my leg, and immediately started spurting blood. The pain was close to unbearable and a black veil threatened my vision, but somehow I managed to pull myself over to the line holding Nacho's boat to *Pelicano* and sliced through it before my lights went out.

When I opened my eyes, which wasn't something I wanted to do because it was pain that woke me, the boat was rocking side to side. A banging sound made me think, for just a moment, that I'd failed to cut us loose, but then I realized the rocking was caused by another source: Po Thang. And the banging noise was Javier's panga knocking against Nacho's. My dog was causing all the turmoil as he frantically tore at a bag with both his paws and teeth, and had managed to make a hole in the tough black plastic of another.

Pushing to seated, I retrieved my filet knife from the deck, butt-scooted, my knee screaming in protest—oh wait, that was me!—to help him. Shoving Po Thang out of the way, I used my knife and made a bigger gash in the bag and shrieked loudly when a small white hand shot out and grabbed my tee shirt.

After I caught my breath, I said, "Johnnie, let me go. I'm here to help."

Big brown eyes met mine. "Mac?"

"We don't know where he is," I said, stretching the truth a bit.

"Water."

"In a minute. I've got to get to these other bags."

"Hetta," I heard Jan say. She sounded weak, and her voice raspy.

"Jan! Are you okay over there?"

"Not…so…good. Maybe…call…help."

Johnnie rallied quickly. "Give me the knife, you get on the radio."

Po Thang heeded Jan's distress, jumped back into Javier's boat, and was licking her face, which was a horrible shade of gray.

Pulling myself up to the captain's chair, I reached past the now-awake-and-cursing Javier, put out a Mayday call giving our boat names and coordinates, and requested medical assistance. I also relayed what I knew about Jan's injuries; she'd suffered a blow to her midsection, probably her ribs, and was having trouble breathing.

By the time I got the call out, Johnnie had cut slits in all but one bag, at least ensuring air could get in. There was movement in most of the bags, so I figured if Johnnie survived, most likely so had the others. I scooted over to another bag, cut a long slit in it and almost passed out again from the smell. Whoever was in there was way past needing a little oxygen.

Drawn by the scent of whatever makes dogs love to sniff really dead stuff, and sometimes roll in it, Po Thang bounded back, rocking both boats. I was way past yelling at him and figured if he wanted to stick his nose into that putrid-smelling bag, so be it.

"Café?" I heard from behind me and turned to see Nacho crawling out of a bag. "What took you so long?"

I would have hugged him, stink and all, but Johnnie called for help as she worked on another bag and was pulling Chino out by his feet. He looked disoriented, but was moving and breathing so I concentrated on the last bag. Wait a minute; Nacho, Chino and Johnnie accounted for three bags and we had two left.

The really smelly one—I was hoping for oysters—was being worried by Po Thang, who was growling loudly as he did so.

Using the knife to carefully open the top, I pulled it down and found Mac, unconscious, but breathing.

"Mac?" I screeched. "But you're dead!"

Johnnie screamed, "Mac's dead? Oh, no!"

"No, no, he's not. But we thought he…oh, never mind. Nacho, are you able to help Jan? She's in trouble over there. And find some drinking water."

Johnnie threw salt water in her husband's face and he finally opened those beautiful green eyes. "Lass," he said softly.

I have to admit I felt a stab of jealousy.

Trying to go see about Jan, I slipped on something, sending yet another wave of pain through my knee. Looking down, a bolt of fear tripped my heart. A long slimy tentacle was wrapped around my foot.

The other end was in Po Thang's mouth.

Someone was in for some serious tooth brushing.

# Chapter Forty-five

Within an hour, our Mayday call brought a small fleet of pleasure boats, two Mexican Navy inflatables bristling with armed Marines, and even a helicopter. We'd decided to stay put on the advice of Johnnie, who had some human medical training as well as being a marine biologist. She was pretty certain Jan had broken a rib or two, and maybe even a nicked lung, so racing back to port in a bouncing panga didn't seem prudent until some real medical attention arrived.

The helicopter was full of PGR guys, called to the scene by Nacho, who actually managed to connect with them via Javier's cell phone using, maybe not so prudently, his speed dial. Two officiously dour types were lowered into Javier's blue panga, which, it turns out, actually belongs to the Justice Department.

Finding their own man, Javier, securely bound and loudly protesting he had been attacked for no reason whatsoever by two *putas locas*—I protested we were not hookers, but let the crazy part ride—didn't exactly bode well for us. Luckily the *Pelicano's* crew started singing like canaries and, along with Nacho's somewhat official status, saved me and Jan from being hustled off to a Mexican federal prison immediately. Later, who knows?

At least, however, the Justice Department guys made a decision to have Jan and Chino 'coptered back to a La Paz hospital while they sorted out who was who on the boats.

Nacho had already instructed us—mostly me, since Jan couldn't do much talking—to only say we were asked by Javier to go to the scene of a nonexistent accident. Realizing we were being kidnapped, we sort of jumped him.

Needless to say, all our weapons were now hidden in a very secure place: in the bag holding a badly mutilated and very dead Humboldt squid that no one, save Po Thang, wanted anything to do with. I'd stowed it under a bench, and with all the other stink left on Nacho's boat, the stench was hardly noticeable. However, I had to hang onto Po Thang lest he drew attention to my stinky stash of guts and guns.

Once Jan, Chino, and the helicopter left, they moved Nacho, me, Mac, and Johnnie to Nacho's boat. Next to us, in the blue panga, Javier and the *Pelicano* crew members cursed at each other and whined to one PGR guy while the other one questioned us.

The Marines I all the pleasure boats away, but some were reluctant to leave until assured I them everything was okay. I appreciated their loyalty, but told them I'd be fine and asked them to keep an eye on *Raymond Johnson.*

That injured knee was swelling badly and throbbing. One of the Marines, bless his heart, found a towel, put a handful of ice into it from a cooler on an inflatable, and Johnnie tied it around my knee. I remembered I'd thrown a first aid kit into Javier's panga when we left *Raymond Johnson*, so I popped a couple of Aleve. What I wanted was something much more substantial. Morphine with a rum chaser came to mind.

After questioning us for an hour, the Justice department agent in our panga made a call and told someone to find and seize *Pelicano* along with the sixth crew member who had taken off in his panga in hot pursuit of the mother ship. Finally convinced Javier and the other crewmembers were guilty of *something*, the agent had the Marines cart them off to La Paz in their souped up inflatables.

Two Marines stayed behind with us and piloted both Nacho's and Javier's pangas back toward the anchorage and my blessed medicine cabinet on *Raymond Johnson*.

I seated myself next to Mac, not totally convinced he was an innocent party, but because he had ended up in a plastic bag, we didn't rat him out to the agent in charge.

I knew the PGR agent couldn't hear me, so I leaned close to Mac. "I'm kind of glad you aren't dead, but I still think you're dirty in some way. Uh, you don't by any chance have some of that stuff you slipped into my tea on you, do you? My knee is killing me."

"Sorry, Hetta. I used all I was given."

I saw the PGR agent-dude eyeing us and shut up, but wanted to ask *given by who. Whom?*

Nacho also noticed us talking and turned an imaginary key on his lips, so we rode in silence, each tiny wave tormenting my leg into a blazing inferno. Johnnie patted my shoulder in sympathy, which was nice, but didn't do much to staunch the pain. Po Thang licked the area around the ice bag and whined. He was either trying to comfort me or he was thirsty. One really never knows with dogs.

When we arrived at *Raymond Johnson*, a panga was tied behind it.

"Oh hell, now what?" I grumbled.

Nacho went forward and said something to the agent, who gave an order to the marine, who moved to the bow and un-slung his gun. I glanced longingly back at Javier's panga, where my own arsenal was riding in that highly undesirable bag of slime.

Nacho took the helm and we circled my boat, but no one was in the panga, or on my deck. So, was someone inside my boat I'd locked up tight when we left with Javier? As soon as we touched the swim platform, Po Thang bounded up on deck, grumble barking but his tail doing a gyro job as though he really couldn't make up his mind if there was a problem as he raced through an open door. A door that was closed and locked when I left.

Another case of fresh Hell?

Getting me out of the panga and up the ladder in any kind of hurry was out of the question, so I was relegated to waiting—something I do not take kindly to—while Nacho, the agent, and one marine boarded to see who was on my boat.

By the tone of Po Thang's bark, I knew he was a little confused whether he was encountering a friend or foe.

A Mexican man I'd never seen before, with Po Thang in hot pursuit, ran screaming from the main cabin, right into the arms of the PGR agent, who took him down. A marine pinned him to the deck with a muzzle to the neck. The man, his hands on his head, was praying loudly while Po Thang danced in for a lick or two. My guard dog: world class licker-to-deather.

I called him away but he ignored me, as usual, and dashed back inside. His barks stopped instantly. Frightened for him, I tried to stand, but the pain quickly reminded me not to do so. Mac did stand, but was waved back down by the second marine's gun barrel.

Agent Pablo, standing on deck, shouted an order to whomever was below, and Jenks came out, hands in the air. He spotted me and grinned.

"As usual, Hetta, never a dull moment."

# Chapter Forty-six

It was dark by the time Jenks and I managed to get rid of everyone.

Jenks was at first insistent that I go with one of the pangas, accompanied by Mac, Johnnie, Nacho, the PGR agent—who by now we were calling Pablo—and the Marines, into La Paz. I stubborned up on him, convincing him since swelling was going down some I wasn't hurting so badly anymore, and we'd return together into port the next morning on *Raymond Johnson*.

I was lying about the pain, but I longed to be alone with him.

Johnnie agreed it was probably just a sprain, maybe a ligament problem, but icing and anti-inflammatories should do the job until I reached La Paz. I did have a pretty good gash but not big enough to require stitches.

Before everyone left I asked to speak privately with Mac, mainly about the pearls he'd left on my boat.

I also still suspected he was somehow guilty of something other than kidnapping me and stealing my boat. And then there was the wife thing.

"Why were those guys holding Johnnie?"

"So I would be forced to help them. They needed someone to convince people of squid attacks, I was the expert, and when Javier saw I was going to exonerate the squid, he took Johnnie so I would change my report and do as he told me. I soon learned there were no deaths at all. Not one. The stories were totally fabricated by him and his mates to ensure no one stumbled upon those oyster beds until he could harvest them."

"But the body with the kilt?"

"Pure fabrication. I think they were setting the scene so when I actually did die, along with the others, they could easily dispose of all of us and no one would be looking because we were already reported as missing."

"So, Javier went rogue. I wonder why? Other than greed, of course, which I can totally relate to."

"His father and grandfather were pearl men back in the day before the oysters died off, and Javier was raised hearing of how the Mexican people were robbed by foreigners. When Javier got wind of the new discovery he wanted to harvest as many pearls as possible before the outsiders learned of the new beds and moved in for the steal. *Pelicano's* captain is his brother and everyone involved is, as far as I can tell, family."

"A family affair. So, in truth, they are guilty of a little kidnapping and pearl theft only because they got caught before any killing started?"

"Yes. Dreams of riches make people crazy."

I stole a crazed glance at the galley, where all those pearls were. "Really?"

He gave me that great grin of his. "Really."

Po Thang was mighty unhappy about being barred from my bedroom, but finally gave up whining and went off to pout.

Jenks had dozed off and I was in an anti-inflammatory, wine, and codeine haze. I know, I'm not supposed to combine all that stuff, but the pain in that knee was much, much better. Or at least I didn't give a damn that it hurt, because having Jenks back on the boat was happy-making all on its own.

I tried to get out of bed but couldn't figure out how without putting any weight on my knee. Sliding off one side of the mattress, I ended up flat out on the carpet.

Jenks looked down at me. "You look like you could use a hand there."

"I could use a sky hook," I growled.

He picked me up—no easy feat, but he did it easily—and asked, "Where to?"

"The head. Just get me there. I can manage the rest on my own."

He looked relieved. "Can do. You hungry?"

"Not so much, but I haven't eaten much today, and we got a mite busy down here before we could cook anything."

"I'll check out the galley, so yell when you need me to come get you."

By the time I managed the toilet and threw water in my face and brushed my teeth, Jenks was back, waiting outside the bathroom door.

"I'm putting together a nice steak dinner. That okay with you?"

"Perfect. And more wine. I need lots of wine."

He gently placed me into a deck chair—no easy task considering that gravity thing—where I tried to make up with Po Thang for locking him out of my bedroom and thereby perpetrating gross animal neglect. I was hand-feeding him bits of chicken breast Jenks found in the fridge when, in mid-bite he suddenly growled and the hair stood up on his neck and back. Rushing the rail, he stared into the dark while barking his, *I'm trying to sound really furious and dangerous but I might be scared,* bark.

"Jenks," I yelled. "Can you turn on the deck lights? I think someone's coming."

Flood lights brightly bathed the area around us with an intense light just as the blue panga pulled up with the PGR agent who had questioned us earlier in the day, Pablo, on board.

"Hush," I ordered Po Thang, an exercise in futility at best.

I waved at Pablo as he brought the boat alongside the swim platform and cut his engines. "Hello, Hetta. I came back to check on you. Is your knee better?" As he was talking, he was stepping onto the swim platform, a little too aggressively for my druthers. Common nautical courtesy requires a, "Permission to come aboard?" request.

"I'm fine," I said, but something didn't feel fine and it wasn't just my knee. Po Thang and I both smelled a rat.

Jenks walked up behind me and put his arm on my shoulder. "Jenks, I think—"

But Pablo was already on deck, brandishing a large handgun. "Where are they?" he demanded.

"Gee, Agent Pablo, I might be projecting here, but aren't you supposed to be one of the good guys? Where are what?" I asked. I had a sneaking feeling I knew what he was after, but I was stalling for time to think.

"Don't play dumb with me," Pablo growled. "The pearls, as you well know."

Po Thang growled as well.

Jenks took a step in Pablo's direction and the agent aimed the gun at Po Thang, who rumbled even louder. "Hold it right there or I'll shoot the dog. I prefer to kill Miss Coffey for being such a troublemaker, but she knows where the pearls are and I don't have time to search the boat."

"If I knew anything about any pearls I wouldn't tell you because you'd just kill us anyway. Did your partner in crime, Javier, tell you there are pearls on my boat? Even if there were he probably took them for himself."

"He did not. Trust me, he would have told me."

Uh-oh, I didn't like the sound of that. Past tense and all.

"You do realize the other boaters can see everything happening on this deck, don't you?" I said, hoping like hell someone was watching. Unfortunately, it was way past Baja midnight—eight at night—and everyone was probably tucked into their bunks.

"Turn off those lights," he ordered.

"The only switch is below," I lied. "I can't walk worth a damn, so Jenks will have to turn them off."

Jenks cut his eyes at me and gave me an almost imperceptible nod. He was reading my mind.

Pablo looked uncertain what to do next then grabbed Po Thang's collar so fast my dog didn't have time to snap off a finger or something more personal.

"Where is the switch? I will turn them off myself, and I will take this cur with me to ensure you do not do anything stupid. I *will* kill him. You have my word on it."

"Oh, I believe you, even though I'm sure your word ain't worth spit. By the way, *Pablo*, what part of the US are you from?"

"None of your concern," he spat, confirming my belief he was a *gringo*. "Do not move, or the pooch buys it."

He backed down the stairs, dragging the furiously struggling Po Thang with him. I winced as I heard my dog's body thump down each stair step. He'd stopped barking and was yipping in pain and frustration.

As soon as they disappeared down the stairs, headed for the light switch in my cabin, I whispered, "Jenks, Nacho's panga! Guns in the black garbage bag!"

Jenks didn't hesitate and with his long legs and reach was back on deck within seconds, dragging the stinking mess behind him. I reached in and grabbed a double handful of squid guts and threw them at the top of the stairs. The smell almost knocked me over.

Pablo must have heard us moving around because he rushed back up the stairs. He'd evidently lost his battle for control of Po Thang for just as he reached the top stair, my dog barreled up behind him and head-butted the backs of the agent's knees like a short, furry linebacker committing unnecessary roughness. Pablo's legs buckled and he went down face first into a pile of slime. Unfortunately, he never lost the grip on his gun. He was quick and well-trained, rolling into a defensive prone position, pointing that mean-looking barrel at us.

I had scooted back and had both hands in the bag again when he managed to get to his feet. "You going to slime me to death, Red? Now where are those damned pearls?" All vestiges of any Mexican accent were gone.

"Po Thang, kill!" I yelled. My dog looked confused and ran over to lick me in the face.

Pablo actually laughed. "Gee, that went well. What is it with you, Coffey? Don't you ever just quit being a giant pain in the ass?"

Jenks shook his head, catching Pablo's attention. The bad-dude agent-in-charge gave him a sympathetic eye raise. "What did you ever do to deserve her, Mr. Jenkins?"

Jenks shrugged. "Guess I'm just lucky."

Pablo turned back toward me and found himself looking down the barrel of an Uzi.

"How about you, Agent Pablo? *You* feelin' lucky?"

# Chapter Forty-seven

We left for La Paz at first light the next morning.

Pablo, wrists and feet plastic tie-wrapped and up to his neck in the stinky black bag with squid parts for company, was chained into his blue panga, which we trailed behind us in hopes of keeping it downwind.

We called Chino, who told us Jan would not need surgery, and was being released from the hospital later that day. She was in for a few weeks of discomfort but would recover nicely.

I also talked with Nacho and told him we were inbound with the so-called PGR agent, Pablo, so he could meet us before we got to the dock, take Pablo into custody and give us time to beat feet out of town until given an all clear to return.

On the way back in, I told Jenks the whole sordid story of how a bunch of human devils framed the

Red Devils while enriching themselves with ill-gotten gains.

"So, they made up the stories to make it look like a squid did it, and for good measure, threw in a tentacle or two as evidence."

"Yep. I feel sorry for that poor squid. It was killed for no reason and hacked up to leave as evidence."

"So, where are the pearls?"

"In the safe?"

"Not those pearls, Hetta. You showed me those. Where is the stash Agent Pablo was looking for?"

"If I tell you I'll have to kill you?"

He gave me that look. The one that reminded me that if I intended to continue life as a serial prevaricator, he was going to get fed up one day. I guess brandishing the occasional machine gun just isn't enough to keep up a man's interest.

"Okay, okay, they're in the freezer. There are three packages of frozen peas. Not peas, pearls."

"Uh-oh. Two."

"Two?"

"Afraid so. Just when Pablo showed up last night I was cooking dinner and dumped a bag of peas in boiling water. By the time I could get back to the galley the water was long gone and they were burned jet black."

"Jenks, they're black pearls!"

"How was I to know? I threw them overboard."

I could almost see my grandmother shaking her finger at me and quoting the Bible. "Hetta," she warned, "the truth will make you free. Someday your habit of avoiding truth by omission will have consequences."

Ya think?

# Epilogue

We drove to Cabo San Lucas right after as we visited Jan in the hospital. She was being released that morning and she and Chino were headed back to Lopez Mateos where his Granny Yee could look after her. They took Po Thang with them so Jenks and I could enjoy the luxury of a fancy beach hotel while my knee healed, and Nacho mopped up the mess we'd left back in La Paz.

Javier had died of unknown causes while in custody.

Pablo was whisked away to heaven knows where by persons unknown.

*Pelicano's* captain and crew were charged with illegal harvesting of pearls, which they admitted to.

However, the location of any pearls they took was unknown.

Unknowns abound.

While languishing around the pool at the hotel I was tagged on Facebook with an article from a San Diego newspaper. Someone had made a spectacular flea market find: almost seven hundred natural black pearls were discovered in the bottom of a Mexican basket of fake fruit. A lucky vacationer, Topaz Sawyer, a Deputy Sheriff from Bisbee, Arizona, would be putting them up for auction in the near future, and experts estimated their value at well over a million dollars.

Mac and Johnnie will continue their circumnavigation soon, but first they plan to stop in San Diego and purchase a bigger boat.

The Mexican Tourist Bureau happily announced squid attack reports were the work of hoaxers, and the Sea of Cortez was perfectly safe for tourists.

Nacho, as always, stole away like the shadow he is, but had reportedly stopped in Bisbee, Arizona to visit my friend, and his reputed one-time fling partner, Topaz Sawyer.

Oh, and Freddie Clark, the missing sailor from *Carpe Diem* ? Seems he, too, tried to really sieze the day by cashing in on the Red Devil attack stories by staging his own death. He was spotted in a bar in Puerto Vallarta. Word has it the IRS and an estranged wife are very interested in talking with him.

Chino generously offered to split his windfall three ways with Jan and me, and plans to spend his part on studies of the giant Humboldt squid, hopefully to remove the stigma of being called Red Devils.

Back on *Raymond Johnson* after two weeks living in the very lap of luxury while the bad guys were bagged and tagged, I was greeted by a petulant pooch, who was returned that morning by one of Chino's cousins.

Po Thang sat on the back of the boat for days, gazing longingly out to sea for his friend, Bubbles, but she never returned. We hope she's fallen in love with someone with fins.

Jenks and I joined the crestfallen Po Thang on the back deck one evening to offer ear scratches, chicken bits, and advice for lovelorn pooches. Kevin and Karen, the cruising couple we'd seen at Partida, walked by with their Poodle, Puddles.

Puddles raised a half-hearted tail wag from the dejected Po Thang—I guess once you stray from the reservation it's hard to get back to your own species—as they nosed each other.

I introduced Jenks.

The couple exchanged a look. "You know, you look so much more Scandinavian than that other Jenks Hetta had on board. See ya."

They walked away, leaving Po Thang whining and me wincing.

Hooboy. Once again, caught between the devil and the deep blue sea, with some 'splainin' to do.

I opened my mouth to do just that, but Jenks held his palm out in a "don't even bother" gesture. "Hetta, I've been thinking about something."

Oh, dear. Once again I opened my mouth and he repeated the *just stop* hand.

Then he smiled. "I don't think you and Jan had to worry about being devoured by those giant squid. You're Texans. They'd probably think you were too hard to clean."

THE END

If you have enjoyed this book, please tell your friends about Hetta, or post a short review on Amazon. Word of mouth is an author's best friend, and is much appreciated.

I have editors, but boo-boos do manage to creep into a book, no matter how many people look at it before publication, and if there are errors, they are all on me. Should you come upon one of these culprits, please let me know and I shall smite it with my mighty keyboard! You can e-mail me at jinxschwartz@yahoo.com

And if you want to be alerted when I have a free, discounted, or new book, you can go to http://jinxschwartz.com and sign up for my newsletter. I promise not to deluge you with pictures of puppies and kittens.

Also, you can find me on Facebook at https://www.facebook.com/jinxschwartz That puppy and kitten thing? No promises on FB posts :-)

Oh, and no sea life was actually harmed in the writing of this book.

Just met Hetta in Just Different Devils? Here are some takes on the rest of the series.

## What people are saying about *JUST ADD WATER,* Winner of the EPPIE AWARD FOR BEST MYSTERY

Hetta Coffey's hilarious string of misadventures after being suddenly plunged into the "yachtie world" is a great page-turner for the quarter berth!— Capt. Pat Rains


A romp of a read, with snappy dialogue and memorable secondary characters, but it is Hetta's story. It's easy to sympathize when she takes her yacht out alone into San Francisco Bay, to nurse her broken heart and start A LIST OF THINGS TO DO AS AN INFINITELY UNATTACHED PERSON. Then, of course, all heck breaks loose. —Pat Browning, Author of Absinthe of Malice


Can't get a man? Just add water.

Hang on tight for a rollicking adventure with Hetta Coffey, a globetrotting civil engineer with an attitude. After a lifelong swath of failed romances, Hetta prefers living with her dog and commiserating her single status with best friend, Jan. But old habits die-hard and one morning while brunching with Jan at the waterfront, Hetta's attention is snagged by a parade of passing yachts and their hunky male skippers. She decides that if she had a boat, she could get a man.

Despite her naiveté of all things nautical, Hetta buys her dream boat and sets about learning to sail. A series of events, including a shadowy stalker and an inconvenient body threatens to imperil her new lifestyle. As her past comes back to haunt her, Hetta must use all of her gritty resources to foil an attempt on her life to figure out who is determined to kill her and why.
—B, Bramblett, for Fiction Addiction

Author Jinx Schwartz will need to change her name to Lucky when readers discover *Just Add Water*. Schwartz has not only hit a home run; her first book is out of the ballpark. Schwartz is a twinkling, bright star on the mystery genre horizon with her witty and sometimes irreverent heroine, Hetta Coffey. Book One of the Hetta Coffey series, *Just Add Water*, is a refreshing antidote to the seriousness of the mystery genre without sacrificing a well-constructed plot, enjoyable story, and colorful characters. Readers will fly through the pages in anticipation of what Hetta will do, and say next. Schwartz ties up all the loose ends at the conclusion of the book, leaving this reader eagerly anticipating Book Two of the Hetta Coffey series.—BookwormBriefing

Made in the USA
San Bernardino, CA
08 December 2015